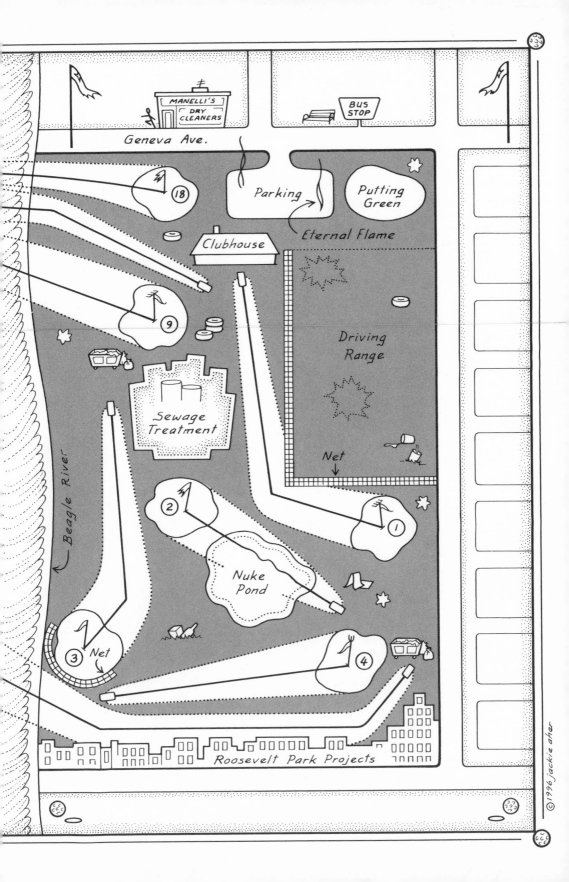

SHANKS FOR NOTHING

Also by Rick Reilly

Who's Your Caddy?
Slo-Mo!
Missing Links
Life of Reilly

SHANKS FOR NOTHING

NOTHING

Rick Reilly

DOUBLEDAY

New York   London   Toronto

Sydney   Auckland

PUBLISHED BY DOUBLEDAY
a division of Random House, Inc.

DOUBLEDAY and the portrayal of an anchor with a dolphin
are registered trademarks of Random House, Inc.

Book design by Kathryn Parise

LIBRARY OF CONGRESS CATALOGING-IN-PUBLICATION DATA
Reilly, Rick.
Shanks for nothing / Rick Reilly.—1st ed.
p. cm.
1. Golfers—Fiction. 2. Golf stories.   I. Title.
PS3568.E4847S48 2006
813'.54—dc22
2005043524

ISBN-13: 978-0-385-50111-8
ISBN-10: 0-385-50111-0

PRINTED IN THE UNITED STATES OF AMERICA

First Edition

1 3 5 7 9 10 8 6 4 2

For Two Down O'Connor, who
has to be toned down for fiction

Acknowledgments

Shanks for everything, Bill (Press) Thomas, Janet Pawson, Michelle Hall and her perfect follow-through, the indescribable Schuyler Grey, the staff at Zaidy's for letting me sit there for hours gulping coffee and pulling out my hair, Rekha Ohal, who made it (and me) so much better, Lenny the Brain, Gene Wojciechowski, who is always there, Kevin Cartin, Mike Bevans, who always pretended not to know I was writing this instead of the column, Sharky, my cool kids, my brother John and his Goons (the Chops' parallel universe), and all those great caddies, especially Sandy at Royal Dornoch, who did the most wonderful thing of all. He introduced me to Macallan's.

SHANKS FOR NOTHING

CHAPTER 1

I distinctly remember the day my life started smother-hooking toward Hell. It was just another day of gentlemanly golfing competition among the Chops at Ponkaquogue Municipal Golf Links and Deli, known across the land as America's worst golf facility. It was our usual fivesome: Two Down, Hoover, Cementhead, Dannie—the hot-tempered, hot-blooded little five-handicap who also doubled as my wife—and me.

"Are those shorts heavily padded?" Dannie asked Cementhead.

"What's it to you?" Cement said.

" 'Cause I'm about to give you a serious butt-kickin'."

Across the way, the hyper Leonard "Two Down" Petrovitz—half-man, half-cappuccino—was locked in mortal combat with me in a game of $20 one-down automatic press bets. Of course, he couldn't have been too worried, since he was beating me like Liza's ex. I'd given him half a shot a hole, plus a hundred-yard head start on every hole, plus one throw a side.

And yet, just because he was beating me didn't mean he was going to stoop to any gamesmanship.

"I see you changed your putter since last time," Two Down observed. "I guess that last one didn't float so good."

"Keep it up, Chirpy," I said. "And you'll be joining it."

Ponky was famous around Boston for three things: 1) Being full of morons who bet way more than they had; 2) Being to golf what Velveeta was to French culinary schools; 3) Being next door to one of the great courses in America, the blue-blooded high-hatted Mayflower Club, whose members were so choosy about who they accepted they simply stopped letting people in three years ago. The line around town was, not even the original Pilgrims could get into the Mayflower now.

Since Ponky and the Mayflower were built in the 1900s, one by Donald Ross and one by *Ronald* Ross—a small mistake made by the city fathers— the two courses had moved in opposite directions from birth until one became the very symbol of posh blue-blood aristocracy and the other of fried-egg SPAMwiches. Now, the only thing that separates the Mayflower and Ponky is a twelve-foot-high redbrick wall, a whole lot of deb balls, and general good breeding.

The Mayflower was so stuck up it had refused to even host a U.S. Open or a PGA or a Ryder Cup, despite being begged. Never, that is, until five years ago, when it agreed to finally lower itself to play host to the greatest players in the world at the U.S. Open, which would descend upon it the following summer. Not that they didn't have events. They had their lavish "Pilgrimage" every year, and their "Heritage Hoopla" and their "Member-Member" (never a member-guest). And whenever they hosted such prestigious events, they rented Ponky's course out to park all the Bentleys that strutted through. For the month after, you'd get tire-track lies in the middle of the fairways. But what could we do? We were privately owned by the cheapest man in the world—Froghair.

Froghair got his name for his length off the tee, which was none at all. He averaged about a buck-eighty. He was straight, though, so we said he led the tour in FIR (Froghair in Regulation). Froghair would rent Ponky out to Islamic Hamas if he thought he could get an extra thirty-seven dollars out of it.

It always delighted us to see those Numerals—you know, your Worth Havermayer III and your Gray Stoneham the IV—get out of their cherry cars and take a look around at the eighteen-hole municipal dump that is Ponky. We loved to watch their faces react in horror at the course we played every day, the abandoned '57 Jell-O green Chevy near the 8th tee, sitting as it did just under the half of a *Boston Globe* billboard that jutted out over the tee box. We giggled to see them hurry away from our battleground practice range, where bad golfers hailed cut, yellowed practice balls at Nuke, our range boy. Froghair wouldn't pay to have the range tractor fixed, so Nuke was out there, eight hours a day, wearing two twinsize mattresses roped together and fitted to his skinny body, a lacrosse helmet with face mask, and a shag bag in each hand. ("Hey," Froghair always said in defense, "the kid's a stoner. He doesn't even *feel* it!") And it gave us a kick to see Boston's gentry get an eyeful of the unshaven community outside the Ponky fences—the pawnshops and strip bars along our 18th hole bordering Geneva Avenue, the ratty blue-collar cemetery out our front windows, the spirited youth who populated the Roosevelt Park Projects off 5 and 13, having their innocent fun with needles and small-arms fire.

Over the last one hundred years, every inch of this part of Dorchester had gone from debutante to drugstore whore except the Mayflower, which just kept building its walls higher and higher until it couldn't see out anymore, which is just how they liked it.

But screw them. I wouldn't have traded one of them for a single Chop. I loved Ponky. I guess because my dad was a member of the Mayflower and, until the last three years, I hated my dad the way mailmen hate Dobermans.

Anyway, on this particular Thursday, it was the usual cast of x-outs and out-of-round humans who probably should've been taken out of play years before.

One hundred and twenty yards behind us, Hoover, our fifth, was taking his sweet time hitting his shot, despite playing against nobody for no bet at all.

"Why don't he hit the goddamn thing already?" Dannie said, exasperated. "He's already pulled a JFK Jr."

"What's a JFK Jr.?" asked Cement.

"Three lost in the water."

"I believe it's your *turn*, Hoov!" Dannie yelled, knowing all the while that there was no such thing as "turns" at a free-for-all etiquetteless joint like Ponky. It'd be like one hyena saying to another over a downed zebra, "I believe it's your turn, Herman!"

But Hoover was back in the fairway, on one knee, holding his latest gadget—the new GPS-enabled SuperTech Bushnell Laser Range Finder 3000—up to his right eye and making sure the yardage was *exactly 176 and not 177* even though Hoover could not hit a green from 17 yards much less 177. He was going to get his yardage all lined up and then smother-toe it left or hosel it right or cold-top it five feet. There was a reason we called him Hoover. He sucked.

"What are you, Patton?" Two Down yelled. "Hit the fuckin' ball!"

Hoover rose and yelled back, "Seven percent of all shots fail due to lack of precise yardage! That was in this month's *Scientific Golf America*!" Then he stepped up and chunked it about twenty yards, or about two yards short of his divot.

"And 93 percent of all shots fail 'cause Hoover sucks like Linda Lovelace," Dannie said to nobody in particular.

So here we were on the 17th, with me down three, down two, and down one to Two Down and needing this hole to have any chance of saving the Claudette Coldbeer fund.

Still, Two Down was lying four. I was lying two right in front of the green. He was taking a long look at his difficult sand shot—all sand shots at Ponky are difficult on account of there being no sand in Ponky's bunkers—when he announced, "I haven't had my throw yet, right?"

I was hoping he'd forgotten.

"Yeah, that's right," I grumbled. "You get one throw a side."

And Two Down got out of the bunker, walked over to my ball, picked it up, and threw it over the twelve-foot-high hedge into the Mayflower Country Club. Then he returned to his shot without comment.

One really needs to think out all bets with Two Down in advance.

As we came to the picturesque 18th hole at Ponky—with its unforgettable view of Manelli's Dry Cleaners on the left—I was down two hundred dollars all day to Two Down. I needed something big on the last hole to bail me out.

"Two, I need a get-even."

Two looked at me and said, quite firmly, "Okay, you know what? *No.*"

"But you haven't even heard it yet," I said.

"Unless the get-even is you chew off your left hand before you play this last hole, I don't want any part of it."

"No, it's better than that. I'm offering you a simple wager."

If there is one thing a true Chop will not turn down, it's the offer of a simple wager. A true Chop will bet on all things at all times. Would that guy eat his ear of corn like a typewriter or in a wheel around it? What odds will you give me that I can't chip one onto the clubhouse roof, run around to the other side, and catch it my mouth? (Odds were set at twelve-to-one against.) One time, on a rainy day, Two Down and Dom bet ten bucks on who would swing first on *Jerry Springer*: the blimp who was about to find out her daughter was screwing her son or the two-toothed dad who was finding out his hunting buddy was in love with him.

Offering Two Down a simple wager was like offering a wolf a pork chop. Half the reason he came to Ponky from his brief exile in Chicago was that nobody would play golf with as many bets on the line as we did. They'd just play the standard two-dollar Nassau. No comp presses, no indies, no greenies, sandies, barkies, or even barfies, in which if the player can finger-barf on command, he can play the shot over. So that's why he came back to us. That, and the fact that his wife divorced his ass.

And so I cast out my bait: "I'm a little longer than you off the tee, am I right?"

"Does Michael Jackson subscribe to *Boys' Life*?" he said.

"Exactly. I'd say I'm about fifty to seventy-five yards longer than you, on average, with the driver, yes?"

"Yeah, and you're about two hundred dollars down to me, too, Mr. Two-Time Massachusetts Junior Amateur Runner-Up. So shut the fuck up and hit."

"Right. Well, here's the bet. I tend to swing only 75 percent with my driver. I think I can be three highway exits past you if I wanted to. In fact, I'll bet you two hundred dollars that you can't knock it past my drive from this tee box in *two* shots. Frankly, I think you'll choke like Mama Cass."

This got Two Down's famous ADD eyebrows to itching. Two hundred dollars was a lot for a guy who was working as the clubhouse assistant at America's only all-women's golf club, Boston National Ladies Golf. Come to think of it, two hundred dollars was a lot for me, a guy who wrote greeting cards at twenty-five dollars a pop.

"Two shots?"

"Two shots," I said.

"Who goes first?"

"Well, it's your honor. We stand on tradition here at Ponky, naturally."

"Naturally," he said. "Two shots?"

"Two."

"You're going to hit your ball and I'm going to hit my ball and neither of us gets to hit the other guy's ball, right?"

"Right."

Cementhead was starting to get annoyed. "Damn, you guys. People have circumcised the globe faster than this."

We both looked at him.

"*Circumnavigated* the globe," I said.

"You sure?" he said.

"I'm sure."

Two Down was back in my face. "*Golf* ball, not any other kind of ball? Not nads, right? Today? Here at Ponky? Right now?"

"Precisely."

"And if I can get past your single shot in my *two* shots you'll pay me two hundred dollars, U.S. legal tender, stacking zops, today, back in the clubhouse, right?"

"Right."

"Bank," he said.

This set off much whooping and taunting and side-betting among the other three members of the fivesome, as is custom. And then Two Down stepped his wiry little Polish ass up to the tee and put his usual unfilmable quickslash on his ball, which produced his usual 190-yard-long, two-feet-high bunny-raping line drive that could go under a 1977 Datsun. "I see you've gone to a higher-lofted driver," I observed, stepping up for my shot.

"Blow me," he said.

I teed my ball up nice and high and began to waggle my driver. I waggled and exhaled and waggled some more. Then I stepped away, pretending to reassess my shot. Then I went around to the other side of the ball and began waggling the club again, only in the complete wrong direction.

"Ray, hole's the other way," Cementhead said.

I said nothing. I just drew it back and slapped the dimples off it, about three hundred yards back up and over the T-tracks, over the group putting out on 17, over the fourteen-foot-high hedge separating us from Mayflower and God knows where from there, perhaps into the matching Louis Vuitton purse of Mrs. Carter Annuity III, playing in the Ladies C-Team Nine-Hole Golf and Tea-Cozy Group approximately 490 yards from Two Down's ball.

I looked at him. He was struck mute. The blood abandoned his face. He looked like a man who'd just been stabbed in the foot with an icepick. Dannie was laughing so hard she was bent over the ball-washer, crying. Hoover was smiling. Cementhead was befuddled.

"Damn, Ray, how's he's gonna catch up to that in only one more shot?" he said.

Two Down turned and stomped off down 18. Dannie was now down on her knees. Cementhead was scratching his thick skull. "Wait, explain something to me."

"Okay, Cement," I said, walking with my arm around his shoulder down 18. "Shall we start with the alphabet?"

As we putted out on 18, we got the usual snide comments from The Voice. Nobody knew the guy. Nobody knew his name. He was supposed to just announce over the PA who was up next—"Crumpacker, eight minutes" and the like—but he could never help adding his little chippy remarks. For instance: "Mr. Finster, you're up in sixteen minutes. Oh, and Mr. Finster? Woodrow Wilson called. He wants his pants back." He was pretty funny, The Voice, until he noticed you. "The group coming down 18?" he announced to us then. "Bad news: There's a job fair coming to town. You can hide at my house."

But the bad news was worse than that and it was very real. It came the next day. I knew it as soon as I saw Blind Bob's face. He was regripping his ball retriever.

"You should sit down."

"How do you know I'm not?"

"Sit."

I sat.

"Froghair's selling."

I started to feel a little lightheaded.

"Selling?"

"Yeah. It sucks huge, doesn't it? He's getting out. He's selling the course and moving to Florida. Joining a nudist colony."

"Selling Ponky?"

"Yeah, Stick. Selling Ponky. Selling P-O-N-K-Y."

I was trying to catch my breath. I guess I completely passed over the disturbing idea of Froghair nude and went to the truly paralyzing news. Ponky was my happy place—five bets riding on every shot, cold ninety-five-cent beer anytime you wanted, and hilarious guys who didn't want to tell you how their Google stock is doing every fucking day. I was happy at Ponky.

"To who?" I managed.

"He doesn't care. Probably won't get much for it. Who wants land that was a fill once? Maybe some cheap-ass developers. Maybe the Mayflower would want it. Pave it over so people have a nice place to park when they hold the U.S. Open next summer. Real nice for us."

I was starting to feel a little queasy.

"Why not to a golf course company?"

"Are you kidding? Golf boom's over, Stick. Golf courses are getting bulldozed every day. Besides, I already asked him. He said Ponky is dead as Bob Hope."

Spots started forming in front of my eyes.

"If you're lying, may God take your hearing, too, you Feliciano fuck."

"I'm not lying! Froghair told a few of us last night. Says he's getting the paperwork together this week. Ponkaquogue is Ponkagone."

I felt like I was going to throw up. I hopped over the golf shop counter—nobody was in this early—and called Froghair at home. Woke his ass up.

"Tell me it's not true," I yelled.

"It's true," he said.

"If you change your mind, I'll loofah you daily. I'll give you free lessons. I'll tongue-bathe your cat."

"I'm done, Ray. I'm going to get out before the EPA starts investigating those gas fissures and condemns me altogether."

"May you rot in hell," I mentioned.

"It'd beat Ponky."

The next day I was trying to write cards, but I just couldn't concentrate. I sat there three hours and could come up with only one.

It was a picture of the pyramids, with the line below it: *The Pyramids are a wonder that has stood for thousands of years.*

And then inside would be the line: *Thanks for building them. Happy Birthday!*

I was depressed. Luckily, depressed in a house that contains my whirlwind three-year-old son Charlie has no life span. Depressed can last only as long as it takes Charlie to find you. He snuck up behind me and scared the piss out of me with a glass-shattering burp.

I tried to suppress a laugh while I said, "Charlie, what do you say?"

"Thank you," he said, obediently.

He was so much like Dannie it was freaky. I met Dannie at Ponky. She was straight out of Little Rock, the spitfire redhead with the hair-trigger temper and the gymnast's body and the five handicap that made her tougher than a Woolworth's steak. Back then, she worked behind the pro shop counter at Ponky, and we found out she loved golf and bets and laughs as much as any guy there.

She and I started out as standard FBs (fuck buddies), but after the margarine and the batteries wore out, we found out we still loved being together and couldn't see anything to do but get married. We begat the insanely athletic Charlie three years ago—the only three-year-old I've ever known who could climb a streetlight higher than you can reach, scaring passersby half to death. He was a born Wallenda—leaping off tables and fence posts and car hoods at every chance—and it was always a guessing game whether you could still catch him and hold on to the groceries at the same time.

It wasn't until later I found out Dannie had had a baby girl eight years ago by some hairball who'd skipped town as soon as he heard the news. But she moved home, had it, gave her up, and started over. That was a wound that stayed with her, though I couldn't get her to talk about it. Only once—and she cried for about two hours on my chest, rocking back and forth and going, "I never got to hold her!" But only that once. Still, I knew it haunted her because she kept a little pink skullcap they gave the baby in the hospital in her bottom dresser drawer, under all the long, cotton pajamas I never let her wear.

Yeah, we were that rare married couple: We still had four-alarm sex. In fact, Dannie's motto was "Waste No Woodies," and she almost never did, bless her horny little heart. I loved her for that, for being as open as a 7-Eleven, not just with her legs, but with her arms, with her heart. She cooked like an Iron Chef, smelled good, and taught me how to hit a blade chip. What more could a guy want? I was having myself a first-class George Bailey wonderful life.

But something changed, just a nudge, about two weeks before all this. She'd gone to see her sister in Roanoke for a weekend and when she came back, there was something a little scared in her eyes. I asked her about it once, but she said I was crazy. But I could tell: There was definitely something. She just wasn't quite as sunflower happy. She was distracted more often. Charlie would say something like, "Mommy, could you shoot me out of a real cannon?" And she'd say, "Maybe later, honey." For the first time ever, she'd occasionally bitch about how little money I made and how little ambition I had.

"Uh, duh?" I said. "Have we met? I'm Ray Hart. I was tragically born without the ambition gene, remember? You used to love that about me. You know, Mr. Happy, Mr. Zen, Mr. Let's Just Screw and Then Have an Erik Estrada Film Festival?"

And she'd give me a courtesy chuckle and put her head on my chest and sigh.

Curious.

CHAPTER 2

Two days later I showed up for the Chops' afternoon Betterment of Society session hoping Froghair was just pulling a hilarious prank on us. The Betterment of Society meetings involved, as usual, a few dozen Claudette Coldbeers and a trayful of Blu Chao's famous ninety-nine-cent fried-egg SPAMwiches—her own tragic invention—and erudite discussions on recent developments in society.

Today's topic seemed to be the three weirdest grocery items anybody has ever bought—in a group—that might make a cashier blush.

"A gallon of mustard, a box of tampons, and nose-hair clippers," tried Hoover.

"Preparation H, Cheese Whiz, and a rolling pin," said Blind Bob.

"A plunger, a zucchini, and a box of birthday candles," said Two Down.

And it was at that moment when Dannie walked in, holding Charlie, looking like she'd just seen a ghost. She let Charlie down and he immediately dived for Resource, who didn't see him coming and went tumbling backward in his chair—beer, cards, Charlie, and all.

"What's wrong, Baby?" I said.

"Ray," she said, "it's your dad."

"My dad?"

"Yeah, Baby. He's dead."

The funeral was nice, I guess. Lots of blue blazers and horn-rimmed glasses. Lots of Numerals with names that sounded more like sweater lines. I met Taylor Hathaway. I said hello to Webber Janzen. And it was good to see Shepherd Lane, Ltd., again.

Hey, at least I went to the funeral. For most of my adult life, I vowed never to go. Never go, never cry, never care. But my relationship with my father thawed a few years ago and he'd even showed up three times at Ponky to play with me and allowed me to be his guest at the Mayflower. It took me ten seconds to discover the first difference between the two courses. The Mayflower prided itself on having no tee times. So did Ponky in a way. Of course, at Ponky, if you wanted to play anytime before noon, you had to get to the parking lot, put your ball in the pipe, then sleep in your car until The Voice called out your name.

My father and I had about as much in common as pigeons and backhoes. We never really saw eye-to-eye on things. I liked people and he liked credit reports. I liked being lazy and happy and satisfied and he liked browbeating me into being what he was sure I should've been, what he'd worked and planned for me to be—a pro golfer. I liked my collection of no-account friends, many of whom thought cotillion was the number that came after *quadrillion*. He thought they would all look better with monitoring bracelets around their ankles.

But we were able to at least speak to each other these last few years, thanks to The Bet.

The Bet was a very bad idea between Two Down, Dannie, and myself to see who could be the first to play a full round of golf at the Mayflower. In trying to win The Bet, I discovered that the father I hadn't seen (or wanted to) in seven years was a member there. Somehow he got mixed up in The Bet and the stakes got ridiculously large. I'm still not sure who won, but I know that at the end of it, Dannie and I ended up married, Two Down ended up nearly dead and had to move back to Chicago, and my dad seemed to be able to at least tolerate playing a round of golf with me now and then, and vice versa.

He was still stuffier than Janet Reno's lingerie drawer and he still refused to sit down anywhere at Ponky—"Uh, Raymond, I really must get to my paddle tennis game," he'd say, looking around at our post-Chernobyl furniture. He still took underhanded shots at my sputtering writing career: "When you finally decide to give up the little writing thing, I'm sure I could put in a good word for you with the boys in Systems Operations down at the bank."

And so we pretty much stayed about as close as the hands at six o'clock. But when he dropped over dead of a heart attack at sixty-one, at least I went. That's more than I can say of my mom, who had this reaction when I called her in San Diego with the news: "He had a heart?"

The cemetery happened to be right across the street from Ponky. You could've seen the procession pull in without leaving the front window. In fact, when Dannie and I and Charlie came back into the Ponky clubhouse, Two Down and Cementhead were paying off on the Cemetery Game, a Ponky original. The idea of the Cemetery Game is to look in the paper to see who's going to be buried that day and bet on how many cars will be in the procession as it enters the gate. If you were reading about, say, a Mr. Horace VanDeVeer, former Elk, member of the Retired Electricians Club, longtime pillar of the community, you'd guess a high number of cars as he had a lot of friends and acquaintances. But if you were reading about Mrs. Gladys Schmertz, homemaker, who had twenty-seven cats and was survived by one child in Walla Walla, a nobody, you'd go low, say, four or five cars. And no fair calling the cops to find out how many motorcycle escorts they were sending (Hoover invented that), or the florist to see how many flowers had been ordered (me), or—my God!—checking with the actual *families* (Two).

Cement was paying Two twenty dollars when we walked in. "How many?" I said.

"Fifty-four," Cement said glumly. "I thought, you know, no disrespect, but that it'd be bigger. I guessed seventy-seven. He said forty-eight."

"Congratulations on profiting on my father's death," I said.

"It's a gift," Two Down said.

And then things just got worser and worser.

It was two days later when we all heard that Resource was busted.

It's a shame how it happened. He was running this beautiful little job at Logan Airport. He'd dust it off whenever he was a little short of spending cash. The idea was to hang a hundred feet or so away from a certain incoming-baggage carousel—something ritzy, like L.A., Miami, Hawaii through Chicago—and wait until everybody had their bags. That left only those bags that had been lost or forgotten. He'd walk up like he was late and snatch the newest, biggest bag left. The trick is, he'd have a razor in one hand and a pair of purple polka-dot thong underwear in the other. Quickly— and blocked from view—he'd cut whatever ID tag was hanging from it with the razor in the left hand. With the right, he'd quickly slide the underwear in any outside zipper pouch of the bag. Then he'd walk out like he'd picked up this bag a hundred times, bored. He almost never got stopped, but whenever he did, the guard would always say, "Claim tag, please?"

And Resource would say, mincingly, "Oh, was I supposed to save that?"

And the guard would say, "ID?"

Resource would show them whatever fake ID he was sporting that day. Then the guard would look in vain for the name tag on the bag.

"Don't you have your name on this bag?"

"Oh, was I supposed to do that?" Resource would say.

The guard would sigh and go, "All right, can you name some items in the bag?"

And Resource would go, "Well, it's kind of embarrassing."

"What is it?"

"Well, I think I have a pair of purple polka-dot thong underwear in there somewhere," and laugh, embarrassed. "Now don't you steal 'em!"

And he'd unzip the pouch for the guard, who'd pull out the underwear, slide it back in gingerly, and send Resource away as quickly as possible, if not sooner.

On this particular day at Logan, everything was going fine until the guard reached into the side pouch and pulled out the purple polka-dot thong underwear—*and* a framed picture of the actual suitcase owner with his wife and kids, all five of whom happened to be freckled and redheaded. Resource froze.

"I'm adopted," he said. "That's my brother's family."

"Uh-huh," said the guard, who opened up the suitcase and pulled out a pair of pants. He held them up to Resource's waist and couldn't help but notice they were about eight inches short of his shoes.

"I am *so* changing dry cleaners," Resource said, sweating a little.

"Uh-huh," said the guard, who then noticed something that raised his eyebrows—a short, redheaded freckled man over by the carousel, scratching his head.

Turns out, a review of airport security videos nailed Resource doing it eleven times that month. Then police, upon raiding his house, discovered not just the ten other suitcases piled up in the corner of his basement, but a few other items looking for the right fence—seventeen car stereos, $100,000 in jewels, nine plasma TVs, and enough fake passports to get half of Cuba over.

It's too bad, too. Resource's goal in life was to break 70 and he was really getting close. In fact, he thought he'd done it once—69—when he realized that on the last hole, upon hitting an 8-iron to a foot away, he'd neglected to pull the pin, simply knocking it in and rejoicing at his feat. Only as he was walking in, The Voice said, "Don't forget to add two shots to your score. Hitting the pin while putting."

They say Resource's black face went white when he realized The Voice was right, and nothing we could do would convince him to write 69 on his handicap sheet. Easily the most principled armed-robbery man I'd ever met.

Anyway, it looked very much like Resource was going away to college for a good, long while and that meant, in this case, Bridgefield State Penitentiary, very much an all-boys school.

"Bridgefield State is that prison with a golf course, right?" Blind Bob said.

"Yeah," I said. "You think they'll let him play?"

"No. You think the prisoners work on the course, though?"

"Yeah, maybe they do. Maybe he could work on the bunkers or something."

"Nah. He's too good at blasting out."

"Ooh, you're good."

And we were all toasting a fresh-squeezed Budweiser to Resource's swift return to Chopdom when a little man walked in through the screen door. He was fairly well dressed, in a natty gray three-piece with a sophisticated yellow tie, Wally Cox spectacles. He was an odd little guy who seemed to need a running start to get any sentence going.

"Oh, uh, well," said the little man, taken aback perhaps at the room's ambience, "I'm looking for a Mr. . . . ."

He reached in his suit for a piece of paper. A few of the Chops started to sneak out. Any intro like "I'm looking for a . . ." makes a lot of Chops nervous, as such a man could be a repo artist, a probation officer, or serving papers.

". . . Mr. Raymond Hart?"

Everybody in the room looked away, as they've been trained. I said, "He hasn't come by here much since that whole incident with the pope," I said. "Can I leave him a message next time he's in?"

"Oh, uh, well," the man said, a little concerned. "Yes, well. I was just told he's always here, but, well, if you'd just tell him it's about his father— William Hart? It's about his will."

"Ohhhh!" I said. "Actually, that's me. I'm Raymond Hart. Ray, really. Ray Hart. I was just being careful, you know."

"Right," said Two Down. "So many eBay hounds tryin' to get the autograph, you know."

"Oh, uh, well," said the little man. "I'd have to see some ID, of course."

I showed it to him and said, "So, what about the will?"

"Oh, uh, well. I've got a copy of it for you here." He opened his brown-leather briefcase and pulled out a thick document. "I didn't think you'd want to read the entire document, so I xeroxed the section that specifically specifies you, which is, well, article thirteen, paragraph five. Shall I read it to you?"

"Knock yourself out," I said.

By now everybody was up the nostrils of the little man—Two Down, Dominic, Hoover, even Blu Chao. My heart was doing a little rumba.

"Oh, uh, well," he said. "Yes, well, it reads, and I'm quoting, 'To my son, Raymond, I leave $250,000—' "

There was much whooping and rejoicing and slapping me on the back by the Chops. But I couldn't help but notice the little man had his mouth still open and his right index finger in the air, as though he had more to say.

" '—providing—*providing*' " . . .

. . . everybody froze . . .

"Uh, you see, well, '*providing* that he qualify for one of golf's major tournaments in the same year of my death—' "

The whooping, rejoicing, and slapping froze solid.

The little man had more. "Oh, uh, well. Quoting again . . . 'the year of my death, providing I die before June 1 in any calendar year. If I should die after June 1 in any calendar year, then the qualification can come in the golf year following my death. Should he not qualify, I hereby bequeath said $250,000 to the Mayflower Club Junior Golf Foundation.' And since he *has* died before June 1—date of passing being May 24—well, then, you must qualify this year."

The only sound you could hear was Blu Chao's burgers burning. We were all struck mute.

Finally, Cementhead spoke up. "Damn, Ray. You oughta keep that money. The Mayflower's got more 'n enough, don't you think?"

Among Chops, there is a universal truth known as the good-bad.

The good-bad is any instance in which you try to look like a good guy when, in actuality, your motives are crooked as a corkscrew. For instance, when you offer to buy a guy a beer when you know he just joined AA, that's a good-bad. You look for your opponent's ball inbounds when you've already spied it sitting out-of-bounds. Good-bad. You finally offer to pay off that twenty-dollar IOU when you know the guy doesn't have change for a C-note. The good-bad.

Until now, the nastiest good-bad in Ponky history was the good-bad Two Down pulled on Cementhead one wintry day over at Franklin Park. Two was into Cement for $140, a lot even for a union plumber such as Cementhead. Cementhead hit a ball that wound up three feet onto the frozen pond.

"Am I allowed to hit it?" Cementhead asked.

"Absolutely," said Two Down with a smile.

There were no "thin-ice" warning signs, so Cementhead gingerly made his way out on the ice and took his stance. That's when the ice split under him, sinking him into the icy water to his knees.

While Two nearly ruptured his spleen laughing, Cement climbed out, dried off a little, fished the ball out with his retriever, took his drop, hit the ball up short of the green, chunked it on, and three-whacked it for seven. Two Down sank a five-footer for his eight.

"At least I beat you on that hole," Cement said.

"Excuse me?" asked Two Down.

"I had seven and you had eight."

"Not quite, MENSA boy," said Two Down. "You made a nine. You grounded your club in a hazard when you fell through the ice."

Two Down would later admit he had been blocking the DANGER! THIN

ICE! sign when Cementhead asked him if he could play it off the ice. Now *that's* cold.

But this good-bad slunk under them all: You make it sound like you're giving your son $250,000 when you know he won't take it. He knew I'd never go try to qualify for a major because it's the one thing he'd always hassled me to do. If I'd wanted to go the great courtesy-car route, driving and flying around, barely making cuts, having to suck up to ass-bag plaid-plagued country-club guys who "sponsor" you, living your life from one Red Roof Inn to the next, I'd have done it years ago. If I'd have wanted to live life as the 124th-best player on the PGA Tour, popping beta-blockers for my nerves and turning the sport I love into something that would compare only to a tapeworm on the FunMeter, I would've. But I never wanted that life and my father could never get over it. So now, from the coffin, he was getting the last laugh. The first-ever from-the-grave good-bad.

And just to rub lemon juice into the wound, he was going to give that money to Junior Golf, the lamest charity ever to exist. Here we have a huge percentage of inner-city kids in America with no health insurance. We have millions of inner-city kids living under the poverty level. And the answer to it all is (ta-da!) Junior Golf. That'll do it! Hey, kid, we know you haven't had a square meal since Tuesday, your dad left two years ago, and your mom is working two jobs a day so you're home alone most of the time. Do you know what you need? You need to learn how to hit a knockdown 6-iron! You need to learn the rule difference between an immovable object and a burrowing animal! You need to learn a game you'll never be able to afford once your six useless Junior Golf weeks are over!

Anyway, I wasn't going after the $250,000, no way, never.

I dropped by Ponky. I bought a beer and flopped down in the chair right under the sign that read KITCHEN OPEN. Underneath it, six guys had signed up.

"Stick, you giant feminine douche!" Two Down cried. "You're scared! You could do this! You're good enough! Hell, most days out here you break par, and anybody who can break par on these piece-of-shit buckled greens and foxhole bunkers and goat-run fairways can break par anywhere!"

"What are you so scared of?" said Blind Bob, who was putting on the carpet, having paced off the distance between the ball and the Dixie cup he was putting into eight feet away. "Finding out your father was right all along and you wasted your life?"

"Thanks, Bob," I said. "Why don't you go fuck a German shepherd?"

Then Hoover chimed in. "Ray, I've done some research into this. And your choices are limited as far as qualifying for a major. You could've tried to win the National Publinks Championship, reserved for players who've never belonged to a country club. That's you. The winner gets an invitation to the Masters. But that's already passed. You could've tried for the U.S. Open, which, as the name implies, is open to players with two handicaps or better. And, according to the computer, you're a plus-two. But entries closed April 28, which was almost a month ago. You could still try to win the U.S. Amateur in August. The winner gets into the Masters. But I think your best odds—and you'd have to hurry—would be to qualify for the British Open. Qualifying begins July Fourth and ends on July 11."

"No problem, Hoov," I said. "I happen to have a really good working knowledge of some of those British Open qualifying courses. Where is it being played this year, Weasel-on-the-Humping or Lower Clottedcream?"

"Actually," said Hoover, consulting his stack of papers, "this year, it's at Silloth-on-Solway, Ashdown Forest, and a course called the Gog Magog."

"Jesus!" I said, tossing my hands up.

The Chops immediately began mulling over life at a course known as the Gog Magog, as I dreaded they would.

"You think after they play, they down a few Grog Magrogs?" said Two.

"Do you think you get a free drop out of the gog?" asked Cementhead.

"Yeah, but not the magog," said Bob, who was now changing the channel on the TV.

"Wonder if there's a lot of fog at the Gog Magog?" asked Two.

Across the way, Dom, the World's Most Sexual Man, seemed to have no interest in the proceedings. He was doing what he was almost always doing lately, mooning over the new luscious in the pro shop, Kelly van

Edelstein, or, as we called her, Kelly van Edible. Kelly was about twenty-five and curvier than the Pacific Coast Highway. She had this long brown hair and green eyes and drop-dead ass that would make the pope crumple his pointy hat. Guys would come in for a bucket of balls and end up leafing through the one stack of flammable Ponky sweaters for an hour and a half just to smell her as she walked by.

Dom, though, king of the swinging dicks, Mr. NeverMiss, the Southie stud who'd gotten more women into bed than Wamsutta, had checked into Monkville with her. Nothing he tried worked, and he'd tried everything—charm, smarm, dirty, clean, lies, love, rock, country, pets, bets. He even tried Christian. Nothing. Nada. Bupkus.

He sighed. "I'd let her run over me in her cah and then eat her tires," he said. "Didn't you rogah Dannie when she was doing this job?"

"Yeah, but I don't think you'd like how it'd turn out," I said. "I ended up marrying her."

He shuddered. The m-word.

Two and I had known Dom since junior high—he was our hero, best jock in high school, only freshman we'd ever known with a fu. I'd never seen Dom defeated, but this one seemed to have no solution. And it was driving him bonkers. Here was Dom, a man whose every fiber and utterance and thought was for, by, and about sex. And here was a woman who oozed sex from every below-the-hip pair of jeans she wore, from every cut-down golf shirt, from the tip of her Pantene hair to her purple toenails and every delicious tan cell in between. And he couldn't crack her safe.

Worse, she always seemed to be especially nice to me. Now, Dom looked like John Travolta's more handsome brother, dark, perfect stubble, bedroom eyes. I looked kind of like Bob Saget with curlier hair, or the guy who gets the second-best-looking girl in a group of three. I'm not bad, but I was no Dom, who would get all three. And yet Kelly was always giving me, "Hiiiii, Ray," and "Wanna go play a few holes, Ray?" And once, when it was just her balancing the register and me trying out a new putter on the carpet, she said, "How come you never wanna see my best up-and-down, Ray?"

Dom had noticed. So had Dannie, and neither was too happy about it. "She knows I'm married and she knows Dom has a crush on her," I explained to my wife. "So she's just torturing him the safest way she knows how."

"I'm gonna torture her," Dannie said once. "You think she likes cattle brands?"

You have to understand, Dom not getting a girl is like the tornado not getting the trailer. He's the best there is. Dom lived for two things—golf and sex, and he always talked about one using words suited to the other. He never broke up with a girl, she'd get "X-ed out" or "I gave her a free drop." Ugly girls were "unplayable" or "out-of-round." Married girls were "230 carries" or "triple breakahs." On the course, he'd hit a bad shot and holler, "Aww, sex fur!" Or, "Chlamydia!" It wasn't long rough, it was "love grass."

He had an all-you-can-eat libido. He'd been hanging around Ponky for two years and I'd never seen it flag. And that's a good thing, because every girl I'd ever seen couldn't wait to be next. Of course, even if Dom hadn't been studly handsome, six-one, dark, and buff, he'd have had his choice of girls. That's because nearly every woman in town knew he lugged around a Dorchester landmark—his cock. It was so colossal it was known far and wide as the Hebrew National. Dannie saw it once by accident at the beach and named it "the ball retriever" because, she said, "That sucker looks like it telescopes." Patty O'Connor, the waitress with the plus-five tits over at Don's Mixed Drinks, told me she called it "the other white meat." We always said if the Sox's Manny Ramirez saw it, he might rub a little pine tar on it and take it to the plate.

Probably half the time he and the Hebrew National found somebody they liked enough to sleep with, it was no more than a curiosity romp for the woman. He knew this firsthand because an electrician buddy of his rigged up a hidden microphone in the women's bathroom at Don's Mixed Drinks one night, allowing us to listen in the storeroom in the back. The highlight of the night was when a girl named Suzi Zwisler was heard to say, "Look, I'm not asking for *all* of it. Just the first eleven inches."

He was not without ethics, though. He had an entire set of rules he lived by. Among them . . .

1. Never expect head from a girl who has too many vowels in her first name—Aimee, Renee, or Merilee. Dom recommended a Patty, a Lynn, a nice Cyndy.
2. Never date a girl with big hands. "Makes yah dick look small."
3. Never stab married whiskers unless they're your last possible chance for that night.

Okay, so he was a few gallons short in his morals tank. One morning we were playing and I asked him who he'd done the night before. He didn't seem particularly proud.

"Well, it got wicked slow last night at Klub Kristal," he began.

"Easter Sunday and all," I allowed.

"Right. And so it was like two, and I had nothing. Zippo. So I hit on this semifat chick. I mean, otherwise, I got *nothin'*. She wants to go back to her place. So I says okay. But *get this*. Her place is a freakin' *boat*. She lives on a boat! In a mariner! Pretty nice boat, though. So we get on the boat, I fire some ink in her, she falls asleep. But now I got the escapes, right? Feelin' clammy. And I know this skank is gonna keep callin' me and callin' me forevah. And I can't have that, right? So what I do is, I sneak out of her bedroom, get off the boat, untie it, and give it a kind of kick with my leg. Last I looked, she was floatin' t'ard Newfoundland."

Everybody stopped talking and just kind of stared at him in disbelief.

He looked at us. "What?" he asked.

Our mouths were agape.

"What?"

"Dom," I said at last. "You pushed a woman, alone in a boat, out to sea? In the middle of the night? On Easter Sunday?"

All eyes were on him.

"Stick," he said to me, imploringly. "I *said* she was fat."

Thin, fat, tall, small, hot, not, it didn't matter. The World's Most Sexual Man had never been stymied. Until now.

"Look at those heatahs, man," he said without taking his eyes off Kelly van Edible. "I call 'em Shock and Awe."

"Still no in-and-out privileges, huh?"

"No."

"Dom, have you just tried being yourself?"

"Yep."

"Damn! You *are* desperate!"

"I can't even get her to *look* at me."

"C'mon, Dom, you've had more pussy than the Boston Humane Society," I said. "Who cares about one you can't have?"

He grabbed me hard by the shoulder. "You don't get it," he said with desperation in his eyes I'd never seen before. "I think I'm in *love*. This is Fort Knox for me. This is my Mount Evarest. Every girl I've slept with 'til now has been nothin' but a bucket of practice balls.

"I just need to split this girl once and I can die happy."

"I thought you said the night that deb jacked you off with a cored peach was your Everest."

"No, this is it for me," Dom finally said, his jaw set firm, his hand on his package, his eyes staring a hole through Kelly's elastically challenged bra. "I'm gonna think of something. Or I sweah on my last condom, I *will* go 100 percent pickle-kissah."

The Chops just wouldn't let this will thing go and Dom needed a drool bucket for Kelly and I'd already played twenty-seven plus an emergency chip-off from the lounge, through the transom window, and off Nuke, the range boy, so I decided to go home. Inside my happy little family room, though, a cold front seemed to have moved in.

"You want me to make Burger Bombs tonight, Babe?" I hollered.

Nothing.

"Babe?" I hollered again, picking up Little Charlie and giving him his usual present, two Genesee beer-bottle tops for his collection, which he stuck in his eye sockets, turned, and knocked over a lamp.

Still nothing.

My God, there were only five rooms in the whole 950-square-foot place. How bad could her ears be?

I went into my Lou Gehrig retirement bit at Yankee Stadium. "This-this-this," I echoed, "is the greatest-greatest-greatest day-day-day of my-my-my life-life-life."

"I believe it," Dannie said walking in, holding the trash, looking like she'd just found socks in her soup.

Uh-oh.

"What'd I do? Run over a puppy?"

She dropped the Hefty bag at her feet.

"You're going to turn down $250,000 because, what, you're so all-fired *proud*?"

"What?" I said. "We're doin' okay."

"You think we're doin' okay? We hardly got two Pampers to rub together! You think I like buyin' dresses at Costco? You think I'm workin' on my new *1,000 Ways to Doll Up Ramen* cookbook?"

"What about that five thousand we have in the CD?"

"We can't touch that, Ray! That's for Charlie's college!"

Nasty silence.

"I mean, would it kill you to take that job at the *Dorchester Bulletin*? That's gotta pay more than twenty-five dollars a birthday card!"

"And what? Cover city council meetings? Garage fires? *Bea Spinsmeister turned one hundred today and celebrated by turning onto her left side?* C'mon, you know I'm close on my novel."

"Yeah, the novel," she grumbled.

Like I didn't see her roll her eyes.

"Look, I don't expect you to understand," I said, but I knew she did. She knew the way my dad had treated me. She knew that he had stuck that in the will only as a way to get in one last dig. He knew I'd never try to qualify for a major. He knew I'd never try because it's the one thing he always wanted me to do, always pushed me, badgered me, mocked me to do. He had my whole life mapped out. When I was nine he put up a big poster board in my bedroom, detailing year by year what my golf career would go like: *Age 10—World Optimist Junior Champ, Torrey Pines. Age 14—U.S. Junior Champ, Pumpkin Ridge. Age 17—U.S. Amateur Champ, TPC Sawgrass.* I wasn't his son, I was the goddamn golf robot he was building in the basement. And so when I finally quit playing competitive golf at twenty-three, he stopped calling. If I wasn't going to be his Golfzilla, then I was dead. And when he died, he tacked up one last poster board on my life: Age 38—sell out self and qualify for major.

"Anyway, I'm not doing it. I'll *never* do it. I don't care about the money. Means nothing to me compared to living my own life."

Dannie stared at her feet the whole time I was talking. Charlie was trying to scale the Amana, falling back hard on his butt, laughing wildly, and trying it again. Now she looked at him and then up at me hard.

"I know you feel strongly about your dad, but what about us? Charlie and me? I don't know if you've been payin' attention, but we aren't exactly livin' like Oprah around here. Okay, Stick, you don't wanna take this lifesaver your daddy threw us, but I haven't noticed many checks cloggin' our mailbox, either. You won't take a regular job. I don't know what to do."

She started to cry. Nothing seemed quite right with her lately.

"Babe, the novel is—"

"Sure! Sure it is!"

She started to walk out. I started to get pissed. Partly because the truth was, I'd already finished the novel and my publisher had rejected it.

"Wait! Let me get this straight. You're pissed I'm not going to let my life be run by a fucking will?"

"No, Ray. I'm just sad that so much of the time it's like you don't *have* any will!"

. . .

The next morning I tried to patch it up. Dannie and those first-place mams were getting out of the shower. That clicked the toggle over on Coach Johnson.

"Hey, gorgeous," I called.

Nothing.

"Baby, let's forget it," I yelled, admiring her breathtaking ass.

Nothing.

I let my head fall back onto the pillow.

"Man, I'd sure love somebody to jump on my face right now!" I hollered, half forlornly.

And then suddenly I heard a wild-Indian scream—"Yeeeeeeahhhhh!"—and opened my eyes just in time to see Charlie's butt falling out of the ceiling onto my face. There was no way to turn. It was over in an instant. The pain in my nose and face felt like a thousand icepicks.

I was yowling in pain, Dannie came running in with a towel around her, horrified. Blood was soaking the pillow.

"Charlie! What did you do?"

Charlie had finally stopped laughing and started to look guilty. "Daddy said! Daddy said!"

I was rolling on the bed in pain.

"Daddy said what?" she asked.

"Jump on Daddy's face! So I did!"

She hadn't quite stopped laughing by the time we made it to the emergency room.

CHAPTER 3

It was bad enough that my nose was broken and my face was covered in bandages, but when I came back from the emergency room and was sitting on the couch wondering how much a guy could get if he sold his child to the circus, Dannie came stomping out of the bedroom hotter than a nine-dollar Rolex.

"What the FUCK is this?" she screamed.

She was holding an opened rubber.

"I found it in OUR bed!"

And all I could think was "Hide and Seek."

Hide and Seek is a very dastardly little game Two Down and I invented in high school. At that moment in my life, I dearly wished we hadn't.

It started out, freshman year, Dorchester High, as a joke. Two put half a joint from the night before on my desk just as our teacher, Mr. Brown, was about to collect a biology quiz. We'd occasionally light one up out on the far-flung 5th hole during golf practice, but now it was on my desk and Mr. Brown was standing right over me with his hand open.

"Let's have it," he said.

And in one very smooth swoop, I picked up the quiz with my left hand, swept the joint off the desk with my paper into my right hand, and handed the quiz up to Mr. Brown.

"Thank you," he said, moving on.

Two was grinning. I flipped him off with a scratch of my head, but now I had the joint. I had the power. I struck back three weeks later during his graduation party at his parents' house. His mom was giving people tours of the home and I wandered up to Two Down, who was happily guzzling a Dr. Pepper, and said, "Wanna play Hide and Seek, Doobie Bro?"

He spat the Dr. Pepper all over the coffee table.

"You *wouldn't*," he said.

"I did," I said.

"Today?"

"Ten minutes ago."

He went sprinting to his room to find, to his utter horror, his mom, Principal Hoback, and the family doctor getting the grand tour of the room he shared with three of his brothers. Two was starting to sweat like a Bikram yogi. I watched from the door with a cantaloupe-slice smile on my face.

Two was looking madly around to see where I'd hidden the joint. Not on his desk. Not on his bookshelf. Not taped to the closet door.

He spun wildly and looked at me like the guy about to take a knife in a Hitchcock movie.

He mouthed: "I'm beg-ging you."

"Sorr-ee," I mouthed back.

"Leonard has won quite a few golf trophies," his mom bragged. (He had—but they were all just "participation" trophies.) She was about to give his dresser the Carol Merrill *Let's-Make-A-Deal* hand sweep when Two Down saw it—I'd taken out the little golf club from one of the little trophy guy's hands and replaced it with the joint. The little guy was at the very top of his backswing, the first golfer ever to use an overlapping grip on a spliff.

Two dived for it, covering the dresser with his entire body.

"Leonard!" his mom cried. "What's *wrong* with you?"

He was trying to look at her while reaching under his body to find the joint.

"Oh! Uh! Well, you know, Mom," he stammered. "I'm kinda shy about, you know, bragging on my, uh, golf."

"Nonsense! Let the principal *see* them."

But Two was staying put. She was yanking back on his shoulders.

"Mommmmmm," he whined desperately. "Don't make me!"

"Aww, show them, Leonard," I said, trying to be helpful.

He shot me a glance that could melt titanium.

"Yes, let us see, son," said Principal Hoback, wiggling his Swiss-clockmaker eyebrows.

His mom and the principal began dragging him away from the dresser by his feet, Two Down holding on to the back with all his might. The trophies started springing free one by one. Soon all five were lying there, toppled and bent, as though they'd been through a war. But none of them had the joint.

His mom straightened them up. "Honestly, Leonard," she griped. "Was that so hard?" The three of them nodded *very nice, very nice* and went on to the next room.

When they'd left the room, I was laughing so hard I was crying. Suddenly Two spun around and opened his mouth wide and stuck out his tongue. And there it was.

Since then, Hide and Seek, like Denny's chili cheeseburger, has come up about once a year. There are only three rules: 1) You have to warn the other guy; 2) If you get caught, you can't rat out the other guy, no matter how hateful your circumstances; and 3) You cannot go longer than a year without playing it. It could be anything. Didn't have to be a joint. It could be any incriminating object. I think I last got him by sneaking a gay *Butt Boys Monthly* into his bag when he was playing somewhere swank. The caddy brought it out right in front of his boss and went, "Is this for tight lies?"

But where the hell was my warning this time? And now I had Dannie, about to turn eggplant purple, ready to rip off my dick and choke me with it.

"Babe, it's not what you think," I began. "It's—"

". . . that slut Kelly in the pro shop, isn't it?!"

"No!"

"I'm sure it is! What game are you and her playin', huh, Stick? Bronc and cowboy?" She barked a few more examples—warden and prisoner?—and then broke up sobbing.

Okay. Screw rules. I was going to be damned if I was going to take a .32-caliber bullet for Two Down's skinny ass.

"Honey, there's a simple explanation," I said calmly. "It's a game Two Down and I have played since high school called Hide and Seek."

"Oh, just shut up, Ray!"

"No, we try to get the other guy in trouble by—"

"Out!" she said, coming at me with the fireplace shovel. "Get the hell out!"

Charlie happily picked up the fireplace tongs and started coming at me, too.

I got out.

So now I had a fractured nose and a flaming wife and when I got to Ponky, the big freeze from everybody there.

I walked in and nobody said a word about my nose, which was pulsing like a marching-band drum. Nothing. From anybody.

"Yeah, it hurts a shitload," I said to nobody in particular.

"Yeah, my son did it. Funny how it happened." Still nothing.

"You're gonna laugh. You are. When I said I wished somebody would come and jump on my face, my son thought he meant *anybody*. Hilarious, no? And he came running up out of nowhere and jumped from about three feet onto my nose! Sure does suck. Damn straight. Thanks for your concern."

Zero love. Even Blu Chao, the Cambodian cook, wouldn't look up at me. I usually at least got an "Enjoy please, Mr. Stick?"

Two Down came up.

"You really want to see this place become a parking lot? After all the great times we've had here?"

"Why is this all up to me?" I said. "And thanks for the Hide and Seek warning, you Iraqi. I'll be sleeping at your place for a month."

His face fell. "You didn't get my text message?"

"No, I didn't get your fucking text message."

He checked his phone. "Shit. I guess I didn't send it. I'm terrible with this damn phone."

"Oh, well, that makes me feel better."

"You can sleep at my new place," he said.

"What new place?"

"I moved into the Sunrise Assisted Living Home yesterday," he said.

"No you didn't."

"Yes."

"You really did? *Really?* 'Cause you are one sick puppy if you did."

"Stick, they make your bed! Three squares a day! Movie every night! Why not? You don't have to be sick or anything. Besides, my cousin runs it and gave me a great deal, 'cause they have too many empty rooms. Plus, I made fifty dollars off Mrs. Pilkrants playing cribbage last night. I coulda made twice that, but she kept falling asleep."

"You're thirty-eight years old!"

"So? There's no age limit!"

"Yeah," Dom said. "Great place to meet chicks."

"You want me to call Dannie or not?" Two said.

"No, I want you to die in a pileup on I-95."

"I'll call her."

"Right. Like she'd believe you. She'll think I force-fed you a bullshit story to tell her."

I took a deep breath and looked around the room. Nobody was looking at me. "Anyway, that's not what I wanted to talk about. Look, the thing is, about Froghair selling, we can find a way out of this. What's Froghair want, anyway?"

"He's asking for $2 million, but he'll never get it," Blind Bob said. "He might get $1.5."

"Okay, so we could go in as a whole, all of us. What would the bank loan us if *we* ran Ponky? All of us?"

"Buncha guys driving '82 K-cars?" Bob said. "They'd want 20 percent down, so that's, what, $300,000?"

"Okay, so that's a shitload. But maybe they'd give it to us for 15 percent down if we make a big stink about losing a valuable community asset and all that. So we'd need, what, $225,000? Okay, everybody, what do we all have saved up that we could put into this thing?"

Everybody was into it except Dom. "Look, I wanna help, but . . ."

"But what?" Two said. "Man, we all need to be part of this."

"Well, I do have fifteen hundred, but I was saving it fah my Winnerbago."

Everyone paused. Dom, the World's Most Sexual Man, a guy who lived in a crappy apartment just so he could drive a used Porsche 911, was going to trade it in for a Winnebago?

"Yeah!" he said. "Check it out! I can bag more wool that way! Get a girl at 10:00, schtoink her, have her back in the club by midnight, get anothah at 1:00, plank her by 2:00, and kick her ass out by 2:30!"

We shamed him into it. So between the five of us—Dom, Cement (credit union account), me (Charlie's college savings), Two (Christmas Club), and Bob (vacation fund)—we had a total of $12,300 ready to invest. And that included $100 in change we were sure we had in our golf bags and couch cushions. That might buy us a golf cart but not a golf course.

"We're so hosed," Dom said.

We mulled over the death of Ponky and how much we hated Froghair.

"Cheap sonofabitch," Two said. "I shared a room with him on the road once. 'Member that little tournament we played in? That bastard would make me go down to the lobby and make calls from the twenty-five-cent pay phone instead of paying seventy-five cents from the room!"

"That's nothin'," said Dom. "Do you realize he unplugs all his appliances when he's not using them, so he can save on electricity?"

"Hell, for a while he was separating the two-ply toilet paper into two rolls!" I said. " 'Til he found out you can buy one-ply."

A silent and deadly gloom descended upon the Chops for a good ten minutes.

Then Two Down's eyebrows shot up as from a catapult. "I've got it! Let's try Cow Chip Bingo again!"

One SPAMwich, a bag of corn nuts, and a handful of ice bouncing off his head later, Two Down retracted the statement. "Hey!" he said, rubbing his forehead. "It was just an idea."

He'd had it about five years ago. We were trying to come up with money for a decent lawyer for Resource, who really and truly didn't do it that time. He may have done it the other 999 times, but this time, honestly, he hadn't done it. We know, because he was robbing somebody else at the time.

Two said he heard about Cow Chip Bingo once in Montana. The idea, he said, was to take a large field—say, as big as the Ponky driving range—and divide it into squares. The driving range was 300 yards long by 50 yards wide, so that was 15,000 square yards. We would divide the range into 10-by-10-yard squares, which means 150 squares.

"We sell each square for $100," Two Down explained. "That's what?"

"$15,000," said Hoover.

"Right. $15,000! It's like a Super Bowl–square pool. You buy your square and hope it wins!"

"Wins what?" Cement said. "The Super Bowl?"

"No, you hope one of the cows dumps on your square!"

Everybody stopped cold.

"What cows?"

"The four cows we release onto the range! We release one cow from each corner of the range. Then everybody waits to see where the cows take a dump first. Soon as a cow dumps, he's done. He's outta there."

"*She's* done," Hoover interrupted.

"Right. She's done. They take the cow off. That leaves three cows and the rest of the square owners. And it goes like that until all four cows have taken their dump on an eligible square and we've got four winners! We give away $1,500 to each winner. That's what—uh—"

"$6,000," said Hoover.

"Right. $6,000. And even if a guy gets lucky and wins two squares, then he gets $3,000, but we still give away only $6,000. And we pocket $9,000! Bam! Just like that! If it works, we go do it at other clubs!"

Again, we all froze and stared at each other.

"Two Down," Dom said. "That's . . ."

". . . so . . ." Dannie said.

". . . brilliant!" I said.

And so the first-ever golf course Cow Chip Bingo game was, uh, formed. Cementhead knew a farmer who would bring in the cows in exchange for four squares. It took two weeks to set it up. In the meantime, everybody had their cow strategies. Me, I was going to take one of the eleven shady squares in the corner. Dannie gauged the wind every day and decided she'd take the squares that were a little lower and more sheltered from it. Cementhead was going to take the squares the farthest from the burger joint across the street, figuring the cows would be offended.

When the big day came, we'd sold every square. And all those square-owners were lined up along the fences and chalk lines we'd laid out to watch the action. For the Chops, this was the most anticipated event at Ponky since the men in the yellow suits came to investigate the underground fissure burning in the parking lot.

But this promised to be even more of a gas. The farmer showed up in a truck and a trailer and led the cows out, one by one, tying each one to a post in each corner we'd planted. Naturally, there were all sorts of cries of conspiracy.

"That's bullshit!" some Southie yelled. "The cow near my squah looks like it's from freakin' Afghanistan! A cow that skinny ain't shittin' shit!"

"Wait a second!" yelled a guy in a tracksuit and a cigar. "The land tilts away from my square! You didn't tell me that, Two!"

"What?" Two said. "You don't scout?"

On the count of three, the farmer in one corner, Froghair in another, me in another, and Cement in another untied the cows, slapped them one time on the butts, and let them roam. If any cow left the grounds, we were allowed to head it back toward the range, but other than that, no touching the cows.

Of course, that's when all these mooks started with their incentives. One guy had a cowbell, thinking the cow might come toward him. Didn't work. One woman had a bunch of hay, which she tried to entice the cow with. Didn't work. One skinny guy went around with an air-horn to chase cows away from the sides he didn't have a square near. Didn't work. Besides, after about ten blows, Cementhead went over and grabbed it from him and threw it in the Dumpster.

And then a very weird thing happened. Three of the cows wandered toward one single square and stayed there. This happened to be Two Down's square, near the far corner. "Yes!!!" Two Down screamed. "Yes, yes, yes!!! Oh, baby! Stay right there! Don't move, you beautiful big bovines!"

And they didn't. And five minutes into it, one took a dump right there.

"Ayyyeeeahhh!!!" Two Down yelped. "Bingo! Bingo Bessie! Yeah, you gorgeous heifer, you!"

The farmer came out and led her off. Three minutes later, another one dumped on Two's square.

"Yeeee-hawww!" Two Down yelped, doing 360s in the air. "Two times, baby! Two for two! Three large, Marge!"

But when the third dumped in his square seven minutes later, we had a revolt on our hands.

"What the hell?" a big guy in a Members Only jacket growled. "I never seen anything like this. Cows don't all cram together like that. Somethin' funny's goin' on." He stalked out to the square to investigate. A few dozen others followed, including many Chops. One of them dragged Two by his arm.

"What?" Two Down crowed. "Jealous? You didn't scout your cows, suckers! I *know* cows, baby! Do you have any *idea* how much milk I down?"

But the big guy was squatting down, digging under the grass, when he found something. "Salt!" he said, yanking out a piece. "There's a buncha salt under here! Somebody buried salt here!"

Two looked like he'd just been caught with the microfiche. "Whaddya know?" he said. "There's salt under that square? How lucky can I get? But I'll bet there's salt under a lot of this land!"

Everybody stared at him.

Two stuck his chin out. "Pay me my money, Froghair. I won fair and square. I just happened to pick the right square. I mean, what are the odds?"

And as he started to walk purposefully toward Froghair and his $4,500 payoff, a curious thing happened. The fourth cow followed behind him, nuzzled his butt, then tried to bite his pocket. Two Down screeched and ran like a schoolgirl. He ran and the cow ran after him.

Two guys on that sideline grabbed him.

"What's in your pocket?" Mr. Members Only growled.

And when they turned it inside out they found—salt.

"Okay, so I like margaritas!" Two said.

Anyway, Cow Chip Bingo was definitely out this time. We were all scratching our heads when Dom leaped up like somebody had electricified his chair.

"Hey!" he yelped. "You remembah about two months ago? When those big-time gamblahs came here, looking for anybody that wanted to bet high? You remembah?"

"So?" Blind Bob said.

"Well, let's take the $12,000 and put our boy Stick here up against their best guy, at Ponky! Anybody that hasn't played Ponky is two shots a side down from the staht. You have to know how to play our volcano-shaped holes, right? And you have to know that on half the holes, the only decent lie you're going to find is in the rough, right? And how many guys know how to hit a tee shot that has to go *under* a *Globe* billboard, like on 8, right?"

"No way," I said. "I don't want to lose people's life savings."

"See? You just don't get it, Stick! You don't realize you're one of the best playahs in the state! But the beauty is, you're such a weird fuck that you never hardly leave Ponky, so nobody knows it."

"I like it," said Two. "We tell 'em you're a two, when really you're a plus-two. That's four shots right there, plus the four Ponky gives you. I'd bet my *house* on you beating those guys and I've *never* said that. I'll start gerry-rigging the computer."

"Two, you already bet your house against the Numerals from Mayflower, remember?" I said. "In the last stupid bet we got into. You, me, and Dannie? Remember? You nearly lost your house? Ring a bell?"

"Oh, yeah."

But the idea was starting to grow on me. I was playing as well as I ever had.

"C'mon, Stick," said Dom. "Dammit. All of us can see it in you. If you wanted to, I bet you could be out on tour right now. What'd you finish on the Hogan Tour that one year, eighth? And you left three-quartahs the way through to be with your brothah, right? I'm telling you, you're good enough to play the big goddamn, courtesy-cah, free-hot-chicks PGA Tour right now, but you're just too stubborn to admit it!"

"Okay, just supposing," I began, "I do win and we run it to $24,000, then what? That only leaves us a paltry $200,000 short. You think the bank would take the rest in range balls?"

"We double up on them," said Two. "Gamblers like these guys will double and double again until they get their money back. It can't miss!"

We all sort of looked at each other, even Bob.

"Gentlemen," said Cement. "Our backs are to the driver's seat."

We all looked at him.

"Backs to the *wall*," I said.

"I don't think so," he said. "You sure?"

. . .

Every day, eight hours a day, our poor pal Resource Jones worked on the Prison View nine-hole golf course at Bridgefield State Prison. The course was the brainchild of the warden, who was always looking for ways to keep the guards around the family quarters compound in case of a riot. That's why the guard families had eighteen lighted tennis courts, four sweet softball fields, and a prison-family bowling alley. But the nine-hole course was the most popular of all. It was full nearly every day, not just of guards but of locals and even some out-of-towners wanting to say they'd played one of the most murderous prisons in the country. It even had big handcuffs that marked the tees, and prison-stripe flags.

It was getting so popular, the warden had to go to computerized lottery tee times, thus making Bridgefield the first prison in history you had to have a reservation to get in.

Seeing that he was an inmate, life wasn't bad for Resource Jones. Outside all day on a golf course. Could chip and putt when things got slow. Could watch women waggle. But Resource Jones is a thinker and the more he worked the golf course, the more it tickled his criminal mind. He was doing ten-to-twenty and that's no small homestand. Each day, he was bent on not doing another.

Guards watched the prison grounds crew, but there were only five for fifteen prisoners; and the five were lazier and fatter than many zoo pandas. They spent much of their time sitting in the shade of the lightning shelter, playing cards and throwing dice. Besides, where were the prisoners going to go? The course was surrounded on all sides by double twelve-foot-high barbed-wire fencing, meaning the only way in or out was by the main guard gate near the parking lot and pro shop. And in his bright orange jumpsuit, that was going to be a very tough exit.

And then one day an idea hit Resource. It thwacked his brain like a lemon meringue. He was watching the same boring twosome he watched every Tuesday, waiting for them to finish the hole so he could get back to work. The first man was a skinny Don Knotts type. The second was a blocky, fortyish black man with teardrop sunglasses and a big Panama hat. They were both dreadful players, but quick, bless their hearts—clunking and skulling and chili-dipping along together, hardly noticing what the other was doing until their balls finally followed each other into the hole. Resource was surprised they didn't knock heads putting out. And then each of them would look up and announce, "That's a nine." Or "That's triple."

But that's not what hit Resource Jones that day. What Resource Jones noticed most was that the black man was his *exact same size and shape.*

I had to spend only two nights on the Ponky couch. (All Chops had a complete set of Ponky keys thanks to Resource.) Dannie let me back home after that, but an arctic front seemed to have moved in. Last-place Iditarod mushers have received warmer receptions. All that week, every answer I got came in two letters.

"Hey, Babe, wanna play nine, loser has to wear the Yankees hat?"

No.

"Hey, Babe. Wanna take Charlie down to the dog park and watch him ride the Saint Bernards?"

No.

"Hey, Babe, wanna put on page six of Victoria's Secret and have some indoor trampoline practice?"

"Yeeaahh!" Charlie screeched, doing a cartwheel across the coffee table. "We're getting a trambomine!"

Dannie gave me a kind of DMV smile and went back to whatever book Oprah decreed she must read next. Seemed like lately it was always a weeper about mothers or daughters or mothers and daughters, all trying to find each other's grooves or pants or ya-yas. I kept wanting to ask her who she was and what she had done with my wife.

At least Two Down was getting somewhere. He needed only that week to set up the game with the high rollers. Since divorcing and moving back to Dorchester, Two Down had trouble getting his old job back at Mass Bell and wound up in the bag room at Boston National Ladies Golf Club, the only women-only golf course in North America. It was started by some woman who got blackballed out of the Mayflower. Oh, men could play Boston Ladies, they just couldn't belong. They had to be with a female member and they had to hit from the one set of tees—the ladies' tees. Oh, and they had to park in the crappy gravel parking lot well back behind the maintenance shed. And if they wanted a beer afterward, they had to go to the tiny six-locker room in the basement behind the bag room, where they could give Two Down two dollars for a beer out of the cooler he kept hidden. They even had drug tests for employees, which was fine for Two Down. The only thing he ever tested positive for was balata.

Anyway, on his way to and from Boston Ladies, Two drove right by Newton Commonwealth Golf Course, which was known to one and all as a place where you couldn't throw a bucket of balls and not hit at least one major golf gambler. He came by a few times, asked a few questions, bought a couple beers, and next thing you know he had set up a game.

The day he told us, we were coming in on 18, with bets and insults flying as usual, all of us savoring what could be our last weeks on the trash-heap links we'd somehow come to love. Hoover was trying his new discovery—putting while looking at the hole, not the ball. "You see," he explained, "golf is target-centric, not ball-centric." He'd already whiffed three putts in four holes and on the third, he went his usual double postal. "I cannot fucking play worse than this!" he screeched. "No goddamn way!"

We all tried to comfort him.

"Don't say that, Hoov," I said. "Of course you can play worse than this."

"Absolutely, Hoover," Blind Bob said. "We've seen you. You can play *much* worse than this!"

Poor Hoover. Once a scientist at MIT, he was a man with a 153 IQ who had helped with the human genome project. Yet golf remained an unsolvable mystery to him. It continuously heaved coconut pies in his face and yanked his pants down in front of the whole playground. So much so that he quit his job just to work on his game, day in and day out. He'd married a French's mustard heir with lots of jing, so he could afford it. Only one time in his life had he broken 100 and that was at night during the famous Midnight Marauder adventure during the famous Mayflower bet. But whatever confidence he'd gained from it, it had all leaked into the ozone. If it was possible, he was actually *worse* than ever, assaulting Ponky with a cringe-making array of smother-toes, shanks, clanks, tops, toeballs, and double-fairway slices. If he had broken 110 in the last year, it could only be because he'd skipped two holes.

None of his gadgets, lessons, videos, books, magazine articles, long putters, spaceship putters, hook-face drivers, cut-face drivers, swing trainers, beepers, and knee and wrist stabilizers did any good. There was hardly a day when you wouldn't see him on the range trying some new gadget, lesson, tool. Good thing he had money, because at the end the day, Hoover always wound up slumped in the puke-orange Naugahyde chair reserved for the day's biggest loser. He was such a regular pigeon, Two often referred to him as Direct Deposit, as in the sentence, "Hey, can we get Direct Deposit to play? I'm behind on the alimony."

Worse, Hoover's wife was now on his case. She insisted he was "wasting his life" playing golf. That it was "useless" to play something and never get better at it. She was even grumbling about "withdrawing as his financial golf-enabler." And since she was the only signer on the checking account, she could.

All this was on his mind as he prepared to tee off.

"Hoov," I said, standing ten feet behind and ten feet to the right of him. "Am I safe back here?"

"May you someday enjoy a Velveeta enema," Hoover replied.

He hit a boomerang that was headed directly for Waldeck Avenue. It would've been out-of-bounds at Yellowstone.

Me: "In-flight press."

Hoover: "You would in-flight a man about to shoot a 119?"

Me: "I would in-flight a USAir pilot with one wing on fire."

That's about when Two Down came flying up in a golf cart looking like he might have an aneurism.

"Ponky is as good as ours!" he yelped.

We gathered around while he reached into the front pocket of the hideous skintight pants he had to wear with a fluffy shirt at Boston Ladies.

"Hey, Two Down?" said Dom. "Do you want us to kick his ass?"

"Who?" said Two.

"The guy who made you weah those pants."

Two stiffened. "Hey, you fucks. I got the call this morning and I raced over here to give you the details. You want 'em or not?"

"Absolutely," I said. "And can we get tickets, too?"

"What tickets?" he said suspiciously.

"To the gay rodeo you're in."

"Fuck you fucks! I'm not giving any of you nothin'!"

"Oh, c'mon, Two," Bob said. "Just dish already."

"Okay," Two said, reading off a napkin. "8:00 A.M. Tuesday. Here. Eighteen holes. Stick versus their guy, Dewey something. Gamblers' rules. $12,000 match play. Press when pissed. Both are twos. No strokes, but since Stick knows the layout, he can't play with his woods."

"What?" I yelled.

"Stick, one of the guys knows who you are! You played with him in some tournament last year and won by four shots. And another guy heard about that 65 you shot once at Mayflower! I had to agree or it was no bet!"

"We're fucked," I said.

"Hell, no. You can get your 1-iron out of your trunk. I've seen you hit that thing on a string, 240 no problem. And you gotta admit, you know every weed, tin can, and bad cup yank-job on this course."

"Why so quick?" I asked.

"I don't know. That's the day they picked. Maybe they've got Bible study."

"What, exactly, are gamblers' rules?" I asked.

"Christ, I don't know," Two said. "The guy said they'd explain them to us when they got here."

"Oh, perfect," I said. "And they'll explain what account they want the $12,000 check made out to when they get here, too?"

"Do you need to borrow some Vagisil?"

"I'm just sayin'."

"You'll be great," said Bob.

"You'll kick their ass!" said Cement.

"You marks are gonna get taken like the last piece of bacon," said The Voice.

CHAPTER 4

When I really wanted someone to look at my swing, I always asked a blind guy.

Bob just had this sense of my tempo that nobody else had, including me. He was like that mechanic who closes his eyes and listens to your engine and then goes, "Gungulator. Definitely, the gungulator." After three or four days playing with Bob, my tempo would be as pure as a metronome's.

"Too quick," he'd say. Or "Sounded weak through the zone." Or, "I could hear you grunting. When you grunt, you tend to pull it. Did you pull it?"

"Yeah, I pulled it," I'd say.

"Swinging too hard, slob," he'd say.

He was to golf as Tommy was to pinball. He could tell from the sound of the club whether it was one of the dreaded four dwarves: Toey or Heely or Toppy or Fatty. And he knew my thumps. You know that really nice thump you get when you hit a good iron shot just right? Bob knew mine by heart. "Nah, just didn't sound right," he'd say. "Try it again." I'd try it again. "Little hollow there. Kind of pushy?"

"Yeah, a little pushy," I'd admit.

"Try it again," he'd say.

He lost his sight in Gulf War I, not in battle, but when some bonehead commanding officer thought it would be funny to juggle grenades in front of the boys. In the face of that kind of tragic idiocy, I don't know how he could always be so damn joyful every day, but he was.

I met him while buying a TV at his little electronics shop in Natick. Just a little place, not even a mom-and-pop. A pop, tops. My kind of place. Not a monster Super Colossal Monolith Wal-Mart that puts everybody in town out of business.

I had no idea, when I met him, that he couldn't see. He was this sturdy guy, maybe thirty-five-ish, dark sunglasses, thick mop of Ronald Reagan hair. "Can you see how crisp the reds and yellows are on the Sony?" he said. "Compare that to the tiny little Hitachi over there. You see? Worth the extra ninety bucks." So I bought the Sony. I realized he was blind only when I saw him "reading" my Visa with his fingers.

"Did you say you could *see* the reds and yellows on the Sony?" I asked, pretending to be pissed.

"I didn't say *I* could," he said, smiling. "I asked if *you* could."

Smart guy.

"How do you know I'm not holding another TV under my arm?"

"How do you know I'm not going to charge you for two more after you leave?"

"Can I ask you something? How does a blind guy end up selling TVs?"

"Oh, that's simple," he said. "There was no profit margin in cameras."

This guy was good.

"Did you meet my wife?" he said.

"No."

"See the great-looking blonde over there, talking to those people?" He pointed to a rather dumpy brunette across the store chatting with a customer. I was kind of flummoxed.

"Uh, I don't know how to tell you this," I whispered.

"What?"

"Your wife's not a blonde."

He looked confused. "You're messing with me, right?"

"Oh, man, I'm so sorry."

"The bitch! Tell me something. Does she look like she could've been on the *SI* swimsuit cover in 1998?"

Okay, so I'd been had.

We got to talking and he said he was into golf. I said that was quite surprising.

"Yeah, broke a hundred once," he said. "But I still think my caddy teed me off from the ladies' tees."

Why didn't he come to Ponky and play with me? I said it was a terrible place if he wanted actual grass under his ball, but paradise if he never once said "Good shot" in his life, unless it was to a bartender.

So he started coming around. His wife brought him the first dozen or so times, then he got used to coming on the 51 bus. They kept his clubs there. The first time I played with him, it took me awhile to get used to helping him, lining up his feet and shoulders and giving him distances. That first day, he was trying to hit a 5-wood, 220 yards, uphill, to a heavily bunkered green. When you play with Bob, you also are his caddy/coach for all his shots. "More to the left, Bob," I said. "Shoulders more open, Bob. Little more to the left. Good. You got it. Pull the trigger." He made good contact on this one and the ball rose nicely. "Awww, Bob," I said. "That was gorgeous. It didn't *quite* get over the lake, but you should feel good about it. You really hit it nice."

And Bob said, "What lake?"

I swallowed hard, looked at my shoes a second, put my hand through my hair, and said, "Okay, that's my bad, Bob. I should've mentioned the lake."

And it took us forever to play. The guys behind us came roaring up on about the 4th hole. Their leader yelled, "Hey, you're not supposed to be teaching out here! You want to teach, go do it on the range!"

And I said, patriotically, "This gentleman lost his sight defending our country in Kuwait." That softened them up. They backed off. But when we were finishing up on 18, Bob came up to my side of the golf cart and said, "Scoot over, I'm driving."

I laughed.

"No, I'm serious, scoot over."

"Are you kidding? You'll get us killed!"

"Not if you give good directions."

So he got behind the wheel and said, "Okay, I want to go back up 18 fairway."

"What? Are you nuts?"

"No. Up 18 fairway."

So I had him turn around and I tried my best to keep us from sideswiping trees. "Uh, left. Left! LEFT!"

"I wanna go right by the guys who were following us," he said. "Close as I can."

"Why?" I said.

"Just get me there."

So I got us heading right past the group that had waited all day. As we passed, with Blind Bob at the wheel, he tipped his cap real friendly and waved at them, hollering, "Thanks again! Thanks a lot!"

You should've seen those guys' faces.

Gotta love Blind Bob.

Tuesday morning came and my house was still Ice Station Dannie. I tried everything. I left her notes, flowers, e-mails. I tried everything but quilting her, "I'm sorry. It was a joke." She never seemed to answer her cell. Girl can be as stubborn as an impacted molar.

I set the Ponky phone back on its hook. Kelly the Edible walked up wearing a T-shirt that read IT AIN'T GONNA LICK ITSELF.

"Need a warm place to bunk down tonight?" Kelly said from behind.

I dared not check out Shock and Awe, not in the state I was in. Instead, I turned away and saw Dom staring a hole at us.

"Why don't you try Dom?" I whispered. "They say he'd make Dirk Diggler kick a hole in his mirror."

"Too easy," she purred. "I like the happily married ones."

"Too late. I'm not happily married anymore."

"Even better," she said.

I shuddered to think what Dannie would do to her if she caught her ear-banging me like this. In her Arkansas days, a girl was hitting on her boyfriend in a pool hall once. "Dannie left her lookin' uglier 'n a sack a navels," Dannie's sister recalled.

Then I shuddered to think what Dannie would to do me if she knew I was playing with the $5,000 we had put away in the college fund for Charlie. So I just tried to put it out of my mind, confident that I could have the $5,000 and then some back in the bank by tomorrow.

"Sorry, Kel," I said, holding up my ring. "I'm kind of a one-owner kind of car, you know?"

"That's no problem," she said, grabbing my thigh. "I just want a test drive."

I laughed nervously.

"Can I get a favor, though?" I said. "Can I write the pro shop a check and get some cash? I'm tapped out."

"Nah, they don't let us do that anymore, sweetie," she cooed. "But I've got cash. You wanna just write it to me?"

So we did a hundred dollars and just then we saw through the window a big Lincoln pull into Ponky's gravel lot. The gamblers were here.

The guys who piled out of that Lincoln bore no resemblance to us Chops. Chops play in jeans and T-shirts. Chops have a two-dollar fine for every logo over the two-logo national logo limit. Chops do not shave regularly. These three guys had the full Lanny Wadkins going—the slick pants with cuffs and creases, the shiny belts, and the hundred-dollar shiny Bobby Jones shirts. They had hats and shirts and belts and pockets that read AUGUSTA NATIONAL and PINE VALLEY and CASTLE PINES and all the other sweet clubs in this country where the only way to join is not to ask.

They had new golf gloves and pure Callaway clubs and big, huge bags that looked like they couldn't be carried by Boeing, much less a caddy.

I was ready for them, just not the way Two Down wanted me to be ready for them. He wanted me to melt all the numbers off my clubs and re-engrave new ones, so that my 4 was actually my 6, my 6 was actually my 7, my 7 was my 4, stuff like that. "Stick, these guys are always checking the opponent's clubs to see what he hit," Two insisted. "You'll completely mess them up!"

"Two, guys like this might *just* be able to know the difference between a 7 and a 4," I said. "My God, Bob can tell that much."

He also wanted me to put a bunch of his fake trophies in the trunk of my car. I was supposed to pull up after they got there, get out, pop my trunk, move a bunch of trophies out onto the parking lot, and then pull my clubs out, as though I had so many trophies I was out of room in my house and was now storing them in my trunk. When I told him no, he looked like a guy who'd just had his little toe lopped off.

"Stick, you gotta get aggressive! They slaughter the lambs, you know. When's the last time you ordered a lion burger?"

I just grinned.

"Mornin'," I said to the gamblers.

The three guys climbing out of the Lincoln just sort of glared at me. One was a stocky little Japanese guy who didn't blink. Another was a salt-and-pepper-haired guy with a friendly face, a little potbelly, and a bit of a limp.

"Nice day, huh?" I tried again.

They looked at me like I was speaking Hindi.

"I'm Ray."

A guy the size of a toll booth got out of the driver's side. He had a dog-leg nose and nuclear-cloud ear hair, a forehead that was annexing his hair, and gin blossoms on his face. You could have cut his forearms in half and made umbrella stands. He looked me in the eye, pulled a huge money clip out, snapped off a twenty, and said, "Have my friendz clubz to put on a cart and have them to range, yez? And alzo, you will tell me pleaz, my friendz and I dezire to have to zomething to eat nearby?"

I had no idea where the hell he was from. He sounded like a Croatian who'd worked as a Paris maitre d'. He set in front of me the biggest fricking bag of clubs I'd ever seen in my life. Had to be, no kidding, forty-two clubs in there.

"Well," I said. "There's a deli in there, although I'm not sure you'll consider it something to eat."

I put the huge bag on my shoulder and my right knee about buckled. Was this guy going to play or hold a yard sale? I mean, Nevada Bob didn't have this many clubs. Still, I figured, why not get a look at your enemy's arsenal if he's stupid enough to let you?

I took it to the range and started going through it. He had three drivers, all different lengths. He had every wood from 2 to 11. He had two 5-woods, one hooked-face that looked like it had the center worn clean out of it. He had a 1-iron that looked like he'd hit maybe one hundred thousand shots with it. He had every iron from 2 thru 9. He had eight wedges, from what had to be a 64-degree down to 46. I figure he had one for every five yards, so he could hit full wedges whenever he needed. He had three left-handed clubs—a 7-wood, an 8-iron, and a 4-iron, in case he had no right-handed stance, I guess. He had one sawed-off kid's club, which I figured he used under trees. He had three putters—long, belly, and short. All three were center-shafted. He had two ball pouches and in one of the pouches all the balls were ice-cold. Smart. Ice-cold balls go farther than regular. He had a bunch of Band-Aids, six good Cuban cigars, two Zippos, the *Rules of Golf, Decisions on the Rules of Golf,* a roll of lead tape, two screwdrivers, some rope, a small hammer, and, curiously, a huge tub of Vaseline.

Where were these guys from, *Deliverance?*

I heard them coming and turned to see some Chops—Two Down, Cement, Dom, and Hoover—walking with the big fella, who was gobbling a fried-egg sandwich.

"Stick, this is Big Alexi," Two said. "Big Al, this is Stick, our best guy."

Big Al gave me a dirty look for having tricked him.

"And, uh, this," said Two, nervous as a bride at her in-laws', "is Yoshi."

Yoshi just stared at me, offering no hand, just a slight bow.

"And this is Dewey. Dewey, this is your opponent for the day."

I stuck out my hand to the gray-haired guy. "I don't shake," he said. "Too many guys try to break your balls."

"Strange place to keep your balls," said Hoover.

The gamblers stared at Hoover.

"Comedian, huh, Stringbean?" Dewey said.

"Actually, no, genetic scientist," Hoover said. "And you, I take it, are an astrophysicist?"

They just stared at him some more.

"Well, Mr. Zcience Person," said Big Al, "how about it iz that you go back to your home on Zaturn and leave uz alone? You copy?"

Dewey laughed.

"Shows what you know," Hoover countered. "Saturn has no solid core."

All the Chops hid their faces in their hands. The gamblers just stared some more.

Big Al sighed. "Let uz now all of uz get immediately to the zet-up of bet. Playing for $12,000 American. We are to play by the well-known gamblerz' rulez, yez? Eighteen holez—"

"Hold on a second," I interjected. "What, exactly, are gamblers' rules?"

Big Al just looked at me like I was chairman of the Dumbshit Party. Then he stared at Two Down. Yoshi and Dewey rolled their eyes and started hitting balls off our sickly-green range mats. "I'm have a hard time thinking of gentlemen like you do not play gamblerz' rulez?"

We both shook our head sheepishly.

"Okay. I prezent these gamblerz' rulez. No gimmez. No out of boundz. If you can find ball, you can hit ball. Anywhere. No handicapz, no ztrokez, none of theze thingz. We prefer the give of the zpotz. You know, zpotz?"

"Spots?" I asked.

"Da, spots! Such az, we get to take away your even-numbered ironz. Or you shall allow to ztart every hole at 150 yardz out. Or we must hit from the blackz teez, thingz zuch az theze. No club limit. And for to allow putting any way which iz required that you can to get ball in hole. Match play. You copy?"

We all nodded.

More staring.

"Okay, now iz the time when I require, with no pun intended toward you, to zee the money," Big Al said.

We all looked at him.

"You know what he means," Dewey said.

Relishing the role of Titanic Thompson, Two Down smoothly reached down to his shoe, pulled up his pants leg, and rolled down his sock to reveal the $12,000, masking-taped to his skinny, white out-of-bounds-stake leg.

"No, I muzt *zee* money," Big Al repeated.

"You can't see it?" Two Down said nervously.

"No, I muzt *count* it."

Two Down had kind of a queasy look on his face. He leaned down begrudgingly and *yanked* the tape off his leg. "Ffffuck me!!!" he screamed.

"Was that your leg hair?" Cement asked.

Eyes glassy, Two stared at Cement. "No," he said. "No, that wasn't my leg hair, Cement. I just hate wasting tape."

"Dude, I got lots more in the truck," Cement said.

Two handed the money to Big Al, who counted it and gave it back to him. Then Al reached into the pocket of his silk pants and pulled out five big rolls of hundred-dollar bills tightly and neatly bundled by rubber bands. He handed one to Two Down.

"Thiz much ten," he said. Then he peeled twenty more Benjis off another roll and showed him. "Thiz twelve." He put the rest back in his pocket.

The Chops hadn't been this impressed since the day Dom brought back a video of him screwing Miss Massachusetts with her sash still on.

Each man had his own cart; three guys, three carts. I walked. Two carried my bag. The rest of the Chops walked. Too cheap to rent carts.

"Pigeons, on the tee," The Voice announced. "Pigeons, please?"

Big Al looked around like he might take out a piece and start blasting, if he could only find where to shoot.

"Funny man, huh?" Dewey said. "Maybe he oughta get a cane and a hat and stand out in front of the circus."

"I'll suggest it," I said.

The Chops couldn't wait to see how these swanky bastards would react when their eyes first took in the glorious cesspool that is Ponky, which is to fine golf what Ripple is to fine wine. It was particularly awful today because the guy who mows the lawns called in drunk and they were fixing some of the tracks for the "T" that ran through every half hour and some of the Filipino immigrants in the projects were hanging their laundry off 13.

"Looks like maybe there used to be a golf course here," Dewey said.

"There was," I said. "Before al-Qaeda bought it."

"Think of it," Two Down said, "as Disgusta National."

"What happened to your nose?" Dewey said.

"A big baby jumped me," I said.

"Yeah, I've run into them kind, too," he said.

We flipped a tee and I won. I had butterflies the size of U-boats in my stomach, but I managed to kind of thin my little 1-iron out there about 250 into the right wispy rough. Dewey took a three-quarter swing with one of his three drivers and the ball rocketed off like nothing I've ever seen. It was straighter than Billy Graham. I mean, it couldn't have moved one yard off line. When it flew by me, it was still thirty yards above ground. He was a good seventy-five yards by me. The Chops' jaws fell open like castle drawbridges. They'd never seen me outdriven, to say nothing of by seventy-five yards.

"Damn!" said Two. "Care to pee in a beaker for us?"

Dewey laughed again. "Everybody's funny at this dump," he said. Then the three of them got in their carts and took off. We Chops suddenly wondered what kind of mess we'd just stepped into.

"My Winnerbago is so doomed," said Dom.

Ponky giveth and Ponky taketh away. Dewey, putting like Sam Snead, croquet-style, missed a four-foot birdie putt on the first because he didn't realize that holes at Ponky are pulled out by a high greenskeeper who yanks them out instead of twisting them, leaving the hole itself a half inch higher than the green around it. His ball actually came up to the hole, looked in, and then rolled *back* toward him.

"Nice Mount St. Helens job there," he said.

"It's home," Dom said.

I made my four and we were tied after 1. And we went on tying every hole through 9, but only because he didn't know Ponky. He didn't know *not* to hit the fairway at 5 because it was buckled and instead to hit it into 4 fairway, much more grass over there. He didn't know *not* to hit it on 6 green, which was harder than Trig 404 and sent every shot flying over it into the fence; much better to miss the green short and try to two-putt. He didn't know *not* to hit it long off the tee on 9, because the decomposing landfill underneath that part of the fairway is starting to leak through and the smell is overpowering.

"Oh, my god," Dewey said, coughing. "What is that smell?"

"Nineteen sixty-three," said Two.

Every time I thought I had the guy, he made some camel ride with that stupid croquet-style stroke. Plus, I just couldn't believe he could hit it that freaking long with that Jack Lemmon ninety-mile-per hour swing of his.

There was something weird about his preshot routine, though. Big Al was handing him his club every time, but Big Al would always touch the side of his cart, then grab the club, then clean off the clubface with his thumb, then hand it to him. But who cleans off a clubface with his thumb? And how does a driver hit pure get dirty every hole? So, on 10 tee box, I made a point to get a look at Big Al's little operation.

And that's when I saw it. He was greasing the clubfaces with Vaseline! I'd heard guys talk about it but never seen it. The idea is that the Vaseline keeps the grooves from imparting spin on the ball, which means it can't hook or slice, which means it goes dead straight. And because the grooves can't put backspin on it, it rockets off the clubface. Big Al had hidden a glob of it on the side of the cart, but it's clear, so you can't see it.

This was so damn illegal as to give Arnold Palmer an instant coronary. The Anal-Retentive Banker, aka my father, made me memorize the rule book before he'd let me on the course. I knew every rule.

"You know that's just slightly more illegal than baby-kidnapping, right?" I asked Dewey.

"Nope. Gamblers' rules. Perfectly legal."

And that's when I decided to do something I'd never done in my life: cheat at golf.

I called Dom over to me. "Hey, man, don't you keep K-Y jelly in the Porsche glove box?"

He looked at me like I was a pervert. "Yeah, but I'm not up for any weird shit, man. We got to concentrate on *this*."

"Just get it for me. Right now."

"Okay, what flavah?"

"What flavor?"

"Yeah, chocolate, buttahscotch, or chipotle?"

"I don't care! It's for my clubs, you freak!"

He was back in five minutes.

The Chops saw me apply a thin layer to my 1-iron. The gamblers looked at each other. Two beckoned me over.

"Are you fuckin' crazy?" he whispered. "That's a DQ!"

"Nah," I said loud. "Gamblers' rules, right, Dewey?"

"Absolutely," he said. "I use more grease than Jiffy Lube."

I hit that next one 325 yards, no joke. It was stupid. I could take lines I'd never dreamed of, over trees, over other greens. It was sick. I drove No. 12, a 376-yard dogleg par-4. By 16 tee I was two up. And then Hoover showed up and everything went full-throttle toward shit.

It wasn't really Hoover, it was the guy with him, a bulbous fat man with a Vandyke, a Hogan cap, a scarf, and a tweed jacket, riding one of those little red electric scooters old people on oxygen ride at Target. He looked like Burl Ives after a weekend trapped in the Sara Lee factory.

"Uh, fellas," said Hoover, pawing the ground with his foot. "This is my wife's brother, Dalton. Dalton, these are the fellas. Dalton is going to be hanging around, I guess, with us."

"Yeah?" said Dom. "Why?"

"Uh—" Hoover started out.

"Well, my good man," this Dalton guy began, "I'm glad you asked. Our hale fellow Hoover, here, as you apparently call him, has finally worn out the patience of his wife, my sister, the long-suffering Evelyn. Far be it from me to judge, but Evelyn tells me he's always out here with you gentlemen instead of at home and hearth with her. Now, Evelyn, being a sporting kind, thinks that would be all right if young Hoover were actually the least bit *skilled* at golf and *enjoyed* golf, but he plainly doesn't. Exhibit A, she says, is the many number of putters your Hoover has hanging from nooses in the garage, their punishment for apparently underperforming."

Hoover turned a little red. None of us had ever been to his house.

"So she has given said Hoover until the day our mother arrives for her monthly visit—that day being July 11—to break 100. If he cannot do that by then, she is taking the somewhat drastic method of cutting him off from any and all golf funding. And since he has quit his job, he will have no choice but to come home and begin extensive involvement in my sister's book club. It is my duty—being 'between opportunities' as we say in the world of dinner theater—to monitor these rounds of young Hoover to make sure they're properly scored and legitimate. I am—how would you earthier types say it?—Hoover's golf narc."

We Chops just looked at each other. I was already sick of this guy and I'd known him only three minutes.

"Hey, Slim," said Dewey, "could you maybe take your one-man Shakespeare act somewhere else so we can get on with our little game here?"

Dalton looked mortified. "Am I keeping you from your contest, sir? Well, carry on, then. I'll simply observe the great battle."

It was my honor. I took a little half practice swing and—

"Missed it!" Dalton said, chuckling obnoxiously. "Hah! Little joke there."

I gave a look to Hoover as if to say, "If you don't suffocate him by sticking a headcover down his throat, I will."

Hoover shushed him. I pulled it back and started down and—

Whirrrr!

It was Dalton goosing the scooter, apparently to get a better view. The ball shanked off the toe and into the lake dead right of the green.

"Goddamnit, Hoover!" I screamed. "If you don't—"

Two Down put his hand over my mouth. "Dalton, you may stay. No problem." Then he turned to Dewey. "Dewey, the box is yours."

I glared at Two Down. What the hell was he doing?

Dewey glanced suspiciously at Dalton, pulled it back, and was right at the top when Dalton said, "Might you gentlemen be—"

Dewey duck-hooked it so far left that it sailed the T-tracks and wound up in the Impenetrable Bog in front of 15.

Yoshi, Big Al, and Dewey came at Dalton from all three sides. Dalton whipped the cart into reverse and was last seen bobbling over Ponky's buckled fairways with Big Al chasing him and screaming, "You are human ztain you are! A fucking human ztain!"

Beautiful. The Human Stain. You just knew that was going to stick.

I looked at Two and he was grinning. Guy is a gambling genius.

So we both made bogey there, but then I greased a 330-yard drive on 17, hit a sweet little 9 off the mound off the green to the left so that it would hop directly right and onto the par-4 green, which it did, to six feet. Dewey hit a good drive, but he had no chance. He hit a lob wedge to within fourteen feet and then missed the putt when his Pro V flew off the tiniest exposed lip of an old buried Folgers can. I stroked my little six-footer for the eagle and the match. The ball went in like it was allergic to daylight.

The Chops roared and came and dogpiled me.

"Twelve fucking grand!" Two Down kept screaming into one ear.

"Can I fellate you?" Dom was hollering into the other.

When we unpiled, Big Al fingered the $12,000 and said, "No pun intended, but iz it that you had never tried the greaze before, yez, Ray?"

"Well, only on Caligula Night here at Ponky," I said, eyeing the zops.

"After zuch a dizplay of achievement, certain to me that you shall give uz a chanz to win our moniez back, for tomorrow, yez?"

I looked at the boys.

"What's he saying? Same game, same place?" I asked Dewey.

"Yeah," he said. "But let's make it $24,000 this time."

I looked at the boys. We huddled for a second.

"Whadda we got to lose?" Two said.

"Twelve grand," I said.

"You got your foot on this guy's neck, Ray! You got grease! And he'll never figure out Ponky! It takes years of double bogeys and obscene amounts of alcohol to figure out Ponky!"

"I think it would be a very astute bet," said Hoover. "I think you are clearly the superior player."

I wondered what they could come up with tomorrow to beat me, but I honestly didn't care. I was flat smoking my ball. Besides, I planned on going into Walgreen's right after dinner and buying the Anna Nicole Smith–size tube of K-Y for tomorrow's round.

"Bank," I said to Big Al. "This means 'I will happily bet you' in this country."

"And I am anxiouz to make zome action for my poor friend Yoshi who is standing here?" he said. "Who among your friendz will not give my poor friend Yoshi a game?"

Well, that wasn't going to work because we didn't have any more money to—

"Jump on me, Froggy," said Two Down, pounding his chest with both hands. "What's his handicap?"

I tried to glare a hole in Two Down's thick skull.

I should've seen this coming. Two Down was the best gambler among the Chops, but thrown in against guys like this, he was the tallest dwarf in the circus. He was miles in over his head and yet he didn't know it. It's like Bob always said, lovingly, of Two Down: "He's like the mosquito who screws the elephant from behind and hollers, 'Take it all, bitch!' "

And now he was taking us all in with him.

"Although it iz we do not partake of handicapz, my friend Yoshi would be known to be about a zixteen," Big Al said, gesturing to the ever-silent Yoshi. "For you to call up the Newton Commonwealth Golfing Club and confirm thiz."

"I'm a twenty," said Two.

"I'll check it," said Dewey.

"And further, we require to play Yoshi ztraight up, becauze of your ob-viouz advantage of knowledge of courze," said Big Al.

"No, that would be cr—" I said.

"Okay," said Two Down, "but I gotta have one thing or it's no deal."

"What iz thiz thing?" Big Al said.

"I get one throw."

CHAPTER 5

Two showed up at Ponky the next morning in an immaculate 1995 baby blue Bentley with white leather interior. This was just slightly different from the puppy-shit-colored Pinto we'd all seen him driving since forever. The Chops just about spit out their morning Sanka.

"Well," I said. "Good morning, Mr. Rockefeller. Will you be having boiled children for breakfast?"

Two looked at the gamblers, who were unloading their bags, and talked out of the side of his mouth. "Don't make a big deal. I borrowed it from the garage."

"The assisted-living garage?"

"Stick, these old coots never drive their cars! They must have seventy-five gorgeous cars in that thing! And they leave the keys in them! It's my duty to drive them just to blow the carbons out!"

"Naturally!"

"Telling you, if Dannie throws you out permanent, you gotta come get a place there with me. Nobody's ever in the pool!"

"And if I got lucky, I could drown in the deep end!"

Dom approached, with Cementhead in tow.

"You know we ain't gonna covah your slappy little dick in this," Dom said. "Our money backs Ray, not you. Yah on your own."

Two was defiant. "Who needs you slobs? I got this guy cold. I will flatten him like a tortilla. I'll send him home in a fucking box by 14."

We looked over at Yoshi, his opponent for the day. He was pulling out a huge bag of clubs, was dressed like Freddy Couples, and was already warming up with a swing that looked suspiciously buttery.

"I'd back out now, Two," I offered.

Cementhead spoke up. "Two Down Petrovitz? Back out? Don't do it, Two! What if America had backed out of Vietnam?"

"We did back out of Vietnam," I said.

"You sure?"

The gamblers seemed slightly less talkative than they had been the day before, which meant they were about as chatty as three anvils.

"Mornin' boys," said Two. "Ready for some action?"

As usual, Big Al did the negotiating.

"We are fine. Here iz how we dezire to be," he said. "Your zcratch perzon here will play my friend Dewey again, eighteen holes, gamblerz' rules, for $24,000 American moniez. Your little fellow here, Too Zad, will—"

"Two Down," corrected Two Down. "As in the bets don't start until I'm two down. Got it?"

"—will engage in action with my poor friend Yoshi here. They can have the game az dezirous of themzelez."

The more I heard about this thing, the more I hated it.

We hit some eggs off the paper-thin mats of our range. They enjoyed the sight of Nuke out there, absorbing many direct hits. I noticed Dewey didn't have nearly as many clubs in his bag this time.

For some reason, even though I whipped Dewey the day before, they didn't want any spots this time; didn't want me to take any clubs out of my bag or let Dewey play from the 150 markers or anything. I think their strategy was to play for so damn much money that I'd choke, but I was swingin' "smoother 'n a gravy sandwich," as Dannie used to tell me.

Back when she was talking to me.

I flat crushed my Vaselined-up driver on 1, blowing it a good forty yards by Dewey. Then Big Al said to Two, "My poor friend Yoshi requirez to know if you will play ze game of dollarz?"

Two had kind of a disappointed look on his face, but the rest of us Chops were greatly relieved. How much could he lose playing dollar nassaus?

"Ah, let's at least play fives," Two said.

Yoshi nodded to Big Al. "Yes, this is fine with Yoshi," said Big Al.

We all four made the turn two hours later and I was already up two holes. But Big Al turned to Two and said, "Fine, Mr. Too Zad, I calculate that you are down $10,415."

The Chops all looked at him like he'd just said, "Okay, Two Down, I have your mother buried in my basement."

"What!!?" Two screamed.

"No pun intended, but it waz clear that my poor friend Yoshi outplayed you most as he won 1, 3, 5, 6, and 9. You tied rest. Those five holez I dezipher to total 2,083 yards. At five dollarz a yard, thiz iz, according to calculation, $10,415."

"Five dollars a *yard*?" Two Down gulped.

"Yeah, you bumped it up to five," Dewey said. "Yoshi just wanted to play dollars."

"Man, we thought you meant 'dollahs' as in 'dollah nassahs,' " Dom objected. "Who's evah heahd of a dollah a yahd? Two can't covah that!"

Big Al wheeled on him, all bulled up. "Underztand pleaze, theze are ze well-known gamblerz' rulez. All gamblerz are in knowing what 'play for dollarz' meanz. And all gamblerz are in knowing that if a gambler can't cover debt, then ze frienz are required the covering of debt for him. And if friendz cannot cover debt for him, then thiz gambler zometimez getz covered with dirt. You copy?"

Dom turtled. Two Down looked sick. Cement was scratching his head.

"Yeah, we fuckin' copy," Dom said.

Two looked at Dom with eyebrows dancing and said, "Screw it, Dom. You don't need to be out here."

"Why?" said Dom.

"You got things to do, I'm sure?" Two Down said. More eyebrows.

"No. Oh! Yeah, yeah I do! You got no chance anyways, Two. Good luck, Stick." Then he left.

Very strange.

We had a Blu Chao corn dog at the turn, but, sadly, Yoshi did not die of it. So off we marched to No. 10, where, just as Yoshi was at the top of his backswing and about to unload, the Bentley's alarm horn went off. Somebody had pulled it right up next to the clubhouse and the 10th tee, like it was some kind of museum piece, and now it was blaring. Yoshi flinched at impact and gave it the full Ann Coulter—way right and nasty—all the way across 18 and up against the Geneva Avenue fence. He turned to Two like he wanted to take out his spleen with his driver.

"Oops," Two said. "Must've accidentally hit it in my pocket."

"Yez," said Big Al, hot. "Aczidental."

Big Al made him hand the key fob to him, then he threw it in the cart.

Me, I had to hand it to Two. He's the only guy that would steal a car based on how loud the alarm horn was.

"Let's see," Two said on 10 green after winning the hole. "That's 401 yards and that's, um, $2,005."

But on 11, Two double-crossed one way left into what is known as Hangman's Field because any ball in there usually results in a hangman on your scorecard, also known as a 7. But when we got there, Two's ball was in a painted white circle, ground under repair, which meant he got to drop it. It was a huge, stupidly happy break. With a much better lie, he hit a nice shot out of there and actually next to the green, where he beat Yoshi again out of 393 yards.

No. 12 is the dogleg left and Two Down was in awful shape. Looked like he was going to lose the hole, until he went to his signature move. "I haven't had my throw yet, right?"

Even pitching Yoshi's ball into the nuclear-waste lake next to the green only got him a tie, since Two managed to four-putt. But it was hilarious to see Big Al nearly fry his cerebellum. "Mr. Zad, you are a man who iz eazy not to like," he grumbled.

"And you're just getting to know him," I added.

On 13, Two flash-fried one toward the fence that separates Ponky from the Roosevelt Housing Project—a very good place to get rolled by some of the young Eagle Scouts who reside therein. But he got *another* amazing break when we got there and found his ball settled right next to a French drain. He got a free drop out of that, as the rules state, hit a decent shot onto the green, and managed to two-putt to beat Yoshi. That was another 389 yards.

But then it all started to turn Janet Reno—ugly for your heroes.

On the par-3 14, with me up in my bet by three holes, a terrible thing happened. Big Al was driving along when Dewey's bag fell off. Big Al put it in reverse to try to go back and get it and backed right *over* the entire bag. Dewey was in the fairway, walking along with his 6-iron, when it happened. You could hear the sickly sound of graphite snapping one hundred yards away.

"Borscht!" Big Al moaned.

"What the fuck, Al?" Dewey said, devastated.

"Dewey, I . . . Thiz was very aczidental. I do not know which I waz thinking."

"You fucking cabbage-eater!" Dewey said, yanking out his now-junior-sized set. "Your only job is to drive the fucking cart and you can't even do that!"

Two Down and Cementhead laughed.

"Hey, Al," said Two Down, "you might want to go forward and back up again. I think you missed a couple clubs."

"Fuck you guys!" Dewey hollered at them.

"Hey, Dewey," said Cement, "what's that club in your hand?"

"Six-iron," Dewey harrumphed.

"Hope you're good with it!"

They laughed some more.

Dewey was pissed. "I guarantee I can kick both of your asses with just this."

"Suuurree," said Two.

"Hmmmm," Big Al said, looking at me. "What about the words which were mozt rezently zaid? Because of my oafishnez, my good friend Dewey iz not going to win thiz bet. But, as a gesture of friendship, what if we made a new bet? We owe you $36,000 in moniez now, but what if you and Dewey play for an additional $36,000, American moniez, him and only 6-iron againzt you and your whole zet of clubz, with my friend Dewey getting—what?—a shot and a half a hole?"

I thought it out a little. I figured Dewey could hit that 6-iron about 180 yards. That meant he'd need three shots to reach three of the four par-4s left. He could probably hit the 364-yard 17th in two. But the greens at Ponky are so hard, you have to come into them high and he couldn't hit that thing high. He'd be terrible chipping with it, too. Putting wouldn't be bad. Hell, I've practiced putting with a 6-iron to work on my stroke. But he'd probably three-putt a bunch.

I looked at Two, who nodded and smiled greedily.

"I'll give him a shot a hole," I said.

"Then you muzt require to make it worth our while," he said. "For we would then dezire to double thiz bet. Let uz play for $72,000."

I looked at Two and Cementhead. They were like puppies who hadn't been fed in days. They were practically drooling. I was just swinging it so good, I didn't think I could lose. I felt two exits past bulletproof.

"We'll start on 15?" I asked. "Four-hole bet?"

Big Al looked at Dewey. Dewey nodded.

"What iz the word here? Ah, yez—bank!" he said, with a grin like he'd just passed his citizenship test.

"Wait!" said Two Down. "I gotta see the 'moniez,' Igor."

Begrudgingly, Al reached into his golf bag, some inner pouch, and produced eight of his tight little rolls of $10,000.

"Bank," I said.

The Chops whooped. They were already counting their $72,000.

Two and Yoshi tied 14, so we came to 15. Dewey had that 6-iron and nothing else. But then he did a strange thing. He put a clump of grass behind his ball on the tee box.

Uh-oh.

The grass did the same thing as the Vaseline. The grass kept the grooves from imparting spin. He was making himself a flyer lie on the tee box is what he was doing. I'd never seen or heard of it before, but it made perfect sense. He put a hook Harley-Davidson grip on it and he must've slapped that thing 240 yards. I was out there 300, but in the right rough. I was a little rattled by what was going on. Dewey had only 160 yards into the 400-yard hole and that was just a three-quarter 6-iron for him. No problem. He two-putted for his par and suddenly I was one down.

"Shit," whispered Cement. "He sure is hanging in there for having only one club."

"Uh, I think he's done this before," I said morosely.

"He has? Well, why does he keep hanging out with this guy if he keeps running over his clubs?"

I was too depressed to explain it to him.

Luckily, Two was still getting every break imaginable. On 15, he hit it into some trees right and *again* was in the white ground-under-repair markings near some trees. When Yoshi saw the lucky break, he looked like he wanted to take out a sushi knife and fillet him. I personally couldn't see any reason the ground was marked under repair, but I'm no stoned greenskeeper. Two took his drop and hit a nice 8-iron short of the green.

Suddenly we heard some yelling in the trees, some branches cracking, and a "Lay off!" Then we saw the sickly sight of Big Al dragging Dom back into the fairway by his shirt collar.

"What the fuck, Al?" I said. "Why you manhandling my guys?"

"Why?" he said, ripping a backpack off Dom's shoulder. "Here iz why my friend." He unzipped it and threw out two cans of white paint and a portable fake French drain.

Everybody looked at Two.

"What are you doing with that stuff, Dom?" said Two unconvincingly. "Are you part of that new volunteer course workers' program the greens-keeper has started? I'll bet you are. That's great!"

Dom looked so guilty he should've said, right then and there, "I did *not* have sex with that woman."

Okay, so Two planted him. It worked for a while. But Yoshi dragged Two back with what looked like a very painful grip on his neck to the last shot and made him hit from that lie, paint or no paint. He topped two out of there, chunked a third, hit a fourth into the bunker, left two in there, and conceded the hole.

Forced to play Yoshi straight up, he managed to also lose 16, 17, and 18.

Come to think of it, so did I. That bastard and his trained 6-iron was the biggest hustle in the history of Ponky. He was a warlock with it. He could hit it high. He could hit it low. He could hit a soft cut with it. He could hit a Chi-Chi chase hook with it. He could putt beautifully with it. Sonofabitch looked like he slept with it.

As I was getting my brains beat in, I realized I'd been conned. I thought about all the signs I should've seen. He showed up with maybe twenty fewer clubs than before. He knew his clubs were going to get broken, so he'd taken all his favorites out. Hell, except for the 6-iron, he was probably play-ing straight out of the Kmart barrel. And then there was the fact that he was walking down 14 fairway with his 6-iron in his hand, even though he was al-ready on the green on a par-3. He should've had his putter in his hand. He had no good reason to have the 6-iron, only a bad one. They'd practically set the wolf trap right in front of my eyes and I didn't even see it. I'd bet they'd run this scam hundreds of times. And all that bullshit about Dewey yelling so ferociously at Big Al. They sold that pretty well, I thought. Bravo,

boys. Oscars all around. I decided if you shook Big Al by his heels, a
Brooklyn accent would fall out. Smartest of all, they did it on 14, knowing
that the final four holes were longish par-4s, where he could hit two full
6-irons to the greens. He wouldn't have to hit any half 6-irons, or hundred-
yard 6-irons, or try to kill one. They played me like a dreidel.

"Gee, that worked out pretty well," I said, leaking sarcasm. "You
played those last four holes one-under with just your 6-iron. It's almost like
you'd done that before."

"Ah, not really," Dewey said. "Just monkeyed around with it a little."

"Is there any way you'd allow me to wrap it around your neck?"

Big Al stepped in.

"My friend, upon the time that it iz that you pay uz our $36,000 moniez,
you can attempt anything for your dezire."

A lump the size of a Maxfli became lodged in my throat. The Chops
looked white with fear. Then Big Al said, "Oh, and Mr. Zad. Az to my calculation, you won the holez 10, 11, and 12 and my poor friend Yoshi won
15 through 18. And we are ignoring the cheating that your friend have
done. So that worked out to 402 yards for Mr. Yoshi. Thiz iz another
$2,010. And then it is required that you owe my poor friend Yoshi a total
of $12,425."

There was a horrible long pause.

Finally I said, "Let's go inside and have a beer and settle up."

Two and Cement and Dom looked at me like I had rabies. "Settle up
with what?" Dom whispered as we walked. "We got $12,000. That's it. We
need $24,000 mah. And Two doesn't have *anything*. Where's he gonna get
twelve lahge?"

"No idea," I whispered. "Except, listen. You got a gun?"

Dom gulped. "Yeah, I think I could get my hands on one."

"I'm kidding, Tupac! We'll think of something."

But I had no idea what.

Then The Voice chimed in: "Uh, the large gentleman walking off 18?
I'm afraid you can't enter the men's grill. We require necks."

. . .

Perhaps the only thing worse than owing somebody $36,000 you don't have is to come back into your clubhouse and have Dalton, the Human Stain, yapping away while you're trying to think of how to get it.

"I repeat again, it was Walter Cronkite!" the Stain was saying. "In the men's room, right next to me, at the Marriott. I urinated next to the great journalist Walter Cronkite!"

That's about when Hoover lost it. He'd shot 128 that day with the Stain following him, and breaking 100 must've seemed at least two galaxies away.

"See, nobody gives a damn who you peed next to!" Hoover was saying sharply. "They don't care if you peed next to Abe Lincoln, okay? They don't!"

Already, there was not a lot of love for the Human Stain among the Chops, on account of he was annoying as gout. Bob charged that he was so fat, he stepped on one of those talking weight scales and it said, "Come back when you're not in your car." He never played golf, but apparently had no problem three-wheeling around in his stupid one-person cart telling Hoover why he should hit 2-iron more often. Hoover can barely hit his pillow at night, let alone his 2-iron.

"Yes, Mr. Cronkite himself," said the Stain. "Sir Walter. And that makes thirty-one celebrities or famous politicos I've peed next to. I dare anyone to match that!"

Dom offered his hand in congratulations. "Congrats, man. You're the most accomplished peckah-checkah in America."

"That's a lie!" the Stain said. "Celebrities are notoriously open about their pubic regions."

"That's very well known," I said to Big Al.

"And now we are requiring of the moniez," Big Al said, looking me menacingly in the eye.

"Yeah, well, about that," I said. "We weren't expecting to play for that kind of money *today*, so we don't have it on us, except the $12,000, of course. But we can get our hands on it, posthaste."

"Yeah, well that ain't gonna fly," Dewey said. "We beat you fair and square. We want our money."

"Yeah, I remember you beating me," I said. "The fair and square part I'm a little fuzzy on."

Dewey wandered over to the puke orange La-Z-Boy, where Blind Bob was "watching" the Sox.

"Losin' again, huh?" Dewey said to him.

"Yeah, we miss Pedro," said Blind Bob.

Big Al was yelling at me and Two Down was yelling at him and I was watching Blind Bob and Dewey and that's when it hit me like a bowl of warm goulash.

A plan.

I cleared my throat. My mind was racing.

"You know, the truth is, Big Al, you and your two stooges really can't play for shit," I said, getting louder. "Dewey is supposedly one of the best players at that candy-ass manicured course you guys play, but he never came close to whipping me, not without pulling that lame-ass one-club setup today. Play me real, no grease, no con jobs, USGA rules, I'd kick his ass by five shots here and I bet I'd kick his ass by ten shots at your place!"

Big Al took a step toward me. "I am now wondering why your courage have juzt now arrived, my friend? For you cannot mean thiz?"

"I'm serious as the gulag, Ivan!" I said, moving right into him. "And do you know why? Because guys who play at precious places like yours don't play true golf. Goddamn, my mother could putt on greens like yours. And anybody can play out of perfectly mown rough, never get a bad lie, imported Italian sand, all that happy horseshit. I've played there, I know. Play here. Punch 8-irons off old Folgers cans because you can't get down through them. Hit putts that weave like a barrio drunk. *Then* you'll learn to play golf. I'll tell you something. I'd bet my life that anybody in this room could beat any of your guys—with *real* handicaps, not like that bullshit sandbagger Yoshi's handicap. Anybody."

"Borscht!" Big Al said, starting to get madder. "It requirez not what kind of courze you play. The golf zwing doez not care what kind of courz under it. You either have ze good zwing or you have not ze good zwing. And you obviouzly have not. We want our moniez."

"It doesn't matter? You care to wager on that?"

"How?"

"You say the kind of course doesn't matter. I say it does. Let's test it. You pick one of your guys and blindfold him. I'll pick a guy and blindfold him. We'll put them in the car and take them to a course they've never played before, neither of them, and we'll just see who's better. Total score."

"You are crazy like lobzter whizling on hill."

"I'm what?"

"Lobster whistling on the hill," Dewey said.

"You're chicken like Colonel Sanders," I said.

Al considered for a moment.

"Anyone?" Big Al said.

"With about the same handicap."

He had to think. I couldn't let him.

"What's wrong, piano-mover? You're worried that I'm right, huh? That the sweet course you play is what makes your guys good, not their swings, huh?"

"Again, I say borscht. I will do it myself."

"Fine. What's your handicap?"

"Twenty-eight."

"We'll check it. In the meantime, we can find a twenty-eight around here."

I pretended to look around and think. Finally I said, "Hey, Bob, aren't you about a twenty-eight?"

Blind Bob froze for a second, never looking away from the TV. The rest of the Chops stood still as statues. Ice hung in the air. I think my heart stopped for fourteen seconds.

"I'm twenty-nine," Blind Bob finally said.

Thank you, Lord, thank you, Jesus.

"You are on, Mr., Mr. whatever you are named," Big Al said. "You will be defeated the zame as your buddiez."

Then the worst possible thing happened.

Cementhead spoke.

"But Bob," he said. "You're—"

"Cement!" I screamed. "Don't start on Bob. He is too a twenty-nine. Check the board. It's right there in black-and-white."

By then Dom had jogged over and slapped Cement hard with a Ping-Pong paddle square in the back.

"Owwwww!" Cement said.

"C'mon, you pussy! When you gonna play me Ping-Pong?" He was dragging Cement out of the room while Cement was rubbing his back. "Damn, Dom! Why'd you do that?"

"Hey, I'm tryin' to watch the Sox here," Bob said, never moving his head. "Do ya mind?"

Bless that man.

"Okay, then, tomorrow morning," I said. "Let's meet here in the parking lot? Say, 8:00 A.M. Double or nothing on the whole thirty-six large?"

"What's wrong?" Dewey said. "Yesterday you wanted to double everything. You don't wanna double this time? Not feeling confident?"

"Fine. Double it—$72,000. Bank."

"You have bank," said Big Al. "But when you are defeated thiz time, you better have moniez or we will dezipher ze exact amount your life azzurance is worth. You copy?"

He and Yoshi and Dewey strutted out. We watched them climb into their Lincoln and drive away before we erupted into the loudest, slammingest, whoopingest Chop-pile since we found out Blu Chao was taking a two-week vacation.

That night, in my suddenly noncontact bed, I was freaking out. My sleep number was zero. What the hell was I doing here? Sure, Bob playing blindfolded was a can't-miss. It was genius—desperation, last-second, buzzer-beater genius. You ever try playing blindfolded? I tried three holes once with Bob. The first couple swings you make decent contact, but the longer you're blindfolded the worse it gets. It's exponential. After a few holes you don't even know which way the ground is. But Blind Bob, he lived this. The worst he'd shoot on a new course was 120, tops. A guy blindfolded all day? He could shoot 150, 200 maybe!

But what if it backfired? We'd be into these bent-noses for $108,000. We had $12,000, but then what? What are we going to do—iron their pants for the next thirty years? All three of 'em looked like they had no problem giving your kneecap the full Tonya Harding. Yoshi looked like he'd snap your arm off and eat it like a Butterfinger, for free. And if any of them couldn't do it, I'll bet they had dyspeptic friends who could. Maybe bust your arm, burn your house, make you wish you had died as a small boy.

What could go wrong? We went over it with Bob a dozen times. He'd be waiting in the parking lot with his blindfold already on. That way they couldn't get a look at his messed-up eyes. Just to make them believe us, we got the blackest, thickest blindfold we could find. And we got one for Al, too. No way he could see through it.

They could be moosing us, but I couldn't see how. There are ways to see if a guy is seeing through the blindfold, but even if they got away with it, no way Big Al could shoot better than 120 seeing just bits and pieces. It seemed foolproof.

And (gulp) what if we won? We'd be up $36,000, everybody would get their money back and then some. I could sneak the $5,000 of Charlie's college money back into the bank and have some money to buy Dannie some decent furniture. We'd have to find some safer way to try getting the $225,000 to buy Ponky that didn't involve guys who looked like they could turn you into complicated lumps. After all, I had a kid now.

There was only one person I could talk this through with—except that person was the curvy mute next to me, pretending to be asleep.

"Baby?" I finally said. "Let's talk this out."

At last she turned toward me.

"I'm still so mad at you I could eat bees," she whispered.

"I know, Baby."

"You're so selfish. Christ, you're selfish enough for twins."

"I know, Baby."

"You won't go out get a real job. All you want to do is play golf. And then when you get a good chance to play golf and earn some real bucks, you get all caught up in your stubborn mule pride."

"I know, Baby."

"And you don't tell me you love me enough."

"I love you, Baby."

"More than Kelly?"

"I don't love Kelly."

"Good job. Trick question. More than you did Maddy?"

Okay, she broke the rule and used the M-word, but what was I going to do, sue? Maddy was the girl I'd dated before Dannie, when Dannie and I were just FBs. She was the cart girl at the Mayflower when I was a caddy there and we did scandalous things in the fog that not only would've gotten us both fired but been a big-seller DVD in the back of *Golf Digest*. I was in love with her, but her dad died and left her rich and she left me for a life in archaeology, digging up kings in East Egypt or somewhere. Kind of a sore subject for my wife. And for me, actually.

"Ten times more," I said.

"Whose condom was that?"

"Two Down's."

"Two Down's. Right. I'm supposed to believe that."

"Yes."

"And you refuse to play for the $250,000. You can't even try."

"No, I can't. But I may not need to."

"Why not?"

"I can't tell you."

I knew she'd figure out that I'd borrow the $5,000 if I did.

"Can't tell me that neither?"

"No, sorry."

"All-righttee then. You know what I can tell you, Sugar?"

"What, Baby?"

"Go screw yourself."

Sadly, already tried that.

CHAPTER 6

The first thing Big Al did when we all met in the parking lot was to fire a golf ball right at a blindfolded Blind Bob, hitting him square in the forehead.

"Owwww!" Bob said. "What the fuck?"

"Fine," said Big Al. "I require knowing you cannot zee through the blindfold."

This left many a chapped Chop ass. A lump was starting to form on Bob's head. The Chops were starting to move in from all angles. I tried to head things off at Brawl Bypass.

"Where we playing?" I asked.

"For that, we dizplay for you here a lizt of courz we could golf upon," Big Al said, handing me a list. They were ten pretty creamy places, courses where you got all the tees and ballmarkers you want, where they handed you mango-scented towels and framed your first divot for you as a keepsake. Chops called them Preposition courses. You know, The Badlands at Cape Swank, and The Experience at MasterCard Acres. Severely suave places where bathrooms are called "comfort stations" and marshals are called "guest relations advisers." Where you could never take the cart off the path and there was a little video of each hole on the in-cart DVD player, with your golf education facilitator, Arnold Palmer. Ponky barely had carts, much less paths. You knew right off that Big Al had played them all.

"We reject all of them," I said, handing him a paper napkin from Blu Chao's counter. "Here's our ten."

He looked at them. They were all muni turd tracks. Fresh Pond, Woburn, and Unicorn. Places like Ponky, places where you took a handful of tees, they charged you a dollar, where you pulled into the lot at 4:30 A.M., put your ball in the pipe, and slept in your car until your name was called at eight, places where bunches of guys hung around on the first tee, swinging clubs and booing crappy shots, places where if anybody came up to take your bag out of your trunk, you better tackle them because they were stealing it.

"We alzo reject thiz," Big Al said.

"I figured as much," I said. I pointed to Cement, who produced the metropolitan Boston phone book.

"Let's just pick a golf course at random out of here," I said. "Bob, just stick your finger on this page somewhere."

"That's perfect," said Cement. "Because Bob's blind—"

"—folded, exactly!" I said. "He can do it. Bob, put your finger anywhere on this page."

I gave Cement a look that would wither iron. Dom stabbed him with a tee.

Bob was still rubbing his head and he had a kind of scowl on his face. Big Al held the book and moved it around and Bob pointed.

"Widow's Walk," I read. "In Scituate. Sounds good?" Big Al nodded. "Somebody call 'em and see if we can get a twosome off. Meanwhile, Big Al, you gotta put on your blindfold."

"Borscht," he growled. "I muzt drive the vehicle."

"Dewey can drive," I said. "It's not fair to make my guy have a blindfold on this whole time and you don't. It gets disorienting. Are you starting to get disoriented, Bob?"

"A little," he said, rubbing his head some more.

"Borscht," Big Al said, relenting.

I tied the blindfold on him and I tied it tight. Immediately Big Al got hit by three golf balls, all at once, hard. One in the forehead, one in the neck, and one right on the nose.

"You fuckz!" Big Al roared.

"Okay," I said. "We had to know you can't see through the blindfold."

He growled something in Croat/Czech/French/whatever.

"Okay, you, me, Bob, and Dewey will ride in your Lincoln," I said. "Just to make sure nobody peeks. Okay, Al? Everybody else can follow. Except you, Cementhead. I need you to stay here near the phone and the phone book in case there's a problem. Can you handle that?"

"Got it!" said Cementhead.

Love the big lug, but the man is so dense, light bends around him. This is a man who, when parking illegally, puts on his wipers so they can't leave him a ticket. This is a man who once got slapped sitting at a bar. A big-meloned girl had come up to him wearing a Guess sweatshirt. And Cementhead said, "44D?"

The drive took forty minutes, which was fine with us. The longer Big Al was in pure darkness, the less of a chance he had, as if he had any to start with.

We knew that for sure when we got to the range at Widow's Walk. Bob hit his first ten balls pretty well. Big Al hit his first three, shanked his next four, and whiffed his last three. I couldn't help but grin.

"Stop grinning," Bob whispered.

"You are a fucking witch," I whispered back, stunned.

What was weird was we couldn't find Two Down and Dom and Yoshi, who were supposed to be riding in Two's auto du jour, a 2001 Cadillac Seville. We decided to start without them.

If they were pulling anything on us, it would show up on the first tee.

My mind was racing trying to see how I was the goose here, not the wolf. But there was nothing. It was still Big Al, not some blind twin. It was definitely a course he'd never been to because nobody lifted an extra finger in the pro shop or on the range to help him. There was no change in the bet— "Eighteen holes, gamblers' rules, medal play, you can never take the blindfold off, the other team can check it as much as they want, seventy-two large, right?"

"Correct," said Big Al.

And so we began a bet that, until all this, would've made my heart stop at the mere mention of $72,000.

Big Al stood on the first tee and whiffed.

He topped the second fifteen yards. Whiffed the third and fourth. Got yelled at by Dewey to "Bend your knees! You're six inches over it!" To which Big Al yelled back, "You are dezirouz to try in my plaze, Mr. Geniuz?" He smacked his fifth two hundred yards dead right, lost that one, had to come back and drop, whiffed another, hit his eighth up fifty yards left of the green, and took seven more to get down from there. Fifteen. Bob made a seven, but only because I made him whiff one.

"But I haven't whiffed in three years," he whispered.

"You're gonna whiff like Reggie Jackson today, pal," I said.

By the third hole, Blind Bob led by seventeen shots. It was a laugher, a gasser. If it were a fight, Big Al would've been counted out, taken to the hospital, and killed by Clint Eastwood by now. But then, as Bob and I were walking down the middle of the fairway and Big Al and Dewey were on some Lewis and Clark expedition looking for his ball, Dom arrived by himself on a golf cart.

"Where's Two Down?" I asked.

"Ah, he and Yoshi decided they'd play anothah match at Ponky," Dom said.

My heart dropped into my large intestine.

"You've *got* to be yanking me," I said.

"No, they did," said Dom.

"He'll get murdered! Why'd you let him?"

"Because! I had to tell you about my perfect idea I came up with last night. And I need Bob."

"Uh, Dom? We're a little busy here. Little matter of seventy-two large?"

"No, but this is about Kelly!"

I sighed. Bob rubbed the lump on his forehead. Big Al and Dewey were so deep in the woods they could've been gnomes.

"Man, when are you gonna give up on her?"

"Stick, it's like knockin' over a Coke machine. You gotta rock it back and fahth a buncha times befah she goes ovah."

"Okay, but make it quick."

It *was* a pretty good idea. The crux of it was this: the Boston Lighthouse, a center for blind people, runs monthly Dining in the Dark fund-raisers for singles. Singles pay a hundred dollars to come to the Lighthouse to eat dinner in the dark with each other. Ten men and ten women arrive into separate rooms, then they're led into a pitch-black dining room for dinner. No candles, no nothing. The blind serve as the waiters and busboys. The singles change seats after every course—appetizer, salad, main, and dessert. No single knows who he/she will sit next to. The idea is the singles get to know each other based purely on the things that matter—what they say, who they are *inside*, the warmth in their voices. In other words, a perfect setup for shallow, duplicitous behavior.

According to Dom, this is where Bob would come in. He would 1) convince Kelly that Dining in the Dark practically oozed studly rich stockbrokers, 2) get her to sign up, 3) sneak Dom in the side door that night, and 4) sit him next to Kelly for the longest session of the night—the entrée. Dom would then seduce her by disguising his voice and whispering sweet somethings into her ear. "I'll say all the stuff that's deepest in my haht," Dom said, "so that she'll finally know the true me and have no choice but to love me the way I love her."

"That's nice," said Bob.

"Yeah," said Dom. "Plus, in the dahk, I'm bound to get some elbow titty!"

They settled on a price. If Bob could get Kelly to do it, Dom owed him ten caddying rounds. "And no bringing a date, like last time."

Over in the woods, Dewey had run Big Al's big bucket head straight into a limb. "Why the fuck?" Big Al bellowed, feeling the blood trickle down his forehead. Coupled with the three lumps the Chops had given him with golf balls in the Ponky parking lot, he was starting to look like he had the mumps.

"Oops," said Dewey. "Didn't realize you were that tall."

By the turn, it was Bob 74, Big Al 123.

Finally, Big Al yelled, "I rezign! I cannot ztand for another moment! I require to zee again!" He ripped off his blindfold.

Suddenly I realized one thing we hadn't thought of. It was clear that Big Al expected Bob to rip his off, too, so that he could know the joy of sunshine and green grass again. If Bob did, he'd see Bob's messed-up eyes and our bacon would be crisped.

Bob just stood there.

"You can as well remove your blindfold, Mizter Bob," Big Al said. "You have dizplayed many good golf thoroughly. I know when I have been conned, no pun intended. I think that you have done thiz before."

"Ah, not really. I just monkeyed around with it a little," Bob said.

"Fine, to take it off already! If it iz that you would like to monkey me, thiz iz what you are doing then, my friend!"

"Ah, well," Bob said. "The truth is, well, I'm not really . . ."

My heart caught in my throat. Dom froze.

". . . ready to take it off. I'd like to see what I'd shoot for eighteen. And we already paid the green fees, right? So do you mind, Ray?"

I could've French-kissed him.

"No, no!" I said. "Glad to go with you. We just need the money from these boys."

Big Al dug reluctantly into his pocket for those delicious, lovely rolls. "You owed me $36,000 moniez from our action yezterday?"

"Yes, American," I said.

"Now I have lozt seventy-two back to you. And therefore I'm down to you thirty-six." He handed me three rolls and then counted off $6,000 in 100s. "But I am quite sure you will be zporting enough to require a revenge action game?"

"Nope," I said, feeling more cash in my hand than I'd ever had before. "No chance. We're done. We'll get a cab back."

But then Bob said, "I don't hear you counting it, Ray."

"Feck you, Mr. Bob. I pay moniez alwayz fairly."

"Well, you don't mind, do you?" I said as I counted the three rolls out. Sure enough, the third roll was off.

"This roll is wrong," I said. "You had a hundred too much in here." I handed a Benji back to him.

For the first time in three days, he smiled. "Many thankz to you," he said, stretching his eyes and looking around. "You know what, my American frienz? It is worth the $72,000 moniez just to remove that blindfold. For it iz true that a man not to realize how much he lovez hiz eyez until it iz that you do not have it for three hourz, am I right, mister?"

Bob just kinda let his head fall toward his shoes.

"Guess so," he said.

If it bothered Bob, it didn't for long. We kept playing for another half hour, giggling, shaking each other's hands, and congratulating ourselves on pulling off the sweetest con since Ernie Broglio for Lou Brock. We talked about how we'd pay off everybody their initial investment, then take the con on the road—New Jersey, Maryland, maybe drive down to Florida—until we had the $225,000 to buy back Ponky. We played until we were sure they were out of sight. Then Bob slipped off the blindfold, put on his dark shades, and we drove back to the clubhouse. God, we were feeling good, like looking under your Christmas tree and finding Halle Berry wearing only a bow.

When we got back to the clubhouse, I went to call a cab. But when I got back, I saw a thing that stabbed little icepicks in my chest.

It was Big Al—standing silently two feet in front of Bob, who was walking right toward him, using his 2-iron as his white cane. Before I could holler, Bob bumped straight into him.

"Oops!" Bob said. "My bad. Didn't see you, man."

"I think you are quite right, Mr. Bob," said Big Al. "I am thinking you do not zee much."

Petrified forests had nothing on Bob at that moment. He was stone still.

I was jogging over to try to get Bob out of there when I suddenly felt a hard hand on my left arm and something very cold and hard in my kidney.

"Wanna go outside and talk?" said Dewey.

"Nah," I said. "I'm kinda talked out."

He jammed the revolver into me some more and cocked it.

"That's okay," Dewey said. "All you gotta do is listen."

Bob was walking in front of Big Al like a man with an endangered kidney, too, and we all wound up out in the parking lot, on the other side of the Lincoln. Odds were good, I thought, that they weren't taking us out there to give us parting gifts.

"You failed to dizplay a little fact about Mr. Bob here, my American friend," said Big Al.

"Oh, yeah, we did," I admitted. "He's a Seventh-Day Adventist."

More kidney.

"Seein' as how we didn't know all the facts," Dewey said, "we've decided we'd like our money back."

"Sorry, gamblers' rules," I said. "Same as not knowing a guy can make a 6-iron do everything but make frappuccinos. It's caveat emptor. Buyer beware."

"Yeah, well caveat this," said Dewey, jamming his gun into me. "It's not gamblers' rules anymore. It's Glocks rule. Give us the fucking money."

Seeing as how I felt like a hole in my back would possibly hamper my backswing, I reached in my pocket and gave him the $36,000. I guess I could be grateful he didn't want $72,000.

"Fuck with uz again and we will put many holez in you where holez were never meant for zuch placez, zuch az in zalt shakerz, you copy?" Big Al said.

"Oh, yeah, we very much copy," I said.

They piled into the Lincoln and started to leave. "Good luck at charm school," I said.

They peeled off. Bob and I were both sweating. Our hearts were racing. We looked at each other wordlessly. There was only one thing to say.

"Borscht," I groaned.

I must've had SPAM for brains leaving Two alone in a car with Yoshi. Because no sooner did they get in the car than Yoshi must've talked him into a little bet right there at Ponky, much more fun than sweating somebody else's match. Where's the glory in that? Wonder what Yoshi's voice sounded like?

Two's eyebrows probably started doing the rumba then. "Explain," he said.

It was retold later by Two Down this way: Yoshi wanted to let him play for double or nothing on the $12,000-plus. Two Down said no way, Yoshi was too good. Yoshi said something about did Two Down have any ideas.

Now, normally, a golfer saying to Two Down Petrovitz "You got any ideas?" is the equivalent of a seal saying to a great white shark, "You hungry?"

Two Down's scheming mind versus anybody else's is usually no contest. This is a man who, the month before, bet five Chops a hundred dollars each that he could get us courtside seats to a Celtics game and spend no more than ten dollars a person doing it. Sure enough, he did it. He bought us the nine-dollar nosebleed seats, snuck six wheelchairs out of the assisted living home, and—voilà!—next thing we knew we were sitting courtside.

This is a guy who, one Christmas, ran a Secret Santa game. Everybody drew a name out of a hat and then secretly gave that guy something small every day for a couple weeks, and then a big gift at the final, big party. Real Christmas spirit, heartwarming stuff. Only problem was, every name in the hat said *Two Down*. So for two weeks, he got candy, presents, new balls from fourteen guys, all of whom thought *they* had the worst Secret Santa in the world, since they were getting bupkus. When the final party came, each guy came into the room with a big present in his arms and said dramatically, "Well, I had . . . Two Down!" And then he was puzzled as to why everybody was laughing hysterically and why Two Down had a giant stack of presents next to him. Yeah, we beat him purple but in an admiring kind of way.

Two almost never lost money gambling. He always insisted that his tombstone should read NEVER MADE A PUTT HE DIDN'T HAVE TO. He was quick on his feet from the day he was born. He was one of eleven kids, eight boys, and on his sixteenth birthday, after his dad died in Vietnam, his mom sat him down at the kitchen table and said, "Leonard, because of budget cutbacks, I gotta let somebody go and you're it. You're the smartest. You'll be fine." And Two went out, got a job, rented a room with an old lady named Mrs. Trumbull, got into her purse regularly playing mah-jongg, and never looked back.

But in this guy, Yoshi, Two Down met his scheming match. He was the Two Down of Japan. He was Two Up. Finally they settled on playing for the $12,000, with Yoshi giving Two a half shot every hole. The only proviso was that Yoshi got to tee it up anywhere on the course, anytime, except on the greens. Wooden tees. Nothing weird. Anywhere he wanted to.

"Bank," Two said.

The only available two-player spot in the schedule just then was with Hoover and the Human Stain and his stupid scooter, so they all came, too. Cement, ever loyal, stayed close to the phone and the phone book.

Two figured out he was in more trouble than Enron right around the second hole. Yoshi topped his drive into a small pond there. When they got to the ball, it was about two feet into the water, unplayable.

"Tough break," Two said. "Just barely rolled in there."

Silently, Yoshi reached into his bag. But instead of bringing out a new ball to drop, he pulled out a three-foot-long wooden tee.

Two's face fell like a gun-club soufflé.

Yoshi stuck the tee into the muck on the bottom of the lake. The top of it stuck about three inches above the water. He took the ball and perched it on the tee, took his stance, and hit a perfectly lovely wedge onto the green. Two Down was so shocked he lost his voice. He kept mouthing words with no sounds. Yoshi made his four, Two Down his five, and U.S. Navy v. Grenada was on.

There was no buried lie, no bush, no bunker lip that Yoshi didn't have a tee to get over. Two Down got the feeling if Yoshi had been behind a tree, he'd have had a tee with a 90-degree turn in it.

Worse, he had to play with the dreaded Human Stain, who was on Hoover like static cling, challenging him on the tiniest of rules. Stuff like: "Actually, my dear brother-in-law, I believe the rule is you must tee up from *behind* the tee markers. That point would be the backmost point of the two cinder blocks. You're in the middle." When Hoover putted with his new can't-miss, sure-cure new putting stroke—standing with his back to the hole, lining the putt up over his right shoulder, standing to the left of the ball, and then hitting it straight-arm with the *back* of his putter—Stain said, "I believe that's a violation."

At one point Two Down couldn't take it anymore. "Screw you, you blimp. What do you care if Hoover breaks 100 anyway? Why don't you just tell your sister he did it and leave us all alone? My God, haven't we suffered enough?"

"A: I have integrity, unlike most of you animals," Stain said, eating one of Blu Chao's Miracle Whip and Bac*Os sandwiches. "B: As I'm 'between engagements' right now, careerwise, I would be a fool to throw away gainful employment. C: I want Hoover to succeed, but the right way."

"And we want you to choke on a kielbasa—the right way."

No wonder that by the turn, Two Down was walking like he had arrows in his back. He came into the clubhouse for his usual—two beers, three Advil, and four Tylenol.

"How're you guys doing out there?" Cement asked him.

"I'm seven down," said Two.

Cement thought about that and tried to be encouraging. "Hey, man, hang in there. You've overcome diversity before."

Two just stared at him.

"*Ad*versity."

"You sure?"

On the 10th tee, Yoshi offered Two a get-even: Two would have to concede the entire first bet and then play him for double or nothing, half a shot a hole, no tees, no spots, no nothing.

Two Down was already embarrassed enough to have lost the money the day before in front of the Chops, who considered him golf's gambling Gretzky. And he believed in the gamblers' rule: You are never too far down to get back to even. And besides, everybody knows that if you play the "double or nothing" game long enough, sooner or later, you will get back to even. A guy can lose 99 straight double or nothings, but as long as he wins the 100th, it's like none of the losses happened. All this was surging through Two Down's beleaguered brain when he heard himself bark, "Hop on, Froggy!"

And Two Down might have done it, too. He might have gotten back to even. After all, he battled Yoshi mightily on that back nine, braced largely by an inordinate number of adult beverages. The more he drank, the slower his swing became. It was always a delicate balance: He could drink eight or ten bottles of "swing oil" as Dannie called it, and play great. But if he didn't stop in time, he could drive that swing off a cliff. He'd get so lubed he could no longer count right, couldn't see the ball well, couldn't remember the point of hitting the stupid thing with these oddly shaped sticks anyway.

So as he came up 18, with the most money he'd ever played for in his life, all the famous Two Down synapses were not exactly firing in order. In fact, it could be said his synapses more resembled a kindergarten class that had just sniffed giant vats of Elmer's glue. The bet was even. Yoshi's ball was tucked nicely and deeply into the bunker right of the green in three, Two had 178 yards to the hole for his third shot. He'd won the last two holes with flag-seeking iron shots and he need only hit this one on the green and he'd win the bet.

But as he looked at his clubs, trying to pick one, he had a problem. He knew that from 178, he usually hit a 5-iron. But he had taken his own advice and removed all the club numbers from his irons and replaced them with fake numbers. The problem was, he couldn't remember what number represented the 5. Was it the 6? Or was the 5 actually the 6 and the 4 the 5? Or did it go the other way? The 4 was the 5 and the 5 was the 4 perhaps? He'd used some formula, but that seemed like two presidents ago. He could vaguely recall that he'd used some very clever math equation, but what was it? Was it all the odd clubs were one higher and all the even clubs one lower? Or was it the evens higher and the odds lower? Worse, because he knew he could play as many clubs as he could carry, he'd put parts of three other sets in his bags, so it was hard now to remember which ones he'd renumbered and which he hadn't.

He could've called Hoover over. He could've even called the Stain over. He could've held them up and got a consensus on which most looked like his 5-iron. But instead he took the 4, waggled over it, crisped it right in the nut, and sent it gloriously on its way toward the flag.

"Wow!" said Hoover in admiration.

"Suck on that!" said Two Down in rapture.

It was headed dead-on for the pin. Then it was headed dead-on for the bunker behind the pin. Then for the Ponky clubhouse behind the green. Eventually it landed with a sickening clatter on the clubhouse's tile roof. It rolled down like a ball in a Japanese pachinko game and dropped down into the old grease fryer Froghair never threw out.

Hoover yelled over, "What club did you hit?"

The Stain trundled over in his scooter to mollify the pain. "You have to hit another one," he sniffed.

Two Down was staring at his club. And that's when he saw it, engraved into the bottom toe-corner of the face, the number: 3. He never thought to check the face of the club for a marking. Until then.

He sank to his knees like Y. A. Tittle and held his haircut in horror at what he'd just done.

"Be sure to use the same brand and compression of ball for your next shot," Stain said. "Anything else is a violation."

To this day, nobody is sure how 135-pound Two Down knocked the Human Stain out of his cart that day, jumped atop him like a rodeo calf-roper, and tried to force-feed the grip of his 3-iron down Stain's mouth. But it is true that it took Yoshi, Hoover, and the group playing behind them to pull his bony ass off the fat man.

Which, in itself, is a shame.

That night, we were staring holes in our drinks at our usual off-site gathering place, Don's Mixed Drinks, wondering how the hell we'd let it come to this and wondering if Froghair would let us move to Florida with him to play nude tennis with octogenarian Swedes.

And then Two Down walked in, with an ice pack on his eye, his collar ripped, his buttons hanging by threads, and both his front pants pockets ripped. He was followed by Big Al, Dewey, and Yoshi.

"Mr. Ray, your friend here Too Zad owez my poor friend Yoshi $48,850 American moniez," Big Al said. "Only he merely had $12,000. Zo you are required to pay to me $36,850 moniez."

This was a banner day for the Chops, you had to admit.

Bob said, "Who is this Two Down you speak of? Never heard of the man."

"Two Down pays his own debts," said Dom. "Got nothin' to do with us."

"Well, if we can't get it out of Two Down," Dewey reasoned, "and we can't get it out of you guys, I guess I can always get it out of Two Down's wife, Big Jane, back in Chicago. I got friends there and they're always looking for freelance work. Whenever they're out of Joliet, that is."

Two Down's eyes got as big as spaghetti plates.

"He'll get it to you," I said. "Give him a couple weeks."

"Sure," said Dewey. "What if I set up a nice installment plan? He can pay me back over five years?"

"Man, if you'd do that," Cement said, "I bet he'd appreciate it."

Big Al took a sip of a fresh-squeezed vodka I'd ordered and dumped it in Two's lap.

"Requiring for me to get the moniez in one week or Jane will be buying all her magazinez from nurzez for future."

They left. We were all staring at each other.

Then Dom leaned over with a lemon and squeezed it slowly over Two's vodka-soaked crotch.

CHAPTER 7

Every Tuesday our favorite student-athlete at Bridgefield State would study his doppelgänger—the man in the big Panama hat and the oversized sunglasses. Resource Jones studied him the way a Doberman studies a butcher-window pork chop.

He knew he pulled up every Tuesday morning in a black Ford Explorer with a small whiskey dent in the back rear wheelwell. His companion, the skinny Don Knotts–looking guy, was always with him. He tracked their tee times—usually 8:00, 8:08, or 8:16. He estimated his handicap to be about a twenty-two. He noticed that the man was a connoisseur of the chili dip, a man who featured divots large enough to recarpet your den. He seemed to have acquired the duck-hook virus and knew of no cure. He always drove a cart, always played eighteen, averaged about 97, according to the scorecard he would always leave on the steering wheel of his cart. One time there was a phone number down on the card and Resource deftly pocketed it. The two of them bet two-dollar Nassaus, with one-dollar greenies and sandies. No presses. The most he'd seen lost was nine dollars. His name, according to his bag tag, was Malcolm Baker. There was no tag on Don Knotts's bag. There were no clues as to either of their hometowns, but if you are playing a shitty prison golf course every week, you cannot live far.

If Resource's plan was going to work, he was going to have to get Malcolm Baker alone, and in a place where nobody could see what transpired between the two. After much research, timing the routes of the four guards, rehearsing the steps, calculating the risks, Resource determined that the place to do it would be at the 1st green. The 1st hole at the Bridgefield State Prison Nine was a downhill par-4, 402 yards, with a roller-coaster drop-off the last hundred yards, so that the green was not visible from the pro shop or the maintenance shed. A guard tower stood about seventy-five yards away, inside the huge barbed prison fence, but most of the time the guard tended to look toward the prison itself. There was a lightning shelter between the 1st green and the 2nd tee. It was just a tiny green shed with a door, a small shuttered window, and a bench inside, but almost nobody ever went in it. That would be very useful, Resource figured.

Slowly, his plan began to form. As millions of prisoners have vowed before him, he swore to himself, "This could work!" If it did, he could be sucking down a plate of *carne asada* in Cabo San Lucas in forty-eight hours, working as a bunker man on one of the rich tourist tracks there within a week and sending for his family within a month.

If it didn't, Resource Jones would probably acquire twenty additional years of lifesuck.

As for me, I really needed that $5,000 back immediately, if not sooner.

It was not going to come from work. With all the crap going on, I hadn't thought of a decent greeting card idea in four days. At twenty-five dollars a pop, that's a real problem. Most days I could come up with eight to ten. But with Dannie giving me the full Ted Williams deep freeze and my beloved awful Ponky getting sold out from under me, I wasn't really in all that funny of a mood. The best I'd come up with in four days was a woman waiting at the instant-photo shop with cobwebs on her, and she's singing:

Someday, my prints will come.

And inside the message: "Luckily, MY prince is already here. Happy Birthday."

That's it—four days, one card. I was a giant useless blob of goo. All the rest were dark, brooding ones on the general theme of depression and death.

Congratulations, graduate! and inside . . .

Now shut up and grab your oar.

I needed money, quick. Now my best friends were tapped out, so I couldn't hit them up for it. I was thinking about how much I could get for a kidney when Dannie herself came busting through the Ponky door like Sheriff Matt Dillon.

"Are you TRYIN' to set the world record for quickest divorce?" she says. "Because, buddy, I'm just the girl that can give it to you!"

Her face was red and her eyebrows were V'd. She looked mad enough to bite a Buick in half. She threw a balled-up piece of paper at me.

"What?" I asked.

"You wanna explain what THAT is?"

I picked it up and uncrumpled it. It was the hundred-dollar check I'd written Kelly.

"So? I was short cash!"

"Read on!"

It read, *Thanks for being there.*

Oh, shit.

I spun around and looked for Kelly, but she wasn't to be found.

"Baby, she's screwing with you!" I pleaded.

"No, she's *screwin'* you, you flyin' turdpile!" She was crying and yelling at the same time. "Is that who you've been goin' to for a shoulder to cry on?"

And she started to stomp out.

"Honey, no! I didn't write that!"

"Oh, bull! That's *exactly* how you write!" She turned and held up one of the purple pens I write with. "And in your precious purple pen, too!"

"No, I mean, I wrote 'thanks' but—"

"Save your breath!" She stomped out and then unstomped right back in. "You know what? I was finally starting to like you again and now you pull this crap. But I'll make it easy on you two! You can come over to the house and bang like minks for all I care. 'Cause I'm takin' Charlie and we're goin' to stay at my sister's."

"—But I didn't write the last—"

The door slammed. I chased her out into the gravel parking lot, but she put her fingers in her ears, jumped in the car, and spun out like Mannix.

"—three words."

The brochure did it. Blind Bob left a single brochure on Dining in the Dark lying around on the pro shop counter and Kelly the Edible picked it up.

The Chops were deeply involved in a game of Sentences That Have Never Been Uttered while waiting for a funeral procession to arrive at the cemetery across the street.

"Would you mind giving me a paper cut in the eye?" Hoover offered.

"Can I taste your spleen?" I said.

"Man, I'd love to nob Dr. Ruth," said Dom.

"Will you take me to Dinner in the Dark?" Kelly said.

"I think that'd be one," Hoover said.

She rolled her eyes. "*Bob*—will you take me to Dinner in the Dark?"

"Ohhhh," Blind Bob said, turning toward her lovely voice. "Sure. Would you like to? I'm working the one tomorrow night. How's that?"

Dom tried not to grin.

Thirty-six hours later, Bob was escorting the delicious Kelly into the women's waiting room at Dinner in the Dark. "I gotta get to work," he said. "I'll see you inside. So to speak."

The women were all between twenty-five and thirty-five, save the blind chaperon who waited with them. They were dressed to slay, even though no man would ever actually see them. And they were bubbling about the night that lay before them.

"Can you imagine, talking to a guy without him looking at your tits the whole time?" the blonde said.

"Oh, they'll still be looking, they just won't see anything," said a tall one.

"I think I'll take my girls out during the whole dinner just for the irony of it," said a redhead.

"The whole thing just really turns me on," said the blonde. "I've been roughing up the suspect all week just thinking about it."

"I know," the redhead said. "This whole thing is so erotic. You can do scandalous things in the dark! I mean, you could screw a guy and never know what he looks like! Don't you think that's totally hot?"

"I think it's really sweet," said the tall one. "What if you fell in love with somebody just for who they are, not what they look like?"

"Yeah, but what if you make a date with a guy and when he comes to pick you up, he's a fat porker?" said the redhead.

"You'll be able to tell," said their blind chaperon, a fortyish woman whose eyelids never opened. "Feel the seat cushion after they get up. If it's totally crushed and warm from corner to corner, you know you've got a blimp butt."

The women shrieked.

"Are you married?" Kelly asked the blind woman.

"Sure," she said.

"That's nice," Kelly said. "You got to pick your husband based totally on how good and kind he was to you, not on looks, right?"

"Pretty much," said the blind woman. "I don't really know how good-looking he is. I had sight until I was seventeen, so when we're doing it, I always picture Richie Cunningham on top of me! From *Happy Days*? He was so cute! I'll bet he's still cute, right? Ron Howard?"

"Are you kidding?" said the blonde. "He's lost all his—"

"—freckles!" said Kelly. "Lost all his freckles and now he's even more handsome. He's still so cute, yes."

"Oh, good," she said.

That's when it was time to be led into the pitch black, windowless dining room, where the décor didn't matter and the presentation mattered even less. Dom stood in a corner, by himself. To substitute him into the ten, Bob had to get rid of one guy, so he said aloud, "Mr. Pearson?"

A voice said, "Yes?"

Bob approached him and took him by the elbow. "I need to speak to you for a moment." Bob took him through the very door he'd snuck Dom through, closed it, then went into the lit waiting room.

"Your check bounced," Bob said. "You're out."

"What?" the guy said. "Well, I'm certainly . . . Hey wait a minute! I didn't pay by check. I paid by Visa!"

But by then Bob had pushed the guy out the door leading to the street and locked it.

He felt his way back and began putting each couple at small two-top tables. There would be ten "courses"—a soup, a salad, a glass of wine, a sorbet, entrée, another sorbet, another cocktail, dessert, coffee, and petits fours. That way everybody could have a session with everybody else. He and the other blind chaperons guided the first set of hands to each other to be introduced. This was when Bob snuck Dom in the side door and sat him at a table.

Dom's first companion was the redhead. Now, if there is one thing in this wide world that Dom can do, it's talk to women. He speaks fluent woman. He could talk a nun out of her habit. He was making the redhead laugh before her soup came. He was making out with her halfway through it. He was supping at her rack by the time the blind chaperon announced, "Now we'll change for the salad."

"No, thanks," gasped the redhead. "I'll have more soup. I really, really like my soup."

Each woman was told to bring at least ten business cards. If they liked was straddling him and The Colossus, which had gone up like the Chrysler building.

"Oh, my God," she said, feeling the beast beneath her. "Is it my birthday?"

"I guess so," Dom said, his hands under her bra. "You wah yah bahthday suit."

Finally, she couldn't help herself from helping herself. She whispered into his ear, "For my present, I want you inside me. Wanna bet I can make your birthday come early?"

"Bank!" Dom whispered back.

Kelly suddenly stiffened like a Kool Pop.

Oops.

Dom's hands froze in their place on her economy-sized cans. He could hear her breathing. He was wondering if she'd heard what he said when there was a bluish light right in his face. It was her cellphone, popped open.

"Asshole!" Kelly screamed, hopping off his lap. The cellphone light had the same effect as pouring a huge tub of cold Malt-O-Meal over the proceedings. Three other women hopped off the laps of their dates. One couple was on the floor. The free-range chicken was going wholly ignored at Dining in the Dark.

"You fucking asshole!" Kelly said.

Across the room a guy said, "You said you were twenty-two!"

Next to them a woman said, "Work out my ass! You're a tub of lard!"

There were three clear slaps across faces, all in a row, like machine gun fire, but the hardest was Kelly's roundhouse right on Dom's blue-lit grille.

"You try any more bullshit like this, and I'm calling the police!" She stomped out, buttoning her blouse as she went.

By then the blind woman had flipped on the light and a sighted supervisor came running in. Everybody stared at Dom, who looked like a chicken caught in a klieg light.

the guy they were talking to, they could hand him one. By the time the entrée came around, Dom had already collected four cards out of four. But here was Dom's big chance. Bob had made sure that the longest segment—the entrée—would pair Dom, the World's Most Sexual Man, with Kelly the Edible. It was the unstoppable force meets the irresistible sex object. It couldn't help but work.

The voice Dom used was kind of a cross between a Southie Harrison Ford and a Southie Julio Iglesias, but it had a spellbinding effect on Kelly. Whatever he guessed she wanted to hear, he guessed right. Plus it was all you could drink for the hundred bucks, and she was getting plenty merloaded.

"This is weird," Dom said, "and I apologize if this sounds fahwahd, but thah's something in yah voice that makes me think that yah beautiful—on the inside. I know, that's crazy, but something about the way you phrase wahds, the breaths in between, I don't know, I just feel peaceful inside listening to you. Wahm, you know? And it's weird, because we just met, but I feel like you have this huge haht—except maybe it's a haht that's been broken a few too many times."

Well, to a twelve-car-pileup luscious like Kelly the Edible, who had spent every day since she was thirteen being ogled by men for her guns, her gams, and her glutes, these words hit her the way a semi hits a phone booth. She was spun. It was all so exotic, the odd and romantic accent, the deep timbre of his voice, the mix of fear at being in such blackness and the elation at being free to be whoever you wanted to be, the way he'd held her hand for that extra second when they met, all of it. It must've put a tingle in her tingler, because the next thing you know, she was saying to this unseen stranger . . . "I'm sorry, but, I just *have* to kiss you."

And that was pretty much the last interest either of them showed in the mustard-grape free-range chicken with ginger-rubbed mesquite-braised asparagus and Sonoma Valley mushroom risotto. You know, Adjective Food. For Dom, finally kissing the woman who'd run from him as if he were conjoined with Stephen Hawking was pure bliss. From there an all-out feelfest broke out, until soon, Kelly had felt her way across the table and

"Boy!" he said, blushing stoplight red. "I guess some people *really* hate it when you eat off their plate!"

When I finally got somebody to pick up at Dannie's sister's house in Roanoke, it wasn't Dannie, it was her sister, Joey.

"Hey, Peckerhead!" Joey said. "Know how I know that? We got Peckerhead ID."

"C'mon, Joey," I begged. "Just put her on for *one* minute."

"Why don't you go cry on your girlfriend's shoulder?"

"I don't *have* a girlfriend, Joe! That was her just trying to get under Dannie's skin! She's playing her!"

"Well, I can guaran-damn-tee ya, Dannie's not playin', Ray. She says she's reconsidering bein' married to a damn goldbrick. How *dare* you shirk your responsibilities to my sister and my nephew!"

"I'm not shirking! I'm working!"

"On your stupid little greeting cards? On your stupid novel that won't never come out? It don't count nothin' if it don't pay nothin', Ray. It's just jerkin' off! Hey, I know, Ray, why don't you tell her you're writin' a whole new Bible, Ray! That don't pay nothin' either."

"Joey, I swear, if you just—"

"Sorry, Dannie can't come to the phone, Ray. She's paintin' herself a Sistine ceiling over here. Should be done any year now. Buh-bye!"

Click.

I guess it was just after I threw the phone through one of the sliding glass doors at Ponky when I decided.

I screamed it so loud the top of my head nearly came off: "Fuck you, William Hart! Gimme my God-DAMN money!"

I called an emergency Choperational meeting the next day. Two Down talked me into having it at the assisted living home.

"It's happy hour, four 'til five, and nobody hardly shows up!" he said. "All the drinks you want, free! Plus those little Vienna sausages!"

The principals were there: Hoover, Blind Bob, Cementhead, Dom (with a purple left eye), Two, and myself.

I drew up a deep breath and said as convincingly as I could, "I'm going to try to qualify for a major."

There was much whooping and yelling, yet not one of the blue-hairs turned to look. It's quite possible they couldn't hear a thing.

"Now, Hoover tells me that there's only one major left now I can qualify for—the British Open. No idea how the hell I'm going to get over there, but I'm going to try. But I'm going to do it on two conditions. One, while I'm over there, you guys have to do everything in your power to stop the sale of Ponky. 'Cause if I go over there and fail—which I probably *will* fail—and my wife gives me a free drop, and Ponky gets sold, I'm just going to stay over there and eat sheep entrails until I die."

"Sounds like a plan," said Blind Bob.

"Second," I said, "if I do qualify and I'm able to buy Ponky, I would then *own* Ponky and run it, nobody else. I would get everybody their initial investment back, and I'd try to loan Two Down as much as I could toward the $36,000, but after that I'd be the owner, CEO, and head fajita at Ponky. Okay? Because my wife thinks I need a job, and that's the only job besides writing that I could imagine stomaching."

"You write?" Cement said.

"Funny. Is that okay with everybody?"

"I think it's a bullshit idear," said Dom.

Everybody laughed.

"No, seriously," he said. "I think you should stay here and help us try to stop them from selling Ponky. You got no chance, Stick. I mean, I love you and everything, but yah just not good enough. Yeah, you throw some 65s and 64s on bums like us heah, but thah's no pressah heah! What are you doin', man? Yah kiddin' yahself! And, besides, what was all that bullshit you said about not givin' in to yah dad? You do this and he wins! He gets the last laugh!"

All of us just stared at him.

"Besides," he said. "I need you to help me get Kelly."

We stared at his purple eye.

"You loosahs don't think I'm gonna quit now, do you? Now that I've got-ten a taste? No way, dude. I *will* drill the fuzzy donut, I promise you."

I tried to gather my thoughts again.

"So, okay, now, Two, you call Froghair and get as much info as you can from him on who's trying to buy us. Fellas, if we stick together, we can do this. Because I guarantee you, we'll never have another Ponky. We'll never find a place that lets us get away with all our crap. We'll never find a place where we can play eightsomes, or play from even-numbered tee boxes to odd-numbered greens, or let ourselves in for midnight Smut 'n Eggs. Yeah, Ponky is a toxic waste dump, but she's *our* toxic waste dump, right?

"So, right now, I need to figure out some way to get on a plane to En-gland, no charge. And somewhere to stay, free. Any ideas?"

"Why don't you stay in one of those youth brothels?" said Cement.

Silence.

"*Hostels,*" Hoover said. "Youth hostels."

"You sure?"

"Where am I going again, Hoover?" I asked.

Hoover stood to address the crowd. He cleared his throat. "The Gog Magog," he said. "In Cambridge, just north of London. It would seem to suit your situation the best—it's the worst conditioned of the three quali-fying courses, it's long, and, since it's a university town, there would be plenty of cheap rooms."

Here we go again, I thought.

"Damn right!" said Blind Bob. "Go flog the Gog Magog!"

"You think there's a dog on the Gog Magog?" said Two Down.

"Oh, Ma Gog, you guys," said Cementhead.

"Okay, shut up!" I yelled. Still, no gray, blue, or purple hairdos turned toward us. "Now—"

"And if I may offer a suggestion to you," Hoover said.

"Uh, that's a five-dollar hackalooski fine," said Two Down, who served as keeper of the list of Ponky fines, a "hackalooski" being a higher-handicapped player giving a lower-handicapped player advice.

"This is not a piece of swing advice," Hoover argued. "It's merely this: I've been watching you hit and I'm not sure if your flex points aren't a little high."

You've got to hand it to Hoover. The man wouldn't say uncle from the bottom of a guillotine.

"Wait a minute, Hoov," said Two. "Who in their right mind would take a golf tip from you? Remember your last one? Remember what happened when it didn't work?"

"I don't recall."

"Oh, yeah, we recall. You got so mad you wound up peeing all over your clubs. Just peed everywhere on them, the bag, the clubs. Even opened up the ball pouch and peed into that."

In his own defense, Hoover said, "I was going to put those clubs in the paper anyway."

"Oh, yeah, those will sell," said Blind Bob. *"Near-new set of Callaways. Only peed on once."*

"Yeah, I can see the ad now," said Two. *"Urine luck! Near-new Callaways! You'll hit the piss out of these!"*

It had turned into the Hoover History Channel.

"Remember the time the pro told Hoover maybe he should learn from the left side?" asked Cementhead. "And Hoover asked him, 'Why? Because it will help me understand the swing better?' And the pro goes, 'No, 'cause you're so fucked up from the right side we need to start completely over.' "

More howls.

"Hey! I was starting to get it on that side, too!" Hoover yelled.

Cement couldn't find his beer, so he held up an especially small sausage on a toothpick and announced, "Gentlemen, here's to Ray!"

When everybody was done laughing, he continued, "No, seriously! Here's to Ray gettin' his wife back, us gettin' Ponky back, and Dom gettin' his dick back!"

And to a man, just to pimp Dom, we all said at once, "Bank!"

I looked at Two, who hadn't been mentioned in the toast at all.

Then a nurse walked in pushing a TV on a cart and yelled at the top of her lungs, "Okay, kids! Who's ready for some *Lawrence Welk*?"

Two Down's world was blacker than Johnny Cash's closet. He would go about his duties at the Boston National Ladies Golf Club—he ran the ladies' tea and card room—but his mind was wondering how he might find a spare $36,000 lying around before having his fingers chopped off without anesthetics.

He'd been taking random routes back to the home every night. He was careful opening his mail. He tried never to walk in the open, alone, which made golf a little hard. He would open his locker in the grubby men's locker room in the basement of the Boston Ladies as though he were 007 light-fingering his way around a bomb. And now he had a new worry to add to "stay alive"—How the hell was he going to stop this sale?

He'd called Froghair, who told him that he was trying to sell it as fast as he could, as he wanted to get down to the nudist colony in Tampa before the big July Fourth dance there. "Apparently the girls all wear lingerie!" he said.

Froghair said he had only one real buyer so far, "but they're very interested"—the Mayflower Club. He said the Mayflower wanted to buy it and pave it over, mostly for parking for U.S. Opens and big events like that. As it was, Froghair always leased out Ponky for people to park on during those events, meaning we had to play a damn tire-track field for a month afterward. If it rained, two months. But even then, that wasn't good enough for the Mayflower snobs. Some of their patrons bitched about the mud and the smell of the methane gas leaking up from the old dump underneath. Picky bastards.

We felt we had God on our side. True, the Mayflower was to Ponky what lobster thermidor was to imitation krab. It was a magnificent course, splendid, huge, epic, gorgeous, manicured as if by toothbrushes, greens like a

Marine buzz cut, double-cut fairways, tee boxes you would happily roll around naked upon. But as much as the course was universally loved, the members were universally despised. Spoiled, privileged, haughty, racist, sexist dandruff balls is what most people thought. And that's just what the members said about themselves. Most of them were so old they'd voted against Lincoln.

As such, when famous feminist Martha Burke started grousing about how the Mayflower's U.S. Open was going to be held at a club that had only one woman member, a lot of Bostonites wrung their hands with glee. Burke had struck out in a protest at Augusta National, host of the Masters, complaining that it had *no* female members, but her whole rebellion fizzled when only twenty-five people came to the rally, one of them holding up a huge sign that read FIX MY DINNER!

Something like that would sell a whole helluva lot better in Boston, a Democratic town like no other. Still, the Mayflower did have one woman member, and that was enough.

And Two Down was thinking about that as he served the women their drinks at Boston Ladies, suffering their butt pinches and leers and come-ons as they stuffed their dollar bills in the pockets of the shorts they made him wear. "What I couldn't teach you in the sack!" said a fifty-something in six-decades-deep mascara. And they'd all giggle. And it was everything Two Down could do not to say, "Everything?"

He was skulking around, a human storm cloud, when he saw somebody who caused his eyebrows to lurch upward and his ears to twitch: Bingsley Colchester.

Bingsley Colchester was nobody new to Two Down. Her real name was Mim Smythe. Colchester was her maiden name and she always hated "Bingsley," so she went by her middle name, Miriam, or Mim. She played bridge most every day at the Boston Ladies. She and her bob haircut never gave him the time of day, harrumphed whenever he said anything to her, and would purposely scrawl NO TIP on any chit he brought her. And yet Two Down couldn't blame her.

After all, for a time, Two Down had stolen her identity.

See, three of us—Two, Dannie, and myself—had our famous Bet to see who could be the first to play eighteen holes at Mayflower, with witnesses. It got out of hand, the money got big, and people got desperate. I snuck on it at midnight, only to fall one lousy putt short. Dannie tried everything up to and including dating a member. But Two Down topped everybody on the insanity parade by discovering the name of a long-lost member who almost never came to the Mayflower—Bingsley Colchester. She was a blue-blood legacy whose father was a member, making her a member. When Bingsley's husband died, the legacy rule was no longer in effect, but it was too late. Bingsley was grandfathered in as a full-fledged member, the only female on the Mayflower roster.

Bingsley then remarried a member and became part of his account. But the Mayflower secretly hung on to her membership under her maiden name purely because they knew that someday, they may need to show they had at least one woman member. Sure, the all-male membership they had now was 100 percent against it, but would they be willing to lose a U.S. Open for it? Probably not. During The Bet, Two Down discovered this little loophole in the membership roster and drove a golf cart through it. He started showing up as Bingsley Colchester—sounds like a man's name anyway. He signed for dinners, signed for clubs, whatever. It all went great until the very day Two Down was supposed to play his first (and winning) round at the Mayflower. Bingsley heard the name being called and sicced the gendarmes on him. And that's mostly how he lost The Bet.

But by the time Two Down was working at the Boston Ladies, Bingsley had been permanently separated from her new husband for a year and didn't want to run into him at the Mayflower, so she spent most of her time at the Boston Ladies, playing cards day after day.

No wonder Bingsley was less than Christian to Two Down. But on this day, her visage was new and wonderful to him. On this day, it hit him like a Boston cream pie that in Bingsley Colchester, he had a real chance to stop the sale of Ponky.

He reasoned: (inhale) If he could somehow force Bingsley Colchester to threaten to quit the Mayflower, then he could use that threat to get the Mayflower to give up their plans to buy Ponky, which meant Froghair would have no other buyers for Ponky, giving Ray time to get back from qualifying at the British Open and buy Ponky himself, at a reduced price, and have money left over to bail Yours Truly out of his current tiff with Glock-bearing ruffians. (exhale)

But how?

He spent the next three days stewing over Bingsley Colchester. He watched her. She was, what, forty-five years old? She never played golf, just bridge. Never seemed to have a man around, only her bridge buddies. Didn't seem to have any hobbies, except bridge. But Lord, she was good at bridge. It was the same old story every time: "Oh, Bingsley, you're just too good at this game!" her opponents would chirp as they paid her their three dollars, or their six dollars, or even their twelve dollars. And every time she'd giggle and go, "I'm just so lucky! No skill at all! Just pure dumb luck!"

But Two Down was not born Tuesday. He knew that people who win all the time and attribute it to luck will also tell you dachshunds can dunk, because luck is how he explained his own wins. "I'm just so damn lucky," he would say with a shrug, "I oughta charge people to rub up against me." But luck runs both ways, and he knew that if you showed him a person who was lucky all the time, he could show you a person who was cheating all the time.

He watched her. She didn't seem all that smart. She'd make dumb bids and then, somehow, get the perfect cards. She had a little blond partner in a pixie haircut named Brie Wollenwebber. The way they could read each other's minds bordered on the occult. They would take on any and all comers and rarely lose. It was as if they were attached at the chakras.

"Well, you two did it again," some poor millionaire's wife would lament as she paid out their $7.50. "You work so *well* together."

He studied her as he vacuumed, swept, and got drinks in his too-tight pants. The more he watched, the more suspicious he got. There had to be some *way* they were doing it. Mirrors or windows or sunglasses, so they could see their partner's cards? Nope. Foot signals? Taps? Nope. Signals? A clearing of the throat? Nope.

He was going out of his mind trying to figure it out when he heard Bingsley yell, "Excuse me! I'm almost out of peanuts here, boy! Do you mind?" There was a tiny bit of a desperate look in her eye. She was slightly pissed and she almost never looked pissed. She always ignored him, but never with vengeance. She always wanted him to keep her bowl of sugar-coated peanuts filled, but he was so intent on studying her that he'd let it slip.

He ran over with a new bowl and set it down. Her shoulders let down a little. She calmed down. Then he watched as she took two peanuts. Across the table, Brie announced her bid: "Two hearts."

The next hand Brie took three peanuts, and immediately Bingsley declared, "Three clubs." Both would take peanuts throughout, even when not bidding, but whenever their bids came around, the amount of peanuts they took was the exact number the partner would bid!

Soon, Two had it decoded. Taking peanuts from the top right quarter of the bowl meant spades. Bottom right quarter—diamonds. Bottom left—hearts. Top left—clubs.

They were telling each other what to bid through the damn peanuts! Ingenious! Cheating their friends at cards for a lousy three bucks when they were tipping the car valet more than that? He loved it! The pettiness of it! The duplicity of it! He was in awe, actually. It must've been like the first time Clyde watched Bonnie shortchange a soda jerk. He nearly misted up.

He walked over and filled their peanuts up to the top, grinning just slightly as he went.

"One thing about peanuts," he said, looking right at Bingsley. "You just can't stop."

He had his plan.

CHAPTER 8

It would be impossible to overstate how badly Hoover wanted to break 100. He wanted it the way a mole wants to dig, a drunk to drink, a Hilton to shop. It obsessed him. It haunted him. Golf was his cruel mistress and she whipped him, beat him, and made him wear plaid pants. He had broken 100 once in his life—with me, in the middle of the night, using flashlights and Glo Balls, as part of my efforts to win The Bet. But when he got home at 4:00 A.M. that night, thrilled as a teenage boy who'd just lost his virginity, his hateful wife only said "Doesn't count at night" and went back to sleep.

Since that night it became his only goal, to break 100 at Ponky. His home course. In daylight. It was more than a golf goal for him. It was the way to finally show his wife he was a real man. It was all he thought about. He was only five-six, 125 pounds, most of that being ears and his little Jackie Stewart racing cap, but he seemed to have bottomless will and energy for attempting this one simple task. And not a single coordinated muscle in his body to accomplish it.

He was a man of science, and yet when it came to golf, he resorted to anything—superstition, religion, the occult. When he bought gas, he would round the cents to 99, for good luck. He shopped daily at the 99 Cent Store. He meditated at night, in the lotus position, visualizing making a three-foot putt on 18 for 99. Some days he would not play golf at all, just drive the course in a car, leaving handfuls of fertilizer at the trees he hit the most, hoping his gift would compel them to spit his balls back into the fairway. Never worked. Ungrateful bitch maples.

And so when his wife put her size-11 foot down and assigned her putrid brother-in-law, the Human Stain, to monitor his rounds—requiring that Hoover break 100 by the time her mother visited on July 11—it only added to the searing pressure.

I would plead with him: "Hoov, just play a few rounds where you don't keep track of your score. Just have fun whacking it and watching it go. You won't believe how much more relaxed you'll be and how much better you'll play."

And he would try it and play better and then, as he came up 16 or 17 or 18, he would not be able to keep himself from going over his round and counting up his strokes. Invariably, he would realize that if he could just make double bogey on the last hole, he would shoot 99. And, like a whore about to address the archdiocese, the enormity of the moment would cause his throat to dry up like Death Valley, his palms and pits to pour sweat, and the demons in his mind to come prancing out in front of his eyeballs. And he would always stub two, chunk one, hook three, until he'd made an eleven and be back in Loserville.

"Couldn't you use the Human Stain to your advantage?" I said. "Let him keep score. Ask him not to remind you of what you're shooting. And then when you've finished the round, ask him what it was. Maybe it'll be something pleasant, like 97, and all this will be over and the Human Stain can leave Ponky forever."

"No, no, no," Hoover said. "You don't understand. The man is constantly on my case. Telling me what I'm doing wrong. Consulting the rule book. Bringing up stuff that only makes me more aggravated and tense."

"Like what?"

"Like who he's peed next to."

"God."

"Not yet. But soon, I'm sure."

A few days before, as it turned out, Hoover had used some new three-hundred-dollar Loomis-blend, resonant-resistant shafts and his third-string set of Titleists to play the front nine in a miracle 46. All he needed was to play the back in anything but flippers and oven mitts and he'd do it. By the time he got to 16 tee, he was on the cusp of heroics. He needed only to double bogey the last three holes to pull it off, a feat possible for even Hoover. He hit his drive, using his patented whippy-takeaway-chicken-elbow-52-mile-per-hour-through-the-hitting-zone-no-finish swing, and cut it right into the lake. His only drop left him behind a typical Ponky tree—half dead, mostly limbless, no leaves. Hoover pulled out his 8-iron.

"What do you think you're doing, my hapless relative?" Stain asked him.

"I'm going through it."

"You, sir, are a functional idiot, do you realize that?"

"Actually, I read in *Avid Arborist* that trees are 90 percent air," said Hoover, who then pulled the club back and was right at the top of his back-swing when Stain added, "So are screen doors."

The ball, crisply hit, smacked the only large branch in his way, came back and hit Hoover in the right knee, and caromed into the lake. If you're keeping score at home, that's one shot with the 8-iron, two shots for touching the ball, and the drop to get out of the lake—four shots in one swing, the rare grand slam. He'd blown his chance at 100 in one fell swoop.

Hoover went triple-platinum O. J. He screamed as though someone had stabbed him in the little toe. He chopped the 8-iron like an ax over and over against the offending tree, threw the destroyed 8-iron into the lake, decided that wasn't enough punishment to inflict on an inanimate object, took his clubs off the back of the cart and heaved *them* into the lake, and drove off, with Stain sitting beside him, wordless. If the bulbous Stain hadn't been about four hundred pounds, Hoover probably would've deposited him in the water as well.

Playing behind him, Cementhead saw the whole thing. "He finished all that and then drove back to the clubhouse," he reported to us. "We kept waiting for him to turn around and come back, but he just kept driving. So we hit our shots. Then, like five minutes later, we see him coming back in the cart, getting bigger and bigger as he's coming toward us. And I'm thinking, 'Okay, he's going to fish his clubs out.' And sure enough, he stops the cart, wades back into the lake, gets the clubs out, throws them up on shore, gets out of the lake, unzips his side pouch, takes his car keys out, zips it back up, pitches the whole bag back into the lake, and drives off again. Classic."

Two Down knew exactly where he would do it.

He waited in his shoeshine room for Bingsley Colchester to come down the hallway to the women's locker room. As she passed, he lurched at her and dragged her into the shoeshine room before she could make much ruckus.

"Ms. Smythe," Two Down said, using her most recent name. "There's something you and I have to talk about—right now."

She and her bob haircut spun on him, hitting him with her Kate Spade purse. "How dare you speak to me! After what you did at the Mayflower! Get away from me this *instant*!"

"Well, ma'am, that's what this is about—the Mayflower."

"You let me go or I'll scream bloody murder!"

"It's about the way you play bridge. Actually, it's about the way you and Ms. Wollenwebber *cheat* at bridge."

She turned and poked a very sharp fingernail into his chest. "Listen, Leonard, or whatever your real name is, you'd best be careful who you're messing with here. I don't like to be accused of cheating in my own club. Especially when we're playing for money!"

"Oh, you don't take your friends for much. Just *peanuts* really."

Her eyebrows jumped to attention. "What are you accusing me of exactly? Because I can get you fired in ten minutes with one call, you understand?" She pulled her cellphone from her purse and began dialing.

"Oh, I'm not accusing you of cheating. I'm *proving* you cheat. See, I had one of those little hidden video cameras in my belt the last week," he lied. "I've got it on VHS: You take two peanuts from the top right of your bowl, Brie bids two spades. She takes three peanuts from the bottom left, you bid three hearts. You take one peanut from the center of the bowl, she bids one no-trump. It's really beautiful to watch. On the videos, I mean."

There was a long silence while she looked him dead in the eye. Two didn't blink. Too many years of lying into the eyes of priests and nuns.

"Okay," she said, "what's this going to cost me?"

Two Down glanced around. Then he said, "One simple phone call."

"What? To whom?"

"To the Mayflower."

"The Mayflower? The Mayflower Country Club? What in the world for?"

"So you can resign your membership."

"You're insane!"

"No. You're going to call Laird Fredericks, president of the Mayflower, and you're going to tell him that you're resigning from the Mayflower because it's a sexist club that treats women like slaves and felons and three-dollar whores. You're resigning over the fact that the Mayflower has all kinds of antiwomen rules: No women can be members, no women can have tee times before one o'clock any day, no women can go in the grill room, the card room, or the bar. You're saying Andrew Dice Clay treats women better. You're going to remind him that your resignation leaves the Mayflower with exactly zero female members. And that you're going to send letters to the *Globe*, the *Herald*, the USGA, and Martha Burke explaining exactly why you're quitting. And you will tell him that your resignation is going to make this next year before the Open at the Mayflower pure hell for him, if he even gets to *keep* the Open, which you now doubt."

"Not to offend you," she said, "but why the *hell* do you care about women at the Mayflower? What are you, Hillary Clinton?"

"Ahh, this is the good part. At the very end of the call, you're going to say, 'On the other hand, Mr. Fredericks, I could be persuaded to remain on as a Mayflower member and burn the letters, *if* the Mayflower would do me one little favor.' "

"Which is?"

"The Mayflower has to agree *not* to buy the golf course next to it, known as Ponkaquogue Municipal Golf Links and Deli, for now and forever, amen. No sale. You want them to kill the whole idea."

"That's it? This whole thing is to keep the Mayflower from buying that ghastly course next to it?"

"Yep. That's it. Make this call and the women of Boston National Ladies Golf Club will still think you're the greatest cardplayer since Amarillo Slim. I'll just go on topping off your peanuts. Don't make this call and I'll make sure every club in town gets a copy of these videos, along with a long letter explaining how you do it. I might even put it in Blockbuster."

Bingsley Colchester went raised-eyebrow-to-raised-eyebrow with Two Down for the longest time. But nobody out-eyebrows Lenny Petrovitz.

"Let's do this quick," she said at last. "Gimme your cellphone."

"I'm not giving you my cellphone," Two said. "I don't want him having my number."

"Well, I sure don't want him having my number."

"We'll use this phone right here," he said, pointing to his shoe-polish-stained phone above his tiny desk.

"Fine."

But just then, Two's cellphone rang.

It happened to be me.

And I said, "Hide and Seek, Miss Petrovitz."

Resource Jones did not believe in violence. He fancied himself a sort of gentleman bandit. So he was in trade negotiations with a friend of his in the sick bay to get one syringe full of some knockout drug or another in exchange for a quart of Legal Sea Foods' Boston clam chowder, the lack of which was giving the sick-bay attendant a facial tic. Resource is not named Resource for nothing, and within a week he had a very complicated exchange system of this-for-that going, of favors-for-secrets between guards, prisoners, and laypeople that worked out and executed the roofies-for-soup deal.

With proper administration of the drug, his sick-bay friend said, a large-sized man could be knocked out for "at least four hours, probably six or seven."

So if the day ever came when he could get his body double, Mr. Malcolm Baker—Mr. Panama Hat and Big Sunglasses—alone long enough to have him take a forced nap, and could drag that man from the 1st green into the lightning shelter behind it, and if he could successfully change into Mr. Baker's clothes in that shelter and then go unnoticed back to Baker's cart, he figured he'd have at least two hours to get away. Plus, according to his detailed calculations, another hour before any guard missed either Baker or him, and another hour to find Baker. That would give Resource Jones about four hours.

So, in order to not draw a single bit of attention to himself, Resource would simply play the nine holes out. Playing by himself, a hole in front and a hole behind the nearest groups, who would think to check under the Panama hat and the glasses? Their size, skin tone, and age were about the same. The guards never came anywhere near the players, and certainly the other inmates working on the course wouldn't rat him out. They loved him. And besides, to do the opposite, to just suddenly go driving back *up* No. 1 and quit, was bound to cause questions. "Everything all right, Mr. Baker?" "Something wrong, Mr. Baker?" The pro was like a prison guard himself. He was just slightly more suspicious than a mafia bodyguard.

No, he would play out the remaining eight holes. He'd dig out the food he'd stashed on some holes—in bunkers and in bushes—and jam those in Baker's bag. He'd finish as unobtrusively as possible, pull the hat low, drive the cart into the parking lot, stop at Baker's black Ford Explorer, take the keys and Baker's cellphone out of the bag, unlock the Explorer, throw the bag in, return the cart to the back of the pro shop, and drive off as normally as possible.

He would take the cellphone out of the bag and ditch the Explorer at the Brockton bus station. He would then purchase a bus ticket to Miami with Baker's Visa card, get on the bus, leave the cellphone tucked into the back-row cushions of the bus, get off the bus before it left, take a cab with whatever cash Baker had left him in his wallet, and light out in the opposite direction. He would steal a car in the first covered parking lot he could find, then start making his way across the northern United States in it until he hit Washington State, where he would take a direct left to Mexico and all-you-can-drink Tecates the rest of his days.

Meanwhile, the police, using the latest technology, would be triangulating Baker's cellphone—using the cell company satellites to get a bead on the phone's exact location without anybody even calling on it. They'd locate it just outside New Jersey, at some rest stop, stopping the bus while *Eyewitness News* choppers hovered above. They'd run aboard with guns cocked, finding no escaped cons, only a cellphone in the back row with a little note taped to it: "Congrats! You found me!"

It was a perfect plan, if he did say so himself. But one sticky problem remained: How was he going to get rid of Baker's weekly golf companion, the skinny Barney Fife lookalike?

When I hung up from my Hide and Seek call, I was laughing the self-satisfied laugh of a man tasting the sweet nectar of revenge. Little did I know I was laughing at my own funeral.

I really hadn't thought it out much. I knew he'd be at work, so I snuck the "surprise" in at his work before he arrived. I honestly thought he'd find it in time, no problem.

"Hide and Seek!" I said.

"Ray!—" he hollered, but it was too late. I'd clicked off. I gleefully imagined his state of mind.

Immediately there came a panic into his eyes that you usually don't see outside of public executions. This Bingsley blackmail was a very delicate operation, and now I'd thrown a squealing pig into the middle of it. It was like a man about to split the Hope Diamond when he suddenly gets a call saying his car is about to be towed. Two was much too deep into the Bingsley sting to stop now, and yet he knew he had to find the hideous Hide and Seek, pronto.

Bingsley could feel the way his manner changed. Why were this wacko's eyes darting like a fox's on hunting day? What the hell was going on now?

In Two Down's overcaffeinated mind, he thought the worst, as well he should. Hide and Seek possibilities riffled through his mind like flash cards. What would it be this time? Faked stolen property in his locker? Drug paraphernalia on the dashboard of his car? Phonied-up pictures of him with young boys?

He snapped out of it. "Make the call," he barked, pointing to the phone on the wall.

"Fine," Bingsley grumbled. "What's the number?"

Hmmm. The number. Good question. He hadn't really thought that far ahead. "Just call the Mayflower and ask for Laird Fredericks."

"Okay. What's *that* number?"

"You don't know that number, either?"

"Sorry," she said, pointing to herself. "Was this my extortion? My apologies!"

"All right, all right. Keep your shirt on."

Two Down began hunting around the room for a phone book. He spied one up on a shelf. He had to move a box in order to climb high enough to get it, but eventually he had it. When he came back, he was presented with a horrifying sight.

It was Bingsley Colchester holding my Hide and Seek.

"Look what I found!" she said.

Two Down swallowed what appeared to be a small-sized Siamese cat in his throat.

I had to admit. It was pretty good. It was called the Original Whizzinator. It was a prosthetic penis used to deliver fake urine for drug tests. In today's world, most tests are administered in full view of the tester, to keep cheats from simply coming out of the bathroom with their neighbor's clean urine. You actually have to be *seen* holding your hose, peeing into the bottle. Well, the Whizzinator, which I found half-price on eBay, actually looked like a human penis. ("Now in White, Latino, Black, and Asian colors!" the Web site bragged.) A tube ran from a pack you wore around your groin that held heated, clean urine. Upon squeezing the prosthetic penis, it delivered that urine ("Now in easy-to-use freeze-dried urine packets!") into the cup for your tester. Very handy for people being tested for drugs at places like Boston National Ladies Golf Club.

And now Bingsley Colchester was holding the entire kit and caboodle, complete with a sticker that read: PROPERTY OF LEONARD "TWO DOWN" PETROVITZ, 571 LINDEN AVE., DORCHESTER, MA, 617-555-2135. RETURN IMMEDIATELY IF FOUND.

Okay, so that's my bad.

Two Down's face went white.

"Ohhh, I think the president of the club would be delighted to see this!" said Bingsley, dangling it with two fingers of her right hand. "Even if she *is* a lesbian!"

"That's a setup," protested Two, reaching out for it. "Who the hell puts their name on something like that?"

He lunged for it. She pulled it away. With her left hand she produced a benzene torch and she was pointing it at Two Down's ski-jump nose. "Take one more step toward me and I'll fry those stupid jumping-bean eyebrows off your face."

Two Down pulled back a foot. She fired it once, just to be sure. It emitted a six-inch-long blue flame, not enough to kill you, but enough to keep him farther than arm's length. She backed toward the door.

"Well, well, well. Now we both have a little secret, don't we?"

Two just swallowed.

"Hey, relax! I don't mind if our card-room boy lights up the occasional doobie. As long as he doesn't mind if our bridge champion enjoys a few peanuts, right?"

They could both hear women chatting outside in the hall. Two could've probably knocked the torch out of her hand and taken the Whizzinator, but Bingsley would've screamed and they both would've been kicked out of the club, one way or another.

He accepted defeat, once again, at the hands of Bingsley Colchester.

"All right, you win," he said.

"Good answer," she said, holding up the Whizzinator by the prosthetic penis itself. "Dickless."

CHAPTER 9

Never had been to England. Never had been to Europe. Never had been overseas. I like sticking to the rivers and lakes I'm used to. When I was in college and busting 70's ass every other day, my father was always trying to get me to go to Scotland on one of his bank-paid "client" father/son golf chartered-air chartered-bus blue-blazer boondoggles. "It'll be so enriching," he said. "Twenty dads, twenty sons, ten from Lake Charles [his club] and ten from Plymouth [another fancy club in town]. If we have you, we'll roast them alive!" Trust me—it wasn't like he wanted to spend time with me. What he wanted was to kill Hibbings over at First National. Real heartwarming, Kodak stuff. I'd always said thanks, but no thanks.

"Raymond, how can you truly appreciate the game if you don't know its origins?"

"I don't know," I'd say. "I'm appreciating this burger and I don't know its origins. Actually, I'm happy not to know its origins."

But now I was packed to go to Cambridge, England, home of the absolutely unheard-of Gog Magog golf course. I felt as ready as I could be. My game felt good. My nose wasn't throbbing much past "kettledrum" anymore. Had my laptop to work on the novel and hammer out greeting cards all the way over. Had one already. Picture of a jet plane with the line: "Ladies and gentlemen, we've attained our cruising altitude of 37,000 feet . . ." and on the inside the line:

And we can STILL see your birthday candles.

Now, there was only the trifling matter of the $1,395 for the ticket. Which I needed by the next day.

I decided to wander over to Ponky to see if I could put the touch on somebody. I didn't like my chances. Going to Ponky to borrow money is like going to a convent to borrow condoms.

Just as I was coming in the front door, I heard The Voice crackling over the loudspeaker.

"Hey, Ray Hart, you look thinner!" it said. "Have you lost wife?"

I paused a second at the door, took a deep breath, saluted, and headed into the Pit of Despair, where all the scholars were deeply into a favorite game amongst Chops—wagering heavily on the National Spelling Bee.

"C'mon, little Rekha!" Blind Bob was yelling. "You can do this!"

"Hey, did Bob pay the extra twenty-dollar Indian surcharge?" Hoover cautioned.

"Yeah, yeah, I paid it!" he grumbled. "But that's bullshit. This girl was born in New Jersey, not New Delhi."

"Doesn't matter," said Hoover. "You pick somebody with an Indian surname: twenty clams extra. Korean or Thai: ten. Any girl: five."

"Who's still in it?" I asked.

"Bob's got this gahl," Dom said. "I got the freckle-faced stuttahah from Omaha. And Hoovah's got the Dominican kid. Although he looks twelve, not ten. But then again, he's Dominican, so he could be fourteen."

"When's he report to the Yankees?" I asked.

"Yeah, if it comes out the kid is married with two kids and a mortgage, we get our zops back!" said Hoover.

The Indian girl spelled "insouciance" flawlessly, causing Bob to do a Tom Cruise on the couch and the others to grouse and mutter. It occurred to me that Blind Bob must've known how to spell "insouciance" or else he wouldn't have known immediately that she got it right, since he couldn't see the word on the set.

Clever guy, Blind Bob.

In the corner, Two Down was sitting in the puke orange Naugahyde recliner, reserved for the biggest loser of the day. Until somebody got in deeper than $36,000, it was all his.

He looked up at me, bitterly.

"Oh, hey everybody," he said. "Here's fucking Osama. Are you *trying* to ruin my life, Osama?"

"Two, I said I'm sorry. How did I know she'd go in the damn shoeshine room?"

"You hairball. We had her!"

Cementhead stood up to leave. "Hey, does anybody know when 24-Hour Fitness closes?"

We all rubbed facial parts.

I stepped up. "Wait. I got something important to ask you guys."

"I know what you're going to say and I agree," said Cementhead suddenly. "None of us want to see Ponky sold. Ponky is our *lives,* man. I mean, I don't have any family in the world except you knuckleheads right here. I eat most of my meals here, play all my golf here, play dice, throw quarters, watch TV here, everything. I've celebrated every big event in my life here."

"That's true," Two said. "We had all three of your last-day-of-senior-year parties here."

"Exactly! Man, I'd miss you guys so bad I don't know what I'd do. I'd probably just curl up and die!"

"That's real nice, Cement," I said, floored by his sudden eloquence. "Anyway—"

"And so," Cement continued, "I've been putting my mind to this thing."

"You *found* it?" Bob asked.

"I'm being serious here!" he continued. "Now, we've been trying to stop the Mayflower from buying Ponky, right? But maybe we need to look at it from a different angle. Maybe we need to find somebody who'll *outbid* the Mayflower for it, you know?"

All of us were sort of stunned. Cementhead was making sense?

"I don't know who you are or what you want," I said, "but what have you done with Cementhead?"

"No, listen! I had an idea of who might want Ponky more than the Mayflower."

We all just looked at each other.

"Go on," laughed Hoover.

"Okay, well, I was fixing a blown toilet over on Chatham Street, right? And this house sat right on the 13th at the Mayflower, right? One of the nice ones inside the walls, right? So I'm fixing the toilet—it was a blown elbow—and I can hear this woman on the phone complaining about her neighbor. Saying awful stuff about him. How horrible he was. How nasty he was. How he was ruining the neighborhood and bothering people at the club. Well, the woman on the other end of the phone must not have known anything about it, so she explained it to her. She said the guy is some filthy-loaded new-money Internet-porn-pioneer dot-com guy who bought this big $3 million house right over the 13th green. But when he turned in his application to join, he got dinged. Blackballed. All it takes is one person to blackball you at these Numeral palaces and your rich ass is out, right?"

"Right . . ." we all said.

"So this dot-com guy just can't believe it, right? I mean, he's sunk $3 million into this house, thinking he's going to be able to walk out his back gate and play one of the greatest courses in the world any damn time he wants, right? And now he's gonna have to just look at it, every day, like a fat lady at a bakery window, right?"

"Yeah . . ." we all said.

"So apparently this guy just loses it, right? He just starts going batshit on the Mayflower. He starts doing whatever he can think of to fuck with them. Like for a while, he gets these huge big concert speakers, just monsters, and points them toward the hole and starts playing, like gangster rap music, like Tupac and Eazy-E and a lot of stuff about johnsons and tits and stuff like that."

"You listen to rap music?" Two Down asked.

"Oh, yeah, you know, in the truck sometimes. So anyway, he harasses them with the speakers for a while, but the police stop him for noise, right? So then he hires two hookers to stand in his backyard, wearing stuff from the Hooker's Secret catalog. And as the golfers come on to the green, he has them dance and strip and yell come-ons to them like, 'Betcha can't get in the hole, big boy!' Apparently there haven't been that many three-putts there since the earthquake. So the cops tell him he can't do that, either.

"So then he put up these horrible fifteen-foot statues, huge mothers, that you couldn't help but notice, you know like Zeus screwing a swan, and a giant finger buried up to the knuckle in a giant nose, and a big one of a cocker spaniel taking a dump. They're so ugly, apparently some of the women start skipping the hole altogether."

"Unbelievable!" we all said, starting to get the idea ourselves.

"But there's nothing the Mayflower can do about it, right? Because there's no law says you can't have ugly statues in your yard. But still, he hasn't got them to give in and let him into the club, which they'll never do, especially after all that. And he hasn't really gotten revenge, either. So, see, I have this idea."

We all leaned forward, ready to learn at the feet of our new, brilliant master.

"What we do is, we go to him . . ."

"Right," we all said, expectantly.

". . . and we ask him, point-blank . . ."

"Yeah," we all say, knowing what's coming.

". . . whether he knows anybody who would like to buy Ponky! You know, just to get even!"

And we all stared blankly at him.

"Is that a good idea or what?" he boasted.

"No, you dork!" said Dom. "That is *not* a good idear. A good idear is we ask *him* if he'd like to buy Ponky!"

We all paused about twenty seconds while Cementhead let this sink in.

"Oh, yeahhhhhh!" said Cementhead. "That's a *great* idea!"

Could we all slap our foreheads in unison?

"And how we convince him," said Two Down, finally jumping to his feet, "is to say, 'Look, you buy Ponky and you can harass them on— what?—four or five holes? That's how many border the Mayflower, right? Yeah, they got a twelve-foot-high fence and hedge up between us and them, but that's nothing a twenty-foot-high loudspeaker couldn't get over. Or a bunch of guys on a trampoline. And maybe you put The Voice over there. Can you imagine what he'd say to those assholes?"

"Uh, sir," Bob said, mimicking The Voice, "is that your nose or are you chewing on a canoe?"

"Right," I said, doing my Voice impression. "Uh, sir? Don't take that swing out of town, because you'll never get parts for it."

"Right," said Hoover. "And he can do all those impressions he's always doing just as you're about to begin your backswing, you know? Johnny Carson, Tom Brokaw, Floyd the Barber as if he's gay. 'Ooooh, Andy! Andy! You got a real purdy mouth, Andy!'"

"It's genius," Bob said. "Cement, how about you and Two go tomorrow and ask him?"

And pretty soon guys were ordering up congratulatory adult beverages and slapping Cement on the back, until I had to scream.

"Heyyyyy! That's not what I needed to talk about! I need to get to England! Tomorrow! I got no cash for the plane ticket or the hotels. Can I borrow some jing from you guys?"

That stopped them cold. The place went quiet as a morgue.

"Telling you, Stick, this is a huge waste," said Dom, continuing on his popular Stick-sucks theme. "You got no chance."

"Great, Dom. And all the best with you and Kelly van Edible. Let me know where you guys register."

"Absolutely, you can borrow some money," said Two Down. "If I borrow $36,000 from you."

"You can if I get to England and qualify, you ungrateful ass," I said. "But if I can't get over there, you're screwed and we're screwed, because Ponky will be under about six inches of cement and you'll be under with it."

"I would," said Hoover, "but, you know, the wife . . ."

"Why don't you guys just stay at one of those youth brothels over there?" said Cementhead.

Jesus.

"Youth *hostels*," I grunted.

"You sure?"

I sighed.

"Besides," said Cement, "this 13th-hole guy is going to bail us out now."

Now I was hot. "Cement, A: What if he doesn't? and, B: I need to get all of our jing back we blew to the gamblers, including my son's college fund, and your Christmas club, and Bob's vacation funds; C: I need to get out of the doghouse with Dannie, and the only way I can do that is to show her that I'm not some derelict who can't put food on the table; and D: Two Down here is about to test positive for dead if somebody doesn't find him $36,000 real soon."

Blind Bob said, "I may have an idea."

All eyes turned to him.

"Well, it's kind of a long shot," he said.

"Forget it then," I said. "We'd *hate* to take a risk now!"

"Well," he said, "I've always wanted to see Britain, and . . ."

The next morning, Two and Cementhead knocked on Mr. Dot-Com's twenty-foot-high gold-trimmed double front doors at 8:00 A.M. Also at 9:00 A.M. And 10:00 A.M. Finally at noon, a six-foot-four, 2-iron-thin, cigar-stenched goof flung the door open in Hooters boxers and glasses akimbo, looking like he'd slept in a dumpster.

"What in Christ do you want?" he growled. " 'Cause if it's magazines or candy bars or God, I'm gonna have to scab you up!"

That tied Two and Cement's tongues for a second.

"Thought so!" said Dot-Com, slamming the door. Or he started to, until Two got his knee in the way. It made a sickening soft thud. As he rubbed it and tried to keep from tearing up, he squeaked, "We want to help you get even with the Mayflower."

Dot-Com squinted harder at them.

"So?"

"If you let us come in and get a bag of ice, we'll tell you," he said.

"You got thirty seconds and I'm so slamming this door."

"Okay," Two Down started, trying not to think about the pain. "Do you know the crappy muni course that's right across the hedge from the Mayflower?"

"Fifteen."

Two started talking very fast. *"Crappy course? You can see it from the road as you drive in?"*

"Ten. That's a golf course? Shit, I always thought it was a motocross track!"

"That's why this idea is so good," Two Down said.

Dot-Com's eyes opened and so did the door.

Two Down explained it all to him, what a great buy it was, how he could sink a few million into it and make it *better* than the Mayflower, how he could torment the Mayflower snobs to his heart's content, how he could keep it public, just to piss off the Mayflower even more, how anytime he or his friends came, they could march right to the first tee, no questions asked.

Dot-Com was practically in Two Down's lap by the time he finished.

"Fantastic!" he yelped. "I'm in! I'm your boy!"

The two Chops could hardly believe their ears. "Seriously?!"

"Absolutely! This is the greatest idea since tits! Whatever they've bid, I'll double it! I'll show those wrinkle-dicks! They'll wish they'd never fucked with me!"

"Wow!" Cement said. "Great! Cool!"

"And we'll have nineteen holes!" he said. "The first hole won't count 'cause everybody sucks on the first hole! And if you're not finished in three and a half hours, I send my Dobermans out for your ass! And one hole will be just a funnel green so you always make an ace on it. That way, first-time dumbshits will have to buy drinks! We'll drink free every day!"

"Perfect!" Cement said.

"And hell yeah it'll be public!" he said. " 'Course, we can't let no fucking women play, except strippers and hookers. And no Jews. And no spics, acourse. No niggers, naturally. And no damn towel-heads. Or Gunga-Dins. And, and—hey, where you fellas goin'? Fellas? Fellas!"

Logan International Airport is not a particularly convenient place to try to sneak on an international flight without a ticket, since two of the doomed 9/11 flights left from there. But, hey, why should anything get easy now?

Blind Bob was set. Since he was an injured battle vet, winner of the Silver Star, he could fly United one-quarter price as part of their Patriot Package. And of course, seeing as how he was blind, he needed an escort down the concourse, which would be me.

"Oh, we can provide an escort," the bouffant-haired ticket agent said. She turned and hollered, "Devonica?"

A young, cheery, wide-eyed black woman in a blue blazer came over. "Yes?" she said.

Bob started going all Rain Man on her. "No, no, no!" he shrieked, shaking his head and rocking back and forth against my shoulder. "Don't let her touch me!"

"Okay, Bob, okay," I said, patting his back. "Don't you worry. These nice people don't want to hurt you." I turned to the bouffant and said, "Something in Devonica's voice is throwing him. I really need to come down with him."

Bouffant snarled a little and said, "Fine. Devonica will go with you."

She approached him again.

"No, no, no!" Bob said.

"Okay, okay," said Bouffant. Then she wrote out a note for Devonica and me to see: *She will follow 10 feet behind.* The "will" was underlined.

Great. More will problems.

Now we had to ditch Devonica before we could swing into Phase II of the plan. We wandered down the concourse until we came to our gate— FLIGHT 4656/LONDON GATWICK—and took a seat. People were already starting to board. Time was getting skinny.

"We're fine," I whispered to Devonica, loud enough for Bob to hear. "You can go back now."

She took a pen and wrote on the back of the ticket, *I have to stay until you're on.*

"No, Devonica, we're fine," I said, "aren't we, Bob?"

Bob began rocking, shrieking, and chewing holes in his ticket. Now the gate was half empty.

"Tell you what, Devonica," I said. "Do you know those little kewpie dolls? The ones with the stick-up hair? Those always settle him down. Here's ten dollars. Be a dear and get us one of those, will you? They're selling them at that little shop just past Security. We'll wait here. But be sure to get a pink one."

Devonica looked worried. "I don't know . . ."

Bob screamed like he was giving birth.

"Go! There's not much time!"

So Devonica hurried off. If she ever thought to wonder about why it was essential for a blind man to have pink, she didn't let on.

I grabbed Bob's carry-on briefcase and we lit out for the bathroom, Bob holding my right elbow. I left him outside the men's room, went in, and changed instantly into a coat, tie, moustache, and dark sunglasses. When I came out, I handed the briefcase to Bob with my right hand and his harmonica to him with my left. He jammed it in the right front pocket of his jacket.

He grabbed my elbow and I took him straight to the victim we'd picked out. College kid. He was wearing a big red backpack, giant Koss head-phones, baggy camouflage cargo pants, and a University of St. Andrews sweatshirt. We were behind him at the skycap and got his name. We even knew what seat he had. He was getting a Mountain Dew out of the pop ma-chine.

I tapped Blind Bob to stop. I walked ten feet farther to the kid.

"Mr. Canwell?" I said. The kid didn't hear me.

I tapped him hard on the shoulder. He quickly turned and yanked off his headphones.

"Mr. Canwell, please stay very calm. Do not make any noticeable move-ments or remark in anything other than a conversational tone."

He looked suddenly petrified, but he nodded.

"Mr. Jake Canwell, traveling to London Gatwick, in exactly seventeen minutes? Seat 34H?"

"Uh," he muttered, looking at his watch. "Yeah, I guess. Whatever."

"Sergeant Petrocelli, U.S. Transportation Agency." I quickly flashed a badge we'd bought at Toys "R" Us that morning and put it back in my coat.

"Oh, dude," he said, his upper lip starting to tremble. "Dude, oh! Man, no! Seriously?"

What the hell was he talking about?

"Yes, Mr. Canwell. Seriously."

"Dude, can't you lemme slide? I didn't even wanna go! It was my girl-friend! She's so anti-Bush! She's a bitch! How was I supposed to know we'd get our pictures in the paper?" Tears began to well in his eyes. "My dad's gonna *kill* me, dude! He thinks I'm in the Young Republicans club!"

This was going to be much easier than I thought.

"Mr. Canwell, we may be able to, indeed, let you slide," I said. "But we'll need your full cooperation. What I'm about to tell you is classified, orange-code information. The USTA—United States Transportation Au-thority—has reason to believe a person associated with the El Hummus Liberation Front is aboard this flight."

"El Hummus?" he whimpered.

"Exactly. Without any sudden movements, notice the man behind me in the dark glasses, pretending to be blind? He is actually an air marshal."

Inside the coat pocket, Bob stuck the harmonica at us, menacingly.

The kid's eyes widened to Frisbees.

"Because of the oversold nature of this flight, there are no seats for this air marshal. Your seat is being appropriated by your country. Do this and things will go much easier on you."

Now he was bawling, but trying not to show it. "Okay! Yes, I will!" he whispered.

"In exchange, you are rebooked on the 7:13 A.M. flight tomorrow from this same gate. You may also have this thousand-dollar Patriot Package travel certificate from United, good anywhere in the U.S. for the next twelve months."

I took out the stupid fake certificate we'd made in ten minutes that morning at Kinko's.

"Oh, thank you! Thank you so much!"

"But Mr. Canwell?"

"Yes?"

"This is very important: You must say nothing of this to anybody. Not a word. Not even to airline representatives or airport officials or USTA officials. If friends or relatives ask, you simply say you were bumped. If you do speak of this, the nature of your un-American activities can and will be reported to Senator Liddy of the United States Congress."

"Oh, uh, absolutely, sir. Not a word."

"Your reservation will be waiting for you in the morning. President Bush thanks you for your patriotism."

"Oh, cool, wow, thank him, Bush, Mr. Bush, President Bush, for me, so much. And sorry about the other thing."

I checked my watch.

"Now, hand over your boarding pass, take a one-quarter turn to your left, and leave the area immediately," I said.

He did so. Then he turned.

"Can I ask one question?"

"Quickly," I said, looking at my watch. Then I saw Devonica fifty yards away and hurrying in our direction.

"This person? Is he, like, dangerous to the people on that plane?"

"Uh, yes, we have reason to believe this person, a woman, is dangerous. We also believe, uh, that she may not have boarded the plane yet. If you see her, do *whatever* you can to detain her without drawing attention to yourself."

"Yes, sir!" he said.

"We believe she's young, attractive, black," I said, talking rapid-fire. "She'll be in a United Airlines 'ambassador' disguise. And she'll be carrying a kewpie doll, probably pink or green, so her fellow spies can recognize her."

"Cool!"

"Go now. Quickly."

He turned and walked right toward poor Devonica. I snatched Bob's elbow and hurried him to the gate. They were about to close the jetway door. We had given our passes to the agent when I took one last look up the terminal, just in time to see the kid stick his foot out and trip poor Devonica, who was running by then. She went flying Pete Rose—headfirst into a rack of magazines. Jake Canwell just kept walking.

He never looked back and neither did we.

Fifty feet down the closed jetway, Bob turned to me with a huge grin and said, "USTA? What the hell? The United States Tennis Association? It's the TSA, you idiot! Transportation Security Administration! Who the hell is going to be afraid of the USTA?"

"Actually," I said, "the USTA can be *very* tough on foot faults."

Onboard, I wanted to do only one thing: Call Dannie. God I missed her. And Charlie. Damn I missed Charlie. I'd do anything to have him projectile vomit on me right then. Land on my head. Do a backflip onto my crotch. Anything.

Calling her on her cell, I finally got her to pick up. I knew I had only a minute.

"Baby?"

"Lemme guess," she said. "You sold the house and you and Miss Ribbed Pleasure are gonna go join the circus."

"That's right," I said. "She does a really cool trick with the elephants."

"You're funny," she said. "Were you ever on *Hee-Haw*?"

"Baby, I miss you. This Kelly thing is bullshit. She doesn't mean *any-thing* to me!"

The lady next to me tried to scoot farther away from me in her seat.

"So you admit you and her did it!"

"No! No! I never once touched her!"

"Are you lying, Ray?"

"I mean, I may have *touched* her, but you know, just to shake hands or maybe she bumped into me."

The lady next to me rolled her eyes.

"Oh my God!" Dannie hollered.

"No! Baby, I swear on Charlie's head! Please come home!"

"No, Ray. I can't come back yet. I don't trust you. And I can't come back until you start taking some responsibility! Don't you get it, baby? You think it's so cute not to have any ambition—well, it isn't! You can't be Daddy to all your loser beer-drinkin' golf buddies and be Daddy to your son at the same time! You got to grow up someday. Life isn't Chuck E. Cheese forever, you know. Your dad's dead, Ray. You can't blame him any-more. It's all on you now."

"Look, Baby, I'm on a plane right now for London. I'm going to try to qualify for the British Open."

Silence.

"Really?"

"Really."

Finally she took a deep breath and said, "You're goin' *now*? You could've been tryin' all summer!"

"Baby, I know. I know. I could've. I was an idiot! But now I'm trying."

"British Open qualifying? Stick, that's the hardest one! Playin' all those postage-stamp little grandma's-attic courses where you can't tell who're the caddies and who're the sheep?"

"Just like Ponky!"

A chunky, muscular stewardess gave me the "Shut off your cellphone" signal with her hands.

"Is it match or medal? One round? Two? Three?"

"Uh, don't know that yet."

"Hey, well, great! At least you've studied this thing out. How are we payin' for all this?"

"Bob's got a plan, won't cost us a thing."

"Even better! Bob's coming! The blind leading the brainless! What's he going to do, drive?"

"He's great with my tempo. And he's smart."

"And what if you don't qualify?"

"He and I will open up a B&B in one of those little towns like Thumping-on-the-Mum or Upper Spleen, something like that. Sell little needlepoint doilies in the living room."

The stewardess gave me the signal again, only this time with big pissed-off eyes.

"Ray, I mean, I hope you do well. I do. But I need to tell you something. See, I've met somebody and—"

Click.

The stewardess snapped my cell shut.

"What the hell?" I said.

"You're lucky I didn't turn you over to the authorities," she growled into my face. "I happen to *know* there's an air marshal on board."

CHAPTER 10

In the Pit of Despair, we played a macabre game. Whenever we read or heard about somebody killing himself, Two Down would always ask the standard: "Whaddya think? Jump, hose, or rope?"

And we'd all coldly and cruelly debate the merits of each.

"Me, I think I'm a hose guy," Two would say. "Not as messy. No pain. Hook that hose up to the exhaust and drift right off to the big dirt nap. Very seamless."

"Nah, you're too ADD to do hose," I'd say. "You couldn't sit still in a car that long. You'd keep hopping up and going back into the house to call us, tell us shit to say about you at the funeral."

"Hey, speaking of that, don't forget, I want a cell phone in the casket with me, just in case. You heard about that Thai guy, right? Woke up three days after they buried him? Had a chicken bone in his throat and it cut off all his vital signs for a while? Make sure I can reach out and touch you guys."

"What? And waste my minutes?"

But now, on this particular bus stop in our lives, it looked very much like all three of us could be the actual subject of "jump, hose, or rope," maybe all at once.

I mean, consider the wash of blues that was cascading over the three of us, all at once.

First, there was Dom.

You can't imagine how obsessed he became with Kelly van Edible. You've got to understand, Dom *never* got rejected. Not once. Ever. He was so handsome he'd make a Chippendale dancer go into the insurance business. Even my wife salivated over him. "That boy is just finer 'n a Safeway chicken," she'd say dreamily. Her sister met him once and said he "could make a girl plow clean through a fence."

And yet he could not, for all of his efforts, get the time of day from Kelly. Forget that, he couldn't get the current month. He moped around Ponky like a sick yak, playing holes but forgetting what he made, staring off into the window of the pro shop, not even going out and getting laid but, like, every third day.

We knew Dom was MIA when Cementhead came up to him with the obit page, looking for a good bet in the cemetery game, and said, "Check this out! I'll bet this has *never* happened before: Everybody died yesterday in perfect alphabetical order!"

And Dom just stared off into the distance and muttered, "Weird."

He was one sagging stud. And then the Human Stain came up to him and said something so shitty that for weeks afterward, Chops stirred his vodka tonics with their schlongs whenever he went to the john.

"What troubles thee, Romeo?" the Stain said, eating his third plateful of Blu Chao's Velveeta wontons. "Juliet won't come out from yonder windowpane?"

"Get bent, Stain," said Dom.

"What's amusing," continued Stain, "is that the young damsel Kelly seems to be free to date anybody in our fair burg save thee."

Dom turned to face him. "What do you mean? Like who?"

"Whom."

Dom grabbed Stain hard by the collar.

"Listen, you oompa-loompa, you bettah dish whatevah news you got on Kelly or I'll pop yah eyes out and eat 'em like olives."

"All right, all right, calm thyself! It's just that I overheard her on the phone. Seems she's got a blind date tonight. Some gentleman friend of her hairstylist. Apparently the girls call him Gary the God. More than that, sounds like Kelly has been hoping to get this date for a while. They're eating at the Blarney Stone. Eightish."

Dom let go of the Stain and a pall fell over his face. "Goddamn! Everybody gets to shaht-ahm her except me?"

Upon much brooding, he set out on a plan only a desperate man could conceive, a plan that would surely be of absolutely no help to him and only damage the chances of others. In other words, he set out on Operation Cockblock.

The Blarney Stone sits in the middle of Belleville Street, only two blocks from the Lawn and Bottle Club, as we like to call the ever-present collection of bums, winos, and scholarly types who hang there.

Seated at the front window was Kelly van Edible, in her new Betsey Johnson dress, and a guy who seemed to be America's largest purchaser of hair product, Gary the God. He seemed to have been bought at the Kevin Costner knockoff store, only taller, younger, and more cut. He was a blond Dom, and he made Dom see green.

It was sometime after the soup when the first bum, reeking of Ripple and Eau de Funk, came storming up to their table and grabbed Gary the God hard by the shoulders.

"C'mon, man!" pleaded the bum. "Please! I need more time to pay! Just a little more time! I'm begging you, man! It's just—ain't nobody else ever charged me a hundred percent interest before!"

Gary the God pushed the vagrant off him. "Get away from me! I don't even *know* you!"

The bum came in harder. "C'mon, dude! Call your boys off me! I got a mama who loves me! I'll pay! I'll pay! Just another twenty-four hours!"

Kelly, flabbergasted, shrank back in her chair. Gary the God looked at her, panicked.

"I don't even know who this guy is!"

He wailed for help from a nearby waiter. "Get this bum outta here! We don't even know him!"

As two waiters dragged the bum off, he hollered, "Why you gotta play me this way, man? You know I got kids!"

Gary the God tried to straighten his shirt and hair, nervously laughing like a guy who's just been caught with a troop of Cub Scouts in the basement. "Wow. Kelly, honestly, that guy, I mean, he so obviously mistook me for somebody else! I mean, you could see what kind of shape he was in! What a freak! I mean, why would I associate with someone of that kind?"

Kelly said she understood and believed him and not to worry about it and wasn't that weird and let's get some more pinot.

But into the meat of their shepherd's pie came a downtrodden woman, eyebrows furrowed, dusty cleavage swaying this way and that out of her nineteen-dollar peekaboo dress. She stomped straight up to Gary the God, threw her hands on her hips, and said, "Penicillin didn't help either, you bastard!" She threw a ring at him and stomped out.

The entire restaurant turned and froze. Mystery Date was speechless, shoulders up, palms up, eyebrows up, trying to laugh but getting nothing to come up.

"I mean, what's going on here?" he said, finding the ring in his lap. "I mean, look at this! This is a two-dollar ring! I, I, I've never seen that woman in my life! This is crazy!"

Kelly had her lips pursed and was looking down so as not to have to see the fifty or so other faces staring at her for her reaction. "Yeeeah," she said through a hard white line that used to be her mouth. "Let's just finish our dinner and go. Before Britney Spears comes in with your baby."

"Kelly, look, I swear! I don't—this is all so—she was just lying! I wouldn't touch a person who—I mean did you see her? As *if* I would even *look* at somebody—"

"Forget it," Kelly said, wishing she could fall through the floorboards. "Eat."

"Kelly—"

"Just shut up and eat! Okay?"

So they buried their heads in their meals and flinched each time a waiter came up. They looked up with alarm at every customer passing them on the way to the restrooms. They finished, paid, and were climbing into his Maserati convertible when the third shoe dropped in the form of a pastel note left under the passenger-side wiper. Naturally, it was Kelly who snatched it up and read it.

Gary. It will never be over for me. Forever, Lance.

"That's it!" Kelly hollered. "Goodnight, everybody! Drive carefully! I ammmm outie!"

She crumpled up the note, flipped it over her shoulder, and started walking with her thumb stuck out.

"No! Kelly! Somebody is trying to screw me over here! This is somebody's idea of a sick joke! I'm *not* gay! Okay? I'm not! And that other woman! What a liar! And that first guy! I mean, come on! Who's doing this to me?"

Kelly's head just dropped as she walked away.

The first car that came along, a red Porsche, screeched its brakes, backed up, and Kelly ran to it. When she saw the driver was Dom, she crinkled her forehead.

"Kelly?" Dom said. "Are you all right? You look freaked out. You need a ride or something?"

And it all added up in her head.

She slammed the door, flipped him off, and started walking the other way, just in time to get passed by Gary the God in his Maserati, cell pressed to his ear. And as she tried to wave at him, she could hear him say, "Lance? You can't mean that!"

Second, there was Two Down, who had never before slowed down in his life long enough to be morose. For Leonard Petrovitz, life was an all-you-can-eat buffet, timed. This is a man who, when attempting a long putt, would send it on its way and then chase after it, hollering "Eleven o'clock news!" just before it dropped in. He was Walter Mitty in golf spikes. His self-image was along the lines of Ernie Els. He'd go to Richmond's Big and Tall Shop, pick something out, and go, "This is perfect. Just take about eight inches off the sleeves and I'll pick it up Thursday."

Two believed life was his oyster and he swallowed it meat, pearl, and tablecloth. He liked to come barreling into the clubhouse after winning piles of stackable jing and holler, "Stop yer cryin', Two Down's buyin'!" And after a monstrously big win, he'd yelp, "Stop yer bitchin'! Two Down's openin' the kitchen!"

His mind was unlike anything God ever strapped to the top of a spinal column. One time he hosted a very large dice game. The pot was just over a thousand when the cops came busting through the door. That's when Two Down quickly slapped the dice off the table, stood up, and announced, "Well, that's very generous of you gentlemen. The Boys and Girls Club will be so pleased!" and scooped up all the cash with both arms, stuffed it in his coat pockets, and left, hollering, "You'll all be invited to the Easter egg hunt!"—leaving the cops and rollers wondering what in the world they could do to stop him.

This was a man who used to go out and get stinking drunk with us, then call a flatbed truck to come get him *and* his car. Who needs taxis? I can still see him, sitting behind the wheel as the flatbed hauled him away, honking at people he knew, flashing the lights, air-toasting them with his fresh-squeezed Bud.

But the man sitting in the puke orange La-Z-Boy, looking like somebody on his way to anesthetic-free dentistry, seemed to bear no resemblance to the real Two.

Luckily, the Human Stain was around to make things worse.

"I have an idea that I think could get you out of this predicament," Stain announced. "May I proffer it?"

"No," Two said, staring blankly. "You may fold it sideways and stick it."

"Fine. Here's what you do. You engage the services of a very good plastic surgeon and get your face completely redone. I mean everything. Change your eyes, your nose, your ears. Get fuller lips, have your eyebrows narrowed, your nostrils widened, your eyelids lifted, your cheeks dropped, the works. Then you change your hair color and your hairstyle. You completely change your look, all different clothes. You move to the other side of town. You change your name, your job, and your friends. You get all new habits, a new car, a new religion. Now you tell me: How are they *ever* going to find you then?"

Two Down just sat in the chair clutching his haircut, trying not to listen.

"True, but then he'd look like some kind of fag!" Hoover offered.

"Yeah," contributed Cement, "but he got all that surgery for free!"

"True," Hoover said, "but now he's gotta get all new friends because his old friends won't recognize him!"

"True," said Stain, "but they can't collect any money you owe them. And besides, now you can have better-looking friends!"

"Okay, let's just assume," Hoover said, rising and crossing the room like Clarence Darrow, "that Two Down is willing to give up all his friends, stop doing the things he likes, go through all the pain and risk of all that surgery. Let's say he's willing to do this and completely change who he is. That kind of surgery would cost $100,000. He doesn't have $100,000. He doesn't have a dollar. That's why he's in the mess he's in. He needs to *get* $36,000, not *spend* $100,000, you halfwit."

Stain sniffed. "How simple my brother-in-law is. Don't you see? How can the plastic surgeon get the money from him if he can't *recognize* him!"

And now Hoover was holding *his* haircut.

Two Down nearly sank *beneath* the La-Z-Boy. This problem with Big Al seemed to be beyond Two Down. He wanted Big Al and his colleagues to understand that he was making every effort to pay him. That's why he asked them to meet at Ponky to hear his plan. When they showed up—all three of them in the Lincoln—they walked up to the clubhouse like Jesse James and his gang.

Two treated them to a cardboard box of Blu Chao's Vietnamese calzones and ice-cold Gennys.

"So, my American friend, what iz it that you are dezired to inform us with?" Big Al said, pushing away the food.

Two Down ran his fingers through his hair and took a deep breath.

"Okay, I know I owe you guys $36,000, and I just want you to know I have some pretty creative ideas for paying you back."

"Such az?" Big Al said, arms folded over his chest.

"Such as, I've decided to let you fellas in on my business plan. Ground floor. I'll cut you in as full partners—until the $36,000 is paid off, of course."

"Not interezted," said Big Al.

"No, but listen!" Two Down said, practically spraining his eyebrows trying to sell it. "This is good. I've come up with the perfect idea: the remote-control bumblebee. Can you imagine? You're betting somebody huge, some guy who needs to make a putt for $50,000. What he doesn't know is that you've got the remote-control bumblebee in your pocket. You discreetly flip it out on the ground, hit the remote, and just as the guy is about to putt, *zzzzzzip*—the bee goes right by his nose. He yanks the putt a foot off line and the bee has paid for itself five hundred times over!"

"Nyet."

"And it wouldn't just be great on the golf course! You could mess with your ex-wife! Kids could screw with teachers! Can you imagine how much you could win in Vegas? The Oklahoma kicker is about to make a field goal that's going to beat you out of twenty-five large, you send the bee after him, it goes up his helmet, Texas wins!"

"No more talk of bumblebee or I break arm."

"Right, right, there would be some development costs with that one. But what about this one? Look out the window. Right there. What do you see?"

"A graveyard?" said Dewey.

"Exactly! All that gorgeous grass, those fantastic trees, the little meandering stream, all going to waste, right? Cities and counties all over America trying to find land to build golf courses on, and the answer is right in front of them—the cemetery!"

"You wanna build a golf course in a cemetery?" Dewey asked.

"Exactly!" Two Down actually leaped in the air at this. "Our company would specialize in the building—in the *respectful* building—of golf courses on cemeteries. 1) They're the perfect size. 2) The land is woefully underused, and 3) No dead person is disturbed! And think of all the advantages! Yardage markers on the gravestones, for instance. You know, 'Here lies Sam Dilbert, 183 yards.' "

"Nyet."

"Although I'm sure we'll all kick ourselves when this idea starts sweeping America," Dewey said.

Two Down's shoulders slumped. He looked like a man watching his new boat sink.

"We require our moniez," said Big Al. "Now."

"Okay, let me work on a few more ideas."

"No more ideaz. We have already given for you the three dayz extra. Pleaz to give us the moniez."

"But, see, I don't have any, you know, liquid funds, available, uh, currently."

"What about the Bentley?" asked Dewey.

"Bentley?" said Two Down, a drop of sweat meandering lazily down his temple.

"The one out in the parking lot."

"Yeah, well, see, that's not mine. That's a friend's."

"Thiz will be fine," said Big Al. "Pleaze to tell him thank you from uz."

"Well, actually, you see, it's a she. Mrs. Wilcox. Mrs. Gertrude Wilcox. And she—"

"Fine," Big Al said, getting up. "Bring uz the—what iz English?—the *title* and the keyz. Tomorrow night. Zix o'clock. We shall at that point be even."

"What? No! I can't! It's not mine!"

"The Bentley or the moniez," Big Al said, pushing his big shoulders through the Ponky door. "Zix. Or elze."

As they swaggered out to the parking lot, the Voice announced: "Attention Ponky visitors! Take advantage of our July Fourth special! Whack one Chop, get the second one free!"

Big Al turned again to look for the source of it.

"Iz funny man, actually," he said. "Should write humor column in *Pravda*."

Third, jammed in the center seat, between Abject Loneliness and Simmering Red Ass, was me.

I met someone.

You'd be amazed how many times you can repeat a single phrase over and over in your mind during one six-hour coach-class flight, each time attaching some new meaning to it.

Could she really have met someone *met someone*? Could she just be trying to make me jealous? Damn right she could be! Could it be just a bluff! Could be—but what if it's not? What if she's trying to tell me that her feelings for this guy are serious and I need to solve our problems or it could be all over? And if that's true, why the *hell* was I on a plane going four thousand miles *away* from her? On the other hand, wasn't this showing her that I was serious? That I *did too* have ambition, despite what every friend, boss, and family member had always told her? Not to get all Tibetan monk on you, but what the hell was "ambition" anyway except a fucked-up capitalistic push for you not to be happy with what you had? A way to constantly want the Saab 9000S when you already had the Saab 9000? A way not to *be* but to *want*? A way to work your ass off all your life so you can retire at fifty-five and play golf and cards with your buddies and drink beer? I had all that *now*!

Why was she so concerned about me fulfilling my potential when I wasn't? Wasn't it my potential to fuck up as I wanted? Everybody was so concerned about me being great at golf, forcing it on me, wanting it for themselves *through* me, that I walked away from it. I resented it. I purposely didn't try, just to say, "You won't control me. I'm not here to live for you."

But then I remembered Dannie saying something once: "That's all bullshit, Babe. What you fear is finding out you *aren't* great. 'Cause it's a helluva lot safer havin' that pretty unopened present sitting under the tree all the time, Ray. Helluva lot safer than opening it and finding out it's just an old lump a coal. Right, Ray?"

"Ray!"

It was Bob, pulling on my shoulder. "Man, can't you hear anymore? I said your name four times! Damn."

"Sorry."

"Okay. Now, read these faxes Hoover gave me. Tells us where we're going and when you play and all that."

I read Hoover's printout.

British Open Local Qualifying

The Gog Magog

Cambridge, England

July 4

One 18-Hole Round

Top Nine (Plus Ties) Move On to Final Qualifying

Medal Play

And then in italics:

Hart, Raymond—USA

Tee time: 2:53 P.M.

"You realize that means we have to get our butt up there as soon as we land, find this place, hit balls and play, all today, without any sleep, right?"

"True," I said. "But what's at stake, really?"

"Nothing, really," he said. "Except Ponky and Leonard's kneecaps and possibly your marriage."

"Exactly," I said.

We rented a crappy little right-hand-drive Fiat on the concept that rental car companies cannot know that you are fifteen hundred in debt on your credit card already. But by the time we pulled into Cambridge, I felt like a hansom cab had run over me forward and back. The left side of the Fiat was scraped from me panicking and pulling so far to the left that I was scratching hedges, fences, and walls to avoid the traffic that was suddenly coming at me down the wrong side of the road. Bob poured two espressos down me, fed me a pork pie—awful little sausage pies that were so bad I was surprised Blu Chao didn't serve them—signed me up, and got me on the range to hit exactly fourteen balls and three putts.

Who needs better prep than that?

The Gog Magog looked a little like Ponky but slightly more manicured. Then again, the city dump is more manicured than Ponky. It was definitely linksy, no trees. It looked like it was mowed once a month by six sore-gummed sheep. There was a sign that read NO ROUND SHALL TAKE MORE THAN 3½ HOURS, which made Blind Bob and me hoot. "We barely make the turn in that," he said.

Lord, it was flat. I could just hear my wife if she were there. "Damn," she'd have said, "this course is so flat you could watch your dog run away for three days."

Sigh.

Made me think of a good greeting card. It would be a woman on the front and she'd be saying:

I've really missed you. I mean I've REALLY missed you. In fact, I'm going to meet you at your airport gate lying on a mattress.

And inside . . .

You better be the first guy off that plane.

And so it was I made my way to the 1st tee, having declined Bob's generous offer to caddy. "I need no help sucking," I said. He said he'd stay on the porch and listen to girls walk by, imagining them all as Elizabeth Hurley. How he knew what Elizabeth Hurley looked like was anybody's guess.

So this was it. The best nine scores (plus ties) out of 141 players were going to make it to final qualifying. Some guys came with professional caddies, some hauling their own bags on pull carts, some with their fathers or brothers or mothers on the bag, some French, some Swedish, some with perfect Ben Hogan swings and some with Hulk Hogan swings. The par was only 70, and there was already a 63 on the board from the morning round, so there went one of the spots. The best after that was one 64, three 65s, and a pile of 67s and 68s. So there was room in there to qualify at 65 or 66 for one very desperate, unlaid, greeting card writer from Dorchester, Massachusetts, if he could somehow play his best round of the year on no sleep, one pork pie, and two No-Doz.

It was threesomes. I was with a thirtyish-looking guy featuring triangle sideburns and spiked blond hair, a cool bowling shirt, and patterned pants. He introduced himself as Desmond. He looked like the sax player in a jazz quartet who gets the good ecstasy. "Pleasure," he said. He had a professional caddy. Guy named Provisional. Dez told me Provisional got his name for always having a backup plan, no matter the situation. Like, if he was out at lunch, he'd say, "I'll 'ave the 'amburger, love, but only with the Muenster cheese. If they don't have Muenster, then I'll 'ave the chicken sandwich, if you please."

The other player was a kid, couldn't have been nineteen, real slick, with the Titleist hat perfectly bent, the wraparound sunglasses stuck on his hat backward, the buttoned-up golf shirt with the sleeves that went past his elbow, the five-hundred-dollar golf pants that broke fashionably twice at his leather FootJoys. His caddy was a man about forty-five-ish, also spiffy, with nicer shoes than I'd worn to my wedding, gorgeous khakis, an alligator belt, and a golf shirt with a Sunningdale logo on it. Perhaps the only Savile Row caddy in history.

"My name's Ray," I said to the kid, offering my hand.

"If you insist," he said in a stuffy British accent, sticking his tee in the ground.

Okay, so *that's* how it was going to be.

Punk Boy took a rip at his drive and flushed it three hundred yards, at least, down the center cut.

"Good shot," I said, teeing my ball up.

"Get used to it," he said.

Cheeky. I hit a kind of high draw out there thirty yards behind him, and as it landed the kid says, just loud enough for me to hear, "Get in a divot."

Nice manners.

Desmond put a pretty swing on his and blew it by both of us, but the end had a tail on it and he wound up in the right rough. I couldn't help notice the punk didn't say a word to him.

As we walked, the kid's caddy said to me, "Where do you join us from, Ray?"

"Boston," I said.

"What propels an American to come over here with the outlandish idea he can qualify for our Open?"

I get it. *Our* Open.

"United Airlines," I said, thinking myself funny.

"I see you have the sparkling American wit so treasured among game show hosts," he said archly. "So you failed in your attempts to qualify for the American Open and are now gracing us with your presence?"

"Nope. Didn't even try to qualify for the U.S. Open. I just came over 'cause I like pork pies."

"Charming," he said, walking away.

From the looks of him and the way he talked to the Punk, the guy had to be his father. It was a two-man show. Like father, like jerkwipe.

I didn't care. I've taken more shit than a fat stripper. Thanks to the Chops, you could run the Macy's parade behind my backswing and it wouldn't get to me.

But Lord knows these two assholes tried.

On 5, to my tee shot, the kid said: "Get out of bounds!"

On 7, just before my birdie putt, the father said: "Knock it close, Ray."

On 8, the kid screamed "Fore!" on both my drive and Dez's when they were headed for nothing but the light rough.

On 9 green, the kid kept backing off his putt. An old codger was watching us play while absentmindedly jingling the change in his pocket. This unnerved the Punk to no end. Finally he walked over to the old guy.

"Sir, have you any change?"

And the old guy, surprised to be talking to one of the participants, stammered out, "Well, yes, yes. I believe I do. How much do you require?"

"All of it," the punk said. "Whatever you have, if you please."

So the guy had like 4 pounds and 73 shillings in his pocket and the punk kid gave him a five-pound note for them. Then the kid took the change and heaved it as hard as he could right over the old codger's head. Then he stared daggers at the old guy and went back to his putt. Very classy kid.

I made the turn in two-under 33, then birdied 10 and 11, very crisply, I thought. All I knew was I was one shot up on the brat and two on Desmond. I don't know how. I was beat like a Persian rug. I was on autopilot, really. Every shot I hit came out of memory, not will or effort. I kept setting up to shots and thinking I was back with my favorite teacher, my Uncle Joe, while he sat behind me in a lawn chair under the old willow at the range at his course. He'd sit and I'd hit for hours, him giving me tips between laughs. I loved golf with my uncle. All he cared about was the purity of the shot, not where it was going to lead me in life. Maybe that's the way I should play every round—so tired that I go there. I was swinging great. If I parred in from there, I'd shoot four-under 66, and I guessed if I could do that or better, I'd make the top nine.

But then came the 13th—a 208-yard par-3. The kid went first and knocked it onto the green, but his ball disappeared over a little ridge and down. I thought maybe he was off the green, but my yardage book said there was a lower level to the green. I hit my 8-iron on the same line and it disappeared over the same little ridge.

As I got to the green, I saw the two balls were about eight feet apart, one of them deeper than the other. The kid and his dad were already at the near one, reading their line. I went to the deep one, marked it, cleaned it, and lined it up again. I hit my putt about four feet past. But I couldn't help noticing that they were both standing and looking at me.

Finally, the father cleared his throat and said, "I'm not sure how they do things in the colonies, but in England, we're not in the habit of hitting our opponent's ball. In truth, it's a two-shot penalty."

It took a second to sink into my jet-lagged cerebellum. *Hit our opponent's ball?* What the hell was he talking about? I looked at the ball and saw, to my horror, that it was a Precept 00 instead of my own Titleist 3. And then it hit me: I'd been suckered.

The two of them were looking away to keep from laughing outright. They'd tricked me. They'd walked to the *wrong* ball and pretended it was theirs. But they'd been careful not to touch it. They just stood over it and lined it up like it was theirs. They'd moosed me into assuming the shorter ball was mine and in my walking coma, I never even checked it. Who goes to the wrong ball?

"You assholes," I said, my mind frying. "You did that on purpose."

Desmond walked over. "What happened?" he said.

"These two bastards, the guv'ner and the prince," I said. "They walked to my ball and started lining it up, so I'd think this other one was mine. I hit the wrong ball."

"Oh, you paranoid Americans," tsk-tsked the father. "Always sure everybody's out to get you."

"Well, what *were* you doing standing by his ball?" Desmond asked.

"Simply seeing what type of putt our opponent had," he said. "Quite within the rules."

"Bollocks!" said Desmond, glaring at him. I had no idea what "bollocks" meant, but from the look he gave him, I'm guessing in Ponkese it meant, "You're so fucking crooked you have to screw on your hat."

I took a step toward the Family Fuck. Don't know what I was going to do, but it would probably involve burying my putter into one of their orifices at least up to the leather. Desmond got in the way.

"You limey shits," I said as Dez held me back.

"I'd love to, old man," said the kid, trying to get me to brawl.

I had to walk off the side of the green and take ten deep breaths to calm myself down. I'm sure I've been more pissed, but I can't remember when.

I was just so torqued off I missed my four-foot comebacker, my first bogey of the day. Well, actually, with the two-shot penalty, my first triple bogey. The kid two-putted and picked up three greasy shots on me, just like that, and led me by two. Not only that, but now I was only one-under for the day instead of four, back in with the huddled masses, and I knew I had to somehow get to four-under to have a prayer. I was madder than Billy Graham in a gay bar.

I walked up to the dad and said, "I *will* get even, hairball. If I have to move next door to you, I *will* get even."

"I see we've gotten under your skin," he said. "You Americans are *so* predictable."

I vowed then and there—I was *not* sending those two a Christmas card.

CHAPTER 11

As a full-ride scholarship student at Bridgefield State, Resource Jones was afforded many an hour to ruminate on his life and plans. These meditations, day and night, tended to center around this Don Knotts–looking character and how in the world to get rid of him for one simple golfing Tuesday.

He already knew that the first man was Malcolm Baker, but how was he supposed to locate this Knotts lookalike without a name, address, phone number, occupation, or background? Furthermore, how would he cancel that person's regular Tuesday golf game without raising suspicion? And furthermost, how could he do it when he was allowed no outgoing e-mail messages and only one phone call per month?

Lesser men than this would've given up. Not Resource Jones. He cinched up the zipper on his bright orange prison jumpsuit and set to it.

He began with a simple idea. He waited for Don Knotts to leave a wedge on the edge of the green while he putted. Then Resource calmly wandered over, picked up the club, and glanced casually for a sticker on the shaft that would have not just his name but his address and phone number, for no golfer wants to lose his trusty wedge.

Alas, there was nothing. Mr. Knotts apparently was not in the habit of leaving wedges lying around golf courses like newspapers in a train station.

"Your wedge, sir," Resource said, handing it to a very surprised and, in fact, petrified Don Knotts as he came off the green. Looking at Knotts, he had such a gaunt face you were sure it was painted over his bones. He had a weak chin, but not so weak that it couldn't have beat the crap out of his formless mouth. The man looked like he tanned with a 25-watt lightbulb.

"Oh! Uh, well, uh, thanks," he stammered.

Couldn't do that again. Prisoners were not supposed to purposely come within fifty feet of the golfers, to say nothing of quasi-caddy for them. He returned to his bunker and began raking again without looking up.

On to Plan B. Resource had one friend in the pro shop, a black second-string assistant pro/cart washer who he'd crack jokes with now and then.

"Hey, wanna get a brew after work?" Resource would say to the guy.

The guy was at first taken aback, but he soon caught on.

"Sure, sure," he said. "And then catch a movie?"

"Sure! How 'bout *Shawshank Redemption*?" Resource said.

This time Resource saw him, sidled over to him the way only a prisoner can sidle, and said, "Hey, man, I coulda swore I saw my fifth-grade math teacher out there on 1. I don't wanna talk to him or anything—he gave me a D—but I just *know* it's him. Could you check the starter's sheet?"

"Uh, sure, I guess," the pro said. "What time you think he went off?"

"I'm pretty sure it was the 8:08."

Ten minutes later the guy was back with the news: "It just says Baker."

"Nobody else?"

"Nope. Just Baker twosome."

"Okay, not him. Thanks anyway."

Just his luck to try to chase two guys who are just slightly more secretive with their personal information than KGB agents.

Plan C: For his weekly half hour of supervised Internet access, Resource Jones had memorized the phone number he'd stolen off Malcolm Baker's scorecard weeks before and plugged it into Google while the guard was at the end of the line. He knew he had thirty-two seconds to do this— from the time the guard generally wandered past his station to the time he wandered back—as he'd timed it out. He hit ENTER as quickly as humanly possible, but the computer was in no such rush and just ambled along, the little blue bar meandering forward like a boy on the first day of school. At last, with the guard eight feet away, Google spat it out: Your search did not match any documents.

"Bummer," he said as the guard looked over his shoulder.

"What were you looking up," the guard asked, "travel agents? Hah!" And he paced on, rejoicing at his wit.

Plan D came to him weeks later, when he suddenly glanced up from his powdered eggs with a look of Eureka! What was the leading export of Bridgefield State Penitentiary—hello?—license plates!

The next day he made it a point to be working near the parking lot fence when the black Ford Explorer arrived. He took one glance at the tag and memorized that, too: 513YZZ. Then he took that number, along with three packs of Marlboros and a promise of dessert for a month, to Porn Stash, the office guy in the license plate office. Hey, if this thing went right, he would be gone within a week and *anybody* could have his desserts as far as he cared.

Within two days Porn Stash was back with the goods on Massachusetts 513YZZ:

MALCOLM W. BAKER
1127 Delpino Way
Fitchburg, MA
978-555-3839
Bought at Fitchburg Ford
May 21, 2001
Paid $19,877.33

Once he had the number, it was only a matter of waiting for somebody to go putt while leaving a cellphone in the front of the cart—and almost everybody brought their cellphone—slipping it into his pocket, then slipping into the lightning shack an hour later and calling Two Down's cell.

There was no answer, so he left the following message, as slowly and succinctly as he could: "Two, it's 'Source. Got a big project for you. Big. My life depends on it. Can you please call one of your guys with Mass Bell and get the last six months of outgoing and incoming calls for 978-555-3839? Guy's name is Baker. When you get the records, see if you can find a number that he calls every Monday or Tuesday morning or a number that calls him every Monday or Tuesday morning. Probably a short call, a minute or less. Call the number and figure out some way to tell if that guy is Baker's golf partner every Tuesday out here at Prison View. You'll think of some way to do it. Maybe you're an MCI salesman, I don't know. When you find his partner, come out to the course. Get a morning tee time. I'll see you. Leave the guy's info under the water jug on the tee box at 5. You do this without fucking it up, you skinny mother, and I'll give you seven shots a side for life, and you know you got no business getting no more 'n four."

Click.

Directions as long and complicated as that would seem more confusing than Father's Day at Woody Allen's house. But for whatever divine reason, it all came off as smooth as soft serve. Two called his friend in the mail room at Mass Bell, who faxed the bills to him at the assisted-living home posthaste. In his examination of the bills, Two, thinking himself Sam Spade, thrilled at finding the number almost immediately. It was the first time in a week he wasn't thinking about which kidney Big Al would knife.

Resource had said *every* Monday, and there was only one call that happened nearly *every* Monday the last six months: 978-555-6671. Just to double-check, Two plugged the number into Google and it came up as a Mrs. Sylvia Hornbecker, who had once volunteered to host a quilting meeting at her house, leaving for the world to see her address, phone, and even a suggestion of cookie types for the Quite-a-Quilt members to bring.

Two Down went to a phone booth, slapped on his best Don Pardo voice, and said, "Is Mr. Hornbecker in?"

"Hold on," said the disappointed teenager.

In a moment Mr. Hornbecker, first name unknown, came on with his squeaky, nervous voice: "This is [throat clear], this is Mr. Hornbecker."

"Mr. Hornbecker! What a pleasure! It's First Sergeant Darrell Dregs over at Prison View nine-hole golf course over at Bridgefield State Prison. How are you this fine evening?"

"Oh, uh, okay I guess."

"Fine, fine! Mr. Hornbecker, I'm conducting a customer satisfaction survey on our Prison View nine-hole golf course here at Bridgefield."

"Oh."

"Now, you ARE a regular at the golf course, am I correct?"

"Well, yes, yes I am."

"—play every Tuesday, according to our records."

"Well, yes—"

"Play with Mr. Baker, am I right?"

"Well, yes. Have I done anything wrong?"

"Wrong? Wrong? Oh, no, Mr. Hornbecker! We're eternally grateful for your business. We just want to ask you one question: Are you happy with the course?"

"Oh, well, actually, as long as you mentioned it, there are quite a few—"

"Wonderful! Thanks so much for your time this fine evening Mr. Hornbecker and remember, the only bad view at Prison View is from the inside! Hah! Little prison humor there, Mr. Hornbecker! Well, again, thanks and goodnight!"

The next day, keeping a low profile to avoid Big Al, Two "borrowed" the drop-dead white 1964 Lincoln Continental belonging to Mrs. Opel Hickenlooper, an early Alzheimer's patient in the Benny Goodman wing. God, she was beautiful—baby blue interior, white trim, suicide doors, and only 32,356 miles.

He drove the two hours out to Bridgefield. The drive would give him time to think about what the hell he was going to do that night at 6:00 P.M., when the Brothers Grim would be sitting at Ponky, expecting $36,000 from him or a Bentley, which, he noticed, was no longer in the basement garage at the assisted-living home. In fact, he even toyed with the idea of dropping off Resource's info and then continuing west until he hit, say, Milwaukee.

He'd played here once before, on a visit to see Resource, but this time he couldn't find him. He played the first six holes, sticking the little envelope containing all the information under the water jug at No. 5 as prescribed. At 7 green, he thought he recognized Resource working on a bunker wall, his back to him. Nobody else was anywhere near, but Two dared not speak directly to him. So as he lined up his putt, his head down, he said, "Nice work if you can get it."

"Shuttup," Resource said quietly, without turning, "Everybody will apply. How you playin', Two?"

"Bad. Had to lay off two trophy engravers. How's the food in this joint?"

"I toss my own salad, if that's what you mean."

"We all miss you, 'Source. You're the only one all of us trust."

"I'll include it on my résumé."

Two putted out and got in his cart.

"You don't got it too bad, you know. In fact, today? I'd trade you places."

"Tell the warden, will ya?"

Two drove off.

Later, Resource got himself a drink at 5, slid the small envelope into his pocket, then looked at it during his grumpy break.

Resource,

You SO owe me, bitch.

Guy's name is Hornbecker. Don't know his first. Home number:

978-555-6671. 2890 Juniper St., Fitchburg. Wife: Sylvia, and at least one teenage girl. Real mousey type. Scared of own sneeze. DOES play weekly w/ Baker.

I get EIGHT a side for this, plus one floating Clinton, you slob.

Huggy Bear

Then and there, Resource Jones decided to raise his success expectation to 85 percent.

While the Father and Son from Hell were ruining my life out on the unfriendly confines of the Gog Magog golf course, Blind Bob was back in the clubhouse, keeping his ears open and asking questions. People love to help blind people. They'd give them piggybacks down I-95 if asked.

So when word filtered back to the clubhouse what they'd done to me, Bob's little ears perked up.

"Excuse me?" he said, looking purposely lost with his white cane in the middle of the clubhouse. "Who are these two men you're talking about?"

Immediately an assistant pro came over to him. "Ah, it's that sod Worstenheim and 'is bratty kid, Phillip. 'E's a big blow'ard with the Royal and Ancient. Or the Royal and Dandruff, as I call 'em. 'E thinks 'is smarmy kid is the next Nick Faldo. 'E ain't bad, but 'e ain't no Nicky, let me tell you! Plus, 'e's got the manners of a sick walrus. If you were t'ask me, I'd be delighted to see the both of 'em 'angin' from that willo' there."

"Oh?" said Bob. "This Worstenheim, what's his first name?"

"Allistair. But most people call 'im Commodore, 'cuz 'e was in the Royal Navy. Falklands. Lot a bollocks. A lot of us know wha' he really done. 'E fucked up is wha' he done. Incompetent bastard. Drove 'is boat too damn hard. Blew the thing up! Coupla blokes came home in pieces, I heard."

Blind Bob decided that was very interesting.

.   .   .

Honestly, at that moment, when I realized I would have to birdie three of the last five holes—all of them long par-4s—and that my ass was probably fricasseed, you'd think every fiber in my body would've screamed, *Quit, you fool! It's hopeless! Go in, get a beer, and sleep in the car for about twenty-two hours!*

People said I had no ambition and, at that instant, they were absolutely right. But I had something better. I had a textbook case of Fire-Truck-Red Ass. I was so pissed at the little trick these two snobs had played on me, I could hardly see. Everything about these guys reminded me of all the reasons I hated competitive golf: the Joan Crawford daddy, the arrogant spoiled kid who either burns out at thirteen from the insane pressure or, worse, begins to believe his father is right, that he *will* be the next Tiger.

I tend to be very lazy when happy and very good when pissed. Not with words or resignation letters or breakup speeches. But with golf, I get all kryptonite when pissed. My swing gets slower, my eyes narrow, my every effort is to stomp on your neck. I have no idea what Desmond shot those next four holes, but I know exactly what I did. I birdied 14 and 15, parred 16, and made a seagoing 45-footer on 17 for birdie. As we say at Ponky, t-t-t-t-take a s-s-s-s-suck of that!

After that putt, I asked the official scorer how the other guys were doing in comparison to me.

"Mr. Worstenheim is five-under. Mr. Casey [Desmond] is four-under. You are four-under."

I guessed I needed one more birdie out of me or one bogey out of Dez or the Punk. I didn't particularly want it to be Dez.

The last hole was a 454-yard par-4 and I painted it down there in such a perfect goddamn place they should've shot the catalog for the hole right then and there. Dez was about twenty yards behind me and the punk was as long as me but in the right junk.

We were walking to our balls when I saw him, wandering out on the fairway, his white cane waggling—Blind Bob.

"Commodore Worstenheim?" he was calling in a shaky Scottish accent, walking right toward us. "Commodore Worstenheim?"

The dad practically spit out his dentures.

"See here!" he said.

"Commodore!"

"See here! Who is that? We're playing a very important golf tournament here!"

Bob just kept coming. "Commodore! It's Nigel! Nigel Smithson, from the boat! Remember? Second Lieutenant Smithson? Maybe you heard about my accident, with the boiler? Just after you left?"

Worstenheim was within ten feet of him now and trying to shush him. His son was getting fidgety, hands on hips, and spitting.

"Of course, of course, my good man," the father said, checking his son over his shoulder. "I remember you well. But could I speak to you after this hole? We're in a tournament, you see?"

Whatever the hell was Bob's play, it was a thing of beauty.

"Ah, Commodore. I was a cracking golfer myself before the horrible accident. North Berwick was my track. Had the front 9 record there for a time, don't you know? What I wouldn't give to swing the club again. May I have a swing of a club, sir? Just to feel it in my hand again?"

"Father, will you get Stevie Wonder out of here?"

"Ah, a son!" said Bob. "You're so lucky. The accident didn't just take my eyesight, you know, Commodore. Put a dent in the ol' wedding tackle, yes?" And with this, he gently tugged at his crotch.

I had to do a 180 not to laugh out loud.

Bob somehow got to the clubs and tried to pick up the bag. "Let me just carry the bag for the boy on this last hole, will you, Commodore? It would just mean the world to me!"

I started to get the idea of where this was going.

"Go ahead, Commodore," I said, just to let Bob know I was there. "That's the only way we're going to get on with this hole."

"Yeah," said Desmond. "That could've been you at the boiler, you know."

"Fine, fine, just a moment," the Commodore said, exasperated. "Let my boy hit this approach shot and we'll work something out."

So Punk Boy hit a decent 8-iron to thirty feet and flipped the club at his dad in disgust. The dad took the putter out and instead of handing it to his son, handed it to Bob to carry.

"Just 'til we get to the green. Then you hand it to my son and simply—and quietly—stand off to the side, understood?"

"Bless you, Commodore!" said Bob, walking. "Ooooh, I remember this feeling well! Nothin' does a man more good than a long walk with his putter, yes?"

Bob held the putter like a band majorette, pumping it as he went, his white cane tucked under his elbow. Old man Worstenheim kept having to herd him in the direction of the green. Twenty feet from it, he snatched it back.

Bob kept saying, "Bless you, Commodore! Bless you! Say, would you have a shilling or two for an old sailor?"

Worstenheim lost it then. "That's what it was about, was it then? Piss off, you!"

He pointed him roughly toward the clubhouse and Bob kept right on, walking to it, his cane waggling in front of him.

All that was left in this Three Stooges comedy was the putting. I hit a perfect putt but it guardrailed on me, cruelly I might add, and I tapped in for par. Dez made his par, too, which left us both with 66s. I couldn't remember playing better.

The kid two-putted for par. I was keeping his card, so I totaled it and handed it to him to sign.

"Sixty-seven?" he said. "You're daft! I shot 65, you twit!"

"Wrong, dude," I said.

"Here it is, you dolt—you've got me for six on 18. I made four!"

"Sorry, ol' bean. You *did* make six."

"Sod off, you old poofter," he yelled. "Change it!"

"What's the problem here?" his dad barked.

"Your son is the problem," I said. "Not only did you not teach him manners, you didn't teach him math, either. He made six on the last hole, not four."

"Bollocks!" his dad said. "He made four! I saw it with my own eyes!"

"Nope. Six. He gets a two-shot penalty for violating the two-caddy rule."

"What?!" they screamed.

"Yeah, he had two caddies on that last hole. You're only allowed one. Right, Dez?"

"Actually, that's right," Dez said, grinning. "You let that blind guy carry the putter while you carried the bag. That's two caddies. Two caddies—two shots."

The two of them looked at each other, aghast.

"Wrong, you sod!" said the kid. "That would mean I'd miss the cut by one!"

"Get used to it," I said, staring right at him.

Dez laughed right out loud. Bless that man.

"Listen, you fucking miserable wanker," said the dad, getting close enough to examine my fillings. "I don't know how you know that man, but you set us up!"

"Oh, you Brits," I said, not moving an inch from his nose. "Always so paranoid."

The scoreboard was clear. There was one guy at 63, two at 64, 5 at 65, and two—Dez and me—at 66. That meant Dez and I were in, since they were taking the top nine plus ties. There were nine guys at 67 and none of them were in, including (so sad) young Phillip Worstenheim and his trained mouth.

"The shame of it is," I said, "without the two-shot penalty, Phil, you would've been in at 65, which would've made nine total, and 66 would have missed the cut. Isn't that a bitch? An American is in and a cocky-shit Brit is out. And on July Fourth, too!"

When Phillip figured it out, he turned red and actually began crying, screaming at his own father, "You stupid shit! *Do* something!"

The elder Worstenheim called in everybody but the Queen Mother to try to get the ruling changed, but it didn't work. Bob was gone, but we'd all seen it happen—me, Dez, and Provisional. Where Bob had wandered off to, I had no idea, but I could've frenched him right then and there.

"See you at St. Haggith?" Desmond said as I trudged toward my car, past exhausted.

"St. Who?"

"St. Haggith, for the final qualifying? That's where the nine of us go."

"Right," I said. "Absolutely. We will kick St. Haggith's ever-lovin' ass."

Made note to self: *Find out where the hell St. Haggith is.*

As I loaded my clubs into the trunk, elated and nearly nauseous with fatigue, a very curious, very tall, very skinny orange-headed man walked up. He was such a bizarre character I wondered if the combination of No-Doz, pork pies, and tense golf was causing me to go completely batshit crazy. He had the thickest eyebrows and sideburns I've ever seen. But it was not that they were just thick. It's that they were the oddest orange I'd ever seen, too. They looked like they were painted with a bad stencil and a can of Day-Glo orange spray paint. They were the color of highway cones or slow-moving-vehicle triangles. You could've safely hunted with the eyebrows alone. The freckles all over his face were that same orange. He featured braidable ear hair, too. The guy looked like he slept under a newspaper somewhere. He wore not one but two plaid sport coats, both hand-me-downs, a shirt under that, a T-shirt under that, old striped pants that finished a good six inches too high, high-top Converse hoops shoes, and a Simpsons hat with Mr. Burns on the crown.

"You've go' a fine game, American," the big galoot said. "But i' 'll never ge' you throo at St. Aggith. Tha's true Sco'ish links there, no' this bollocks English pish! Ih-ull eatcha alive, mon! You've no *clooo* how tae hi' the Musselborough Skitter, and tha' would've saved you a sho' a' least on 6! And maybe 18, too. And tha way you hi' your irons so high mi' work at Firestone but no' at St. Aggith! Those greens are faster'n Oprah on a wa'er slide! They don' hold grass, much less yer golf ball! You'll need t' learn the punch-and-run, the Texas wedge, the Elmer Fudd. And tha's just the beginnin' o' your troobles!"

"Oh?" I said, too tired to care. "Who are you, Orange Tom Morris?"

"The name's Sponge," he said, offering his orange-freckled hand. The man had to be six-eight. He looked like Ichabod Glasgow. "Bes' caddee in

Sco'land. I could see you throo tae the Open champeenship. If ya had a brain in your daft haid, you'd take me on nex' week."

"Yeah? If you're so good, why don't you have a bag already for the final qualifying?"

"Acchh," he said. "My man today couldna made the cut wi' a gian' pair a novelty scissors."

This guy was too much.

"So, wha' you say?" he said.

I said nothing.

Suddenly he was Richard Dawson from *Family Feud*: "Ohh, good answer, good answer! Survey SAYS . . ."

And he held his hands out, palms up, like it was my line.

". . . Uh, survey says I don't have the first pound to pay you, Sponge, so thanks anyway."

Now he was doing a flawless Ronald Reagan, "Wail, now, thair you go again."

And with that, I tipped my hat, crawled into my car, locked the door, cranked the seat back, put my hat over my eyes, and prayed for Scotland's Robin Williams to leave.

Resource Jones had to make a couple calls, but saying that in prison is a mouthful. He had to wait until the exact right time, Monday night, had to find a phone, and had to make the calls perfectly or the whole thing was sunk. There were no second chances at this.

That Monday he stole a cellphone from a cart, slipped it into his pocket, then into his shoe so that it wouldn't be found in the daily search as he reentered the prison. He knew he wanted to make the calls at 9:00 P.M., but he couldn't allow himself to be heard, so he paid each of the inmates on both sides of him to start yelling loudly to each other, from one cell to the other, so that it would cover up the sound of his calls.

And so they did:

"I'm finna kick your *ass* tomorrow," said the neighbor on the east.

"My ass?" said the west. "You don't even know the rook-castle swap! How you finna kick my ass?"

With the racket in place, Resource dialed a Mr. Hornbecker of Fitchburg, Mass. It was 9:01.

"Mr. Hornbecker!" he began in his whitest voice. "This is groundskeeper Wallace at Prison View Golf Course up here at Bridgefield? Yes, yes, how are you? Sorry about the noise, Mr. Hornbecker. Yes, well, we've had a bit of an incident out here tonight. Yes, sir. We've had information of a possible breakout attempt tonight. Not to worry, not to worry. We get these rumors now and again—chatter we call it—usually amounts to nothing, but we're shutting down the course for twenty-four hours. We've informed your playing partner, Mr. Baker, and he wanted us to tell you that you guys will just skip a week and resume your regular game next week. All right? I woke him up, poor guy, but he did say to tell you, he's only giving you half a shot this time! Hah! He's a jokester, Malcolm is. He says he'll call you tomorrow night about it. Anyway, all the best. Fine, fine. Goodnight!"

He flipped the phone closed and wiped the rivers of sweat pouring off his bald head. The shouting went on, unabated.

"Spassky? You think Spassky was better than Bobby Fischer? You're the Spazz-ky!"

"Oh, fuck you! Spassky could beat Fischer with one lobe tied behind his back!"

Resource breathed deeply again and dialed the next number.

"Mr. Baker? Yes, this is Officer, uh, Wallace of the Fitchburg Police Department. Yes, excuse the noise, Mr. Baker. Some drunks, as usual. Mr. Baker, I need to go ahead and inform you that Mr. Hornbecker was involved in a single-car accident tonight. Yes, sir. Yes. Well, he's fine, but he's being held at the hospital for an indefinite time for observation. He wanted us to go ahead and call you and tell you that he certainly is sorry, but he won't be able to make your golf game tomorrow. But he said to be *sure* to go ahead and play without him. He says he wants you to go out and break 90 out there at Prison View and let him know how you did. Says it'd mean the world to him if you played your round and then reported back to him hole-by-hole. Says if he can't *play* golf, he wants to at least *hear* about some golf. Yes, right, right! Also, the hospital is requesting that family and friends go ahead and let him rest, a day or so, and then he should be able to have visitors. Yes, yes! Well, then, all the best, Mr. Baker. Goodnight!"

He snapped the cell shut, turned it off, hid it under his mattress, breathed a huge exhale, and then realized he hadn't called his neighbors off.

"Andrew Lloyd Webber? He wrote a *musical* called *Chess*, you moron! He didn't *play* chess!"

"I'm a moron? You wouldn't know the Ruy Lopez Opening from the Trini Lopez!"

"ALL RIGHT!" Resource screamed. "Shuddup now!"

All three collapsed back on their mattresses, spent.

Finally home from his prison mission, Two Down pulled up to a red light at Crosley and Winchester in front of the assisted-living home. It was 1:30 A.M. Whatever happened, he decided, he'd at least gotten through that 6:00 P.M. deadline without getting robbed, killed, or both.

And that's when he couldn't help notice a shiny black Lincoln Continental in front of him with its hood up. And Dewey opening his front passenger door. And Yoshi opening the driver's side rear door. And Big Al coming back to him, looking nothing at all like the Massachusetts AAA.

They did not want to rub up against Two Down for luck. What they wanted to do was throw him out onto the pavement, nose first, and steal his car, a task they achieved in just less than six seconds.

Both Continentals—new and old—were starting to pull away when Two Down heard Big Al yell, "We shall zee you in the funny paperz, Too Zad!"

Two was about to ask if he could at least get his clubs out of the trunk, but as the blood trickled into the corners of his mouth, he realized the traitorous bastards had gotten him in all the trouble in the first place.

CHAPTER 12

With only four days to go facing 99-or-wife, Hoover was sure he'd found the Hope Diamond, the lost city of Atlantis, and a cure for eczema all at once.

After much research into back issues of *Tension Analysis Quarterly,* Hoover was positive he'd finally found a method to relieve the tension that caused his golf balls to hook, dive, slice, sky, scatter, and bury themselves in ponds in shame.

He demonstrated it to the general public one day at Ponky. With Cementhead, Dom, and the nonplaying Human Stain along, Hoover set up at the first tee and settled into his waggle. Then he dropped the club and held his arms out as far as he could to the side, then brought them slapping together three times as hard as he could. Then he loosed three successive whoops from the very bottom of his whooper. The strength and volume of these whoops were alarming. Hoover stands only five-four and goes

125 pounds, but the strength of these three *WHOOOP! WHOOOP! WHOOOP!*s sent squirrels scurrying into trees and caused passersby to frantically roll up their car windows.

Then Hoover picked his club up, addressed the ball, and hit a perfect 195-yard drive down the middle, a sight as rare as a Bush sticker on a VW van. The three witnesses were stunned, as much by the clapping and whooping as by the unprecedented sight of Hoover hitting a good shot.

Hoover was still standing heroically, like Walter Hagen, admiring his work.

"You can stop posin' now, Hoov," said Dom. "The photographahs only covah the last three holes."

"What the *hell* was that, Hoov?" asked Cementhead. "A moose call?"

"Yes, Hoover," said Stain, slurping one of Blu Chao's miso mock-shakes. "You put one in mind of a Hindu fertility ceremony I once saw on Discovery Channel."

"I don't know if it's gonna help yah golf any," Dom added, "but I'll bet you get laid by at least three egrets today."

"Who asked any of you simpletons?" said Hoover. "For your information, the rhythmic fury of the clapping and deep vibrational tone of the whooping release tension in all four life/karma groups: the body, the mind, the chakras, and the soul. It frees me from the residual stress and tension that all of us live with every day—for approximately eight seconds."

The three stared at him as though a sumo wrestler was sitting on his shoulders.

But Hoover was too happy to care. After years of waiting at life's bus stop, his day had finally come. He would break 100 clap-by-clap, whoop-by-whoop. His wife would, by agreement, have to continue to bankroll his golf, and, not least, he'd be rid of his horrid, bulbous, sniffing, faux-Shakespearean brother-in-law.

And despite ridicule, Hoover stuck with it, clapping three times and whooping three times before every shot, be it drive, approach, chip, or putt. It was funny at first, then unusual, then just annoying. Dom left after seven holes. Cementhead after nine. But, by contract, the Stain was stuck with Hoover and vice versa. Although, the way Hoover was playing, not for long. He shot an astonishing 44 on the front, his lowest nine ever. All he needed to break 100 was 55 on the back or better, and golful as he was, he was very capable of that. In fact, by the time he got to 13, he was on pace to shoot 93 and make all his fondest dreams come true in vivid bursting Technicolor. Sisyphus was not only going to push the rock to the top of the hill but down the other side to crush the devil himself. Joy was imminent, if not closer.

On that 13th tee box, Hoover clapped and whooped as usual, but as he was picking up the club to hit, the Stain said, "How do you know it lasts only eight seconds?"

"What?"

"How do you know the calm only lasts eight seconds?"

"Because that's what the researchers who discovered this phenomenon found."

Hoover quickly tried to bring the clubhead back and swing, but now the Stain had introduced new tension and he discovered it at the moment of impact, when he suddenly threw in an epileptic lurch, which accompanied a sudden Joffrey Ballet *demi-pointe* in his feet, which sent the ball shanking dead left, immediately toward the very vulnerable ankles of a group of Jenny Craig dropouts on the fifth green, who jumped just in time, and barely high enough, one after another, like a line of out-of-shape Bahamian fire leapers. The ball hid itself in the Beagle River, which cuts Ponky in half.

"Uh-oh," said Stain, "your magic whoop has abandoned you."

Hoover suppressed the urge to insert a driver from one end of Stain to the other and roast him, as on a spit.

"No," he said, grit-teethed, trying to calm himself. "It was simply because you delayed my routine so that I wasn't able to swing within the allotted eight seconds, you jerk."

"*I* delayed you?"

"Yes, *you* delayed me—by speaking to me. So just, from now on, shut up! Please!"

But Hoover's next three attempts to try to play away from the fence met disaster and he wound up making goalposts (an 11) on that hole. Suddenly his sure-thing 99 was in jeopardy. At 14 he clapped and whooped without interruption, but just as he got his feet set, the Stain said, "I think it's whoop, then clap. You did it backwards."

Hoover was irritated, but responded politely as he could, "No, it's clap, then whoop." And he started to pull it back.

"Fine [pause], but it was whoop-clap before."

This produced in Hoover a spinout so fierce that you were sure Hoover would end up eight feet deep in the tee box. He didn't just spin out with his left foot, he spun his whole body around it, like a giant drill bit. The ball, for its part, simply limped off the tee about six inches and then stopped, perhaps exhausted from laughing.

"Goddammit, Dalton!" he said to the Stain. "Stop talking and delaying me! I can't get my shots in within eight seconds!"

"Oh, folderol! That was easily within eight seconds! Your secret has failed you! It's been exposed as just another mind-crutch that collapsed in the white-hot heat of battle!"

"It's not a mind-crutch, you hackneyed pus-filled boil! It's a tool for the body and soul!"

"Acch, loser talk."

Hoover turned to him, red in his eyes and brandishing his 7-iron. "So help me, Dalton. If you say one more word to me the rest of this round, I will plant this club in your fat skull like a rutabaga bulb, brother-in-law or no brother-in-law."

The Human Stain, seeing Hoover in a new light, did shut up from that moment forward, for the rest of the round. And the calming nature of the clapping/hooting weirdness seemed to take hold of Hoover's tortured soul again. He managed to make triple bogey on 14, bogey on 15, double on 16, and a bogey on 17. That left him with the 18th to play, needing only a double-bogey six to break 100 and rid himself of his demons—mental, spiritual, and those riding in personalized three-wheeled scooters alongside him.

Now, the 18th at Ponky borders Geneva Avenue, the kind of street that could use a shower and a shave. It featured check-cashing joints, nail parlors, and a strip bar, known among the Chops as "the shoe show." As Hoover prepared to hit the most crucial tee shot of his life, it happened to be about 6:00 P.M., time for the shift change at Pom-Pons, the strip bar that sits thong-by-jowl next to Ponky on Geneva Avenue. This seminal moment for Hoover arrived at the exact same time as the very statuesque Ms. Mystique Sanchez emerged from her Range Rover, accompanied by her boyfriend, the bodybuilder Justin (Juice) Shaughnessy. It was well known to the regulars at Pom-Pons that the one thing in life you do not want to do is show disrespect to Mystique when in the company of Juice, who, in retaliation, might in turn decide to transform your head into an easy-open can.

The problem was, Hoover did not know Ms. Mystique nor Juice, nor their reputations. Nor did he see them. He was focused on the essential task at hand, which was to calm his nerves and somehow get this drive down the fairway or even into the light rough and make the most glorious double bogey (or better) of his life.

And so it was, as Mystique and Juice walked toward the employee entrance at Pom-Pons, Hoover went into his tried-and-true tension reliever, as described in *Tension Analysis Quarterly*.

First came the three huge seal claps. Then came the monstrous and guttural *whooops!*

Sadly, Juice Shaughnessy misinterpreted an innocent tool meant for the body and soul and found in it something much more sinister. He thought Hoover was wolf-whistling his Mystique in a most unctuous way. Juice does not understand golf, but he does understand tension, and the emotions wrought forth in Juice at that moment released in him a textbook raving 'roid rage.

"Oh, no you didn't!" Juice screamed as he ran to the fence separating Hoover and himself. "Dude, I'm going to rip your lungs out!"

The speed and alacrity Juice used in climbing the fence would've made an Army Ranger jealous. Mystique hollered, "No! Baby! No!" Hoover, suddenly cognizant of the world around him, turned with shocked eyes and yelped, "No, sir! No! I meant nothing untoward—! It's merely a golfing—!"

But Juice was not in the mood to listen. He was at the top of the fence and yelled, "Oh, *fuck* no you didn't!"

Stain had already pulled away from the scene and was driving away like Jeff Gordon. Hoover had jumped into his cart to follow when Juice landed, grabbed the moving vehicle from behind, swung himself into the passenger seat, and, with one businesslike punch, turned Hoover's right eye into a kind of overripe eggplant. Then he dragged Hoover to the fence, smooshed his face up against the steel, and insisted he apologize sincerely and immediately to Mystique.

"Abtholutely, ma'am," Hoover said, the flesh of his face forming a pattern of diamonds through the fencing. "I [ungh] meant no dithrethpect. Ith actually thomething [ooomph] I do when I theek to relieve tenthion—"

"Gross!" screeched Mystique, turning away.

"Oh, *Christ*, no. You didn't!" Juice roared.

Flump! went Juice's knee into Hoover's nuts, doubling him over like a tortilla. Juice added a kick with his pointy cowboy boots into Hoover's guts for good measure, then scaled the fence again, hopped over, took Mystique by the hand, and stomped through the employee entrance.

As you can imagine, with a closed eye and in the position of a man hoping to find quarters on the sidewalk, Hoover did not make his double bogey on that hole. Nor did he make triple. In fact, he did not make anything. He picked up lying thirteen in the right front bunker and started limping to his car.

"Golf: 10,863," said The Voice, "Hoover: 0."

When Blind Bob came out of hiding at the bar across the street from the Gog Magog, we set out for St. Haggith, Scotland, by all accounts a toxic golf dump hard by the Glasgow electric generating station. We had a quarter tank of gas, no money, no place to sleep, no food, and no idea where we were going, but our hearts were light.

"My God, I got no shot," I said, scraping the poor Fiat along the bushes and rock walls as we went. "I had to practically *cheat* to get through the first round. What chance do I have to get through the best of the best?"

"You pussy," said Bob. "Just get us there. We'll find a way."

Along the way, I tried every method known to man to reach Dannie, although I dreaded what might come after the words, "I've met somebody—"

I tried calling home, collect, from one of those red-box phone booths. When offered the chance to accept the charges, Dannie's sister said, "Operator, we're a little short a spendin' cash. Do you accept half-finished greetin' cards?"

I found a little cyber coffee shop and e-mailed her, but when I sent my brilliantly written treatise, I got a message back from Earthlink: *Account Closed; Balance Due.*

Oops.

I tried from my cell and Bob's cell. Verizon doesn't do Scotland.

"Ahh, don't sweat it," Blind Bob said. "Just 'cause a woman says, 'I met somebody,' that might not mean—"

"Don't even try, Bob."

"Good point."

It was about then we pulled into St. Haggith and found Ponky's parallel universe. It was a craphole, undermaintained and overplayed. It was ugly, hideous, and an affront to golf itself. Man, it was good to be home.

The course itself looked as though it had once been a very good layout, but then again Elizabeth Taylor was once hot. St. Haggith probably was one of the best courses in the region, fifty years ago. Now it was burnt out, grown over, carved up, run down, and in need of being plowed under. There was a cinderblock clubhouse with an open-air parking lot *underneath* it, so it looked like some kind of 1963 attempt at space-age cool that was now so homely it was fireproof—no flame would lick it.

"Welcome tae St. Aggith," a voice cooed behind us. It was none other than Sponge, the orange Wilt. "We locals refer tae i' as St. Aggus. For you Americains, it'd be the equaivalen' of staying a' a Mo'el 5."

It was hard to hear him as the M3 highway traffic rushed by us.

"Nice," I said, gazing out on the brownish black mess in front of us. "How often do they test the missiles here?"

"Thairsdays," Sponge said.

Just from a glance around, it looked a little like Dr. Kevorkian's home track. The 1st hole, for instance, appeared to be a blind tee shot up a huge hill. The flagstick on 18 not only had no flag, it wasn't really a flagstick. It appeared to be an old mop handle with a Handi Wipe stapled to it. And the guys playing 18 were doing something I'd never seen. They were picking up their ball in the fairway, laying down a one-foot-by-one-foot piece of Astroturf, putting the ball back on that, and hitting.

"Saves on divo's," Sponge said. "But you'll nae be doin' tha' for the tairnamen'. Tha's a local rule. Charming, though, eh?"

"Bob, for the first time in my life, I envy your blindness," I said.

We wandered over to the registration table.

"Hart?" I said to the woman at the card table. "Raymond?"

The woman went rifling through her envelopes and found nothing. Then I noticed a man standing behind her, watching me—Commodore Allistair Worstenheim himself, arms folded, a slight grin on his face, wearing some cheesy Royal and Ancient blue blazer, complete with pocket crest, and a very large nameplate: TOURNAMENT SECRETARY.

"I see you two know each other," he said, pointing to Bob.

Busted.

"Well, I know him," I said. "But he never seems to recognize me."

The woman shrugged her shoulders. "Terribly sorry," she said, "but I can't seem to find you. Where'd you qualify?"

"The Gog Magog," I said. "Home of sportsmanship."

Worstenheim stared right back.

"Oh, that's lovely then," she said. "Yes, I see your name here, but for some reason I don't have a housing envelope for you. We're wanting hotel rooms here, so a lot of the locals are putting players up at their homes. Bit of excitement in that, of course."

"Well, I'm sure somebody would take us in regardless, yes?" said Bob.

"Oh, I'm sure—"

Worstenheim whispered something in her ear. The lady looked shocked.

"Oh, well, no," she said, suddenly jittery. "No, I'm sorry. We can't be of help. I'm sure you'll find something suitable." Flustered, she handed me my registration packet. "Good day."

I gave Worstenheim the evil eye and we started to walk off.

"Will you give the Commodore a fuck-you stare for me, too?" Bob said.

With no room at any inn, the poor couple wound up back at the Fairmont Fiat, both of us barely fitting into it, sleeping sitting up because the seats wouldn't go back, knees against the steering wheel, starting the car every half hour to keep warm, your basic Westin Heavenly Bed.

From there, things just started to come apart like a wet jigsaw puzzle. I had three days of practice, each worse than the last. I played with Desmond once and he beat me by six strokes. My back felt like a broken Slinky. I needed a caddy but couldn't afford one. St. Haggus proved to be even *worse* than Ponky, if that's possible. There was an old Renault off the 12th green somebody had burned to a crisp. There was a cardboard mansion some poor slob lived in among the trees behind 14—a bunch of refrigerator boxes duct-taped together, tarps over that, and a little fire scar. Lovely. The weeds off the fairway were sometimes five feet high, so I guessed the weed mower was broken. And, like St. Andrews, six of the greens were in fact double-greens, serving as the green going out for one hole and the same green coming back in for another. The only problem was—unlike St. Andrews—they were not nearly big enough, so you were constantly marking on your green so some other guy could putt to his green. It was like trying to play golf in a photo booth.

Worse, I couldn't get ahold of Dannie no matter how many ways I tried. And we were down to Bob pretending that some awful person had switched all his credit cards in his wallet for hotel key cards so that people would buy our dinner in sympathy. Our Pride-o-Meter was on zero.

And every now and then I'd look up and see His Orangeness, watching me and shaking his head, wearing that same outfit with the same Simpsons hat. One time I got lucky when I skulled an 8-iron that should've sailed over the green but instead hit the flagstick and settled next to the cup for a leaner.

"Tha's an incest sho'," Sponge said as I walked to the next tee.

"What's an incest shot?"

"Yoor all the way oop there bu' you really shouldna be."

I double-crossed one deeply into the gorse on the next tee box and he happened to be behind me again. "Not if it were covered in boys' underwear could Mary Kay Letourneau find it."

Who the hell *was* this guy?

Finally, after I'd bogeyed three straight holes, I went up to him and asked, "How much?" As if it mattered. I had four pounds in my wallet and a Finagle-a-Bagel Frequent Muncher card.

And he launched into his TV voice-over mode: "Caddy for two days: $300. Sho's of Macallan for him each nigh': $24. Qualifyin' foor the Bri'ish Open: Priceless."

I just stared at him.

"You're from here, right? You're not from Sheboygan and just faking that Scottish accent, right?"

Suddenly he was a dead-on Christopher Walken. "I don't appreciate the *slanderous* accusation!"

"So how do you know all this American shit?"

"CNN. I only drink where they have CNN. Or, failin' tha', where they have whiskey."

I stared at him some more. Sponge really was very absorbent.

"Just do it, Yank," he said.

"Just bite me, Sponge," I said.

To make matters worse, my own personal tormentor, Herr Worstenheim, was on me like the mumps. He'd only given me a caddy parking pass, not the player one. He made sure my name was spelled wrong on all the sheets and entry boards. He gave me the last possible tee time for the first round of qualifying, 5:52 P.M. Even with the late sunset, I'd be finishing in the dark with the Toro lawn mowers up my ass.

"Hey, thanks for all the great hospitality, Mr. Goebbels," I said when I saw him.

"You richly deserve it," he sniffed without looking at me.

"Gee, I wonder if some of the boys at the Royal and Dandruff would like to hear about some of the tricks you and your fine son, Lucifer, enjoy pulling on the golf course?"

"Perhaps as much as they'd like to hear about your handicapped friend, Bob, and his acting prowess."

"He's not handicapped, he just can't see. Then again, I guess he's lucky. I met your wife."

He suddenly bulled up, chest out, and spat "Cretin!" and walked away.

And so I was the least surprised person in Scotland when I went out on the hairy St. Haggus for Day One of the final qualifying and fired me a crappy little one-under 71, putting me six shots behind the leaders and in a very nifty 39th place out of 144, only three of whom were going to go on to the British Open.

"I'm quitting," I told Bob that night in The Spoon, the homey tavern where we drank poly-Guinness on the tab of somebody whose favorite aunt was blind.

"I recommend it," he said, taking a large slug of his beer. "That really is the smart thing to do, risk going to Guantánamo under the Patriot Act, come all the way over here, nearly get us killed at the Gog Magog, have us sleep in a goddamn Matchbox car for six nights, let Ponky go down the drain, and, not to mention your marriage, forget Two Down. Yep, I think that's the right course of action."

"Bob, I never *wanted* this," I said, about to get all preachy. "I went against my heart coming over here. Everything about this—everything!— has reminded me how much I hate competitive golf. Why, hell, I know I could've been good! And yeah, for a while, I really thought maybe pro golf was something I wanted. But not anymore. I'm fine saying, 'You know what? I really *don't* want it. In fact, I *hate* it.' I do! I hate the way golf becomes this *life* instead of what it should be, which is this *joy*. The way this Worstenheim gargoyle would sooner slice you open forehead-to-big-toe with a divot repair tool than see his precious kid get beat fair and square. Man, I wasn't *meant* for this life. I know all you guys want me to be your Phil Mickelson, but *I* don't want that. I'm sick of everybody having all this ambition for *my* life!"

Bob straightened up. "Stick, listen to me: If you ever want golf to be a joy again, you need to do this tomorrow. If you want life to ever look like what it was for you, you need to play like you've never played in your life tomorrow. You just need to nut up one last day. Tomorrow, you just need to go out and shoot 66—"

"That'll *never* do it."

"Okay, 64, and prove to yourself—and everybody else—that you have what it takes. What you do with it after that is your call. Shred it. Ride it. Smoke it. I don't give a damn. Doesn't matter. But you owe you, us, everybody, this one last great Ray day. Because we'd all sell everything we have just for the *chance* to try for what you seem to want to throw away!"

I flipped my last three pounds on the bar. "Yeah. Great. Except I happen to blow right now. And now I'm going home to get a good night's sleep in the Fiat junior suite. Hey, what's my sleep number?"

I walked out, thought hard about drowning myself in a wee burn, and got halfway to the car when I realized I didn't have the goddamn keys. I'd given them to Bob to lock it up. But when I got back, Bob was still at the bar, talking to Desmond. They didn't see me, but I was surprised to hear Bob telling him all this stuff I'd never heard.

He was talking about how his little TV shop was about to close and he wasn't quite sure what he was going to do for work. He said his wife had been away a lot, at her dying mother's, so it'd been a rough couple months for them. He told Dez how the only thing that really kept him going was Ponky, how he knew he could always get laughs there when he needed them, how he couldn't believe how accepting everybody there had been of him, how the Chops were the first guys who ever gave him shit. How we'd ask if he had any idea how butt-ugly he was, or tell him that the ten-dollar bill Two Down had just given him was just actually a sliced-up Target ad.

"That's the first time since Kuwait, you know?" Bob told Dez, "when I really felt like I *belonged*. Where I wasn't just this Special Olympian everybody was feeling sorry for all the time." He told Dez that Ponky was the first golf course that didn't mind how slow he played, probably because Ponky was slower than he could possibly play anyway. And he said that's why he came with me to Scotland, because the Chops meant more to him than beer and Van Morrison combined. "And with everything else in my life in a fried-egg lie, I need Ponky right now a whole lot worse than it needs me."

I backed out and came back into the bar again, much louder, said hello to Dez, good-bye to Bob again, and got the keys. And then I ran out of that bar and started running. Because I knew I had to do something bigger than myself, something bigger than I knew how to do.

Back at Ponky it was pouring down rain, leaving the Chops blue, especially because they'd played just seven holes before they had to stop, and bets only pay through nine holes, according to Two Down's list of Rules, Regulations, and Fines taped to the Formica table in front of Blu Chao's window (for example, Ernest and Julio: $5—Excessive Whining), along with a few Sanctioned and Proved Provisos, such as:

It ain't a gimme if you're still away.

You only get 18 shots. If you need more, try Jarts.

No posting rounds played with wife.

Nonchalant putts count the same as chalant putts.

When accompanied by Stain, nobody has to listen to his stories
every hole, alternate odd and even.

Any ball you can see in the spinach from 75 yards away is not yours.

No newspaper 5s. No "handicap" 5s. No Donald Trump 5s.

Fifteen-picture limit on vacation snaps.

Guys faking injuries should limp with same leg all the way around.

Any new Hoover putter must be pre-approved for aerodynamic safety.

There's no such goddamn thing as a "circle 4."

"Well, that was a two-hour lifesuck," Dom said, cursing the rain and open-ing a two-day-old *Globe*. Since Gary the God, Dom's mood had turned no-ticeably south, approaching Chapped Ass.

"Lifesuck?" said Two Down, who was breathing easier that nobody was missing a 1964 Lincoln Continental at the assisted-living home.

"Yeah, lifesuck," Dom continued. "Time you'll nevah get back. Life that's been wasted, sucked up, nevah to return. Lifesuck."

"Like, people telling you about their dreams?" Two Down tried.

"Exactly," Dom brooded. "Like yah girlfriend tellin' you about her aunt's cats."

"Guys going over their round," Two said, "*with* swing thoughts."

"Stewardess safety briefings," Cementhead said.

"The first 399 laps of any Coca-Cola 400."

"Waiting for Hoover to hit."

And then Cementhead got up in his new congressional way and began to hold forth, importantly.

"Gentlemen, I have thought long and hard and I have formulated an idea."

"Cementhead speaking," somebody muttered.

"No, I'm serious. As long as we have this time on our hands, I have a subject to discuss that is very important to speak about."

Somebody hit him with a half of one of Blu Chao's Korean corn dogs, which suspiciously had the taste of real dog.

"C'mon, I'm serious! We all know Ray is over there, trying to save Ponky. And we all know how that's going to come out."

There was some awkward face rubbing and rug-examining.

"It's up to us, and we're just sitting around here doing nothing! We've got to think of some way to stop this sale!"

"Holy shit!" Dom said as he stared goggle-eyed at the paper. "This is it!"

"Great!" Cement said. "What you got?"

But Dom had already sprinted out of the Pit of Despair and was jumping in his car.

The Chops read the article he was so gooey about and didn't see the connection.

"Pair Holds Up Restaurant; Forces Sex," Two Down read.

"What the hell?" Cement said.

Two Down read on: "Two masked gunmen robbed the Hungry Dutchman Restaurant in Hyannis last Friday night, but they didn't stop at taking money and jewelry. Locking the door behind them, the men forced the 12 late-night customers to have sex with each other on the tabletops and on the floors. The men did not rape anybody, the restaurant's owner said. Quote—'They just seemed to want to get their jollies watching'—unquote. The entire incident lasted twenty minutes. The gunmen have not been apprehended."

"So?" Stain said.

"Is that considered breaking and entering?" Two asked.

"Guys, c'mon! We've got to concentrate on Ponky here. We're smarter than those guys at the Mayflower. Don't they put their pants on one day at a time?" Cement asked.

This froze the assembly.

"One *leg* at a time, you moron," Hoover said.

"You sure?"

"Okay, well, I'll tell you what I know so far," Two said, stalling while he searched his wallet for a folded-up clipping. "This is the guy who's spearheading the purchase of Ponky. It's mostly all his idea, they tell me. I cut his picture out of *Business Week*. Name's Laird Fredericks, the big-money genius at the Mayflower apparently. Owns about five hundred radio stations."

He showed the picture around to the assorted Chops paying attention.

"Ohhh!" the Human Stain yelped. "You mean 'Fredericks of Hollywood!' "

"What?" Two said.

"Yes, that's the moniker I chose for him. I peed next to him once."

"You know this guy?"

"Yes, well, he's on my C list. That's the lowest grading—business types, local weathermen, and such. I peed next to him at the Department of Motor Vehicles. He's apparently huge in the cable industry here."

"So you remember him for his, uh, cable?"

"Him, I shall never forget. The gentleman wears panties! He had on a pink thong!"

Everybody fell out.

"I swear it to be the God's truth. You know, I've peed next to thirty-one famous people now—"

"We know, Stain, we know," Two said.

"—and it's always interesting to see what they wear underneath. Says a lot about a person—boxers or briefs. Window to the soul, sort of. Usually they're very secretive about it all, but he seemed most proud. His mind was wandering and I was able to get a good look. It was a pink lace thong with little flower inlays."

To a man, each Chop looked like he'd been given a word problem in which a train traveling from Toledo at ninety miles per hour is heading straight for a train traveling to Toledo at fifty miles per hour. It was just a matter of waiting for the crash.

"My God!" Two Down said. "I think I know how we can do this!"

You wouldn't think it'd be hard to find the Jolly Orange Giant, but I couldn't do it. "He lives off 14 green," one of the caddies told me in the

Topple Inn, but I went to every flat and house and they'd never heard of
him. Took me two hours. I came back and the guy was still sitting there.

"I thought you said Sponge lives off 14 green," I said.

"He does," the guy said.

"Hell he does. I knocked on every door around there."

"He doesn't have a door."

"What?"

"He lives in that cardboard mess in the trees behind 14."

It really wasn't bad once you were inside it. Very clean. He had a
lantern in there and a battery-powered radio playing Chopin. He even had
a little wire fruit basket hanging from the ceiling.

"Sponge, I need you," I said.

"Oh, Chris', man!" he spit. "I'm no' tha' way!"

I gave Sponge the deal of his life. I told him about the $250,000. I told
him if I qualified, I wouldn't give him $300, I'd give him $3,000.

"Put 'er there, podner," he said in his full John Wayne. "But the
Macallan scotch, that there's a dealbreaker. You got me, pilgrim?"

He handed me his empty flask. "You fill this wi' the Macallan—the
twelve-year is fine—and you give i' tae me tomorra morning. Wha' time
dae we gooo?"

"3:42."

"Shite! You give i' tae me on the practice tee or I'll no' be goin' ou' with
ya."

"Deal."

And the minute we shook hands, the skies opened. It rained like you
read about. It rained so hard I thought his little compound was going to
wash away, but it stayed perfectly dry. It damn near washed away the Fiat,
though. It gave me a great idea. I ran to it, started it up, got out my travel
kit, pulled it behind a crummy inn on the edge of town, stripped buck-
naked, threw all my clothes in the Fiat, and had myself the greatest shower
of my life.

Okay, drying off with my golf towel wasn't wonderful, but I felt completely renewed.

It rained all night and was still raining the next day when I found Sponge at The Spoon and told him to hop in. I handed him his flask full of Macallan which, I'll admit, I had snuck out of the back room of The Spoon ten minutes before. Hey, God forgives the desperate.

"Take me somewhere," I said. "Teach me everything you know about golf. They'll never play today. This is the break I've needed. Tell me everything."

And so he did. We went to a little linksy course called King's Meadow and we played thirty-six in the pouring-down rain. Not a soul out there but us. And I learned more from Sponge in that one day than I learned from anybody since Uncle Joe under the old willow tree.

He taught me the Musselborough Skitter, which is a half-topped 7-iron that runs along the ground "li' a shor'-legged weasel," Sponge said. I learned to putt from fifty yards off the green. I learned that Sponge can read greens like a Rothschild reads stocks.

We were over about a ten-foot putt when Sponge said, "Ay, this one here is a Lance Armstrong—one ball ou'."

I learned that a "Calista Flockhart" was a shot that was thin but still pretty. Not to be confused with a "Kate Winslet—fa' bu' otherwise pair-fec'!" A Joan Rivers: "Thin and scary." A wicked slice was a Lorena Bobbitt. A shot fat and left was Michael Moore. Fat and right, Rush Limbaugh. A putt that lipped out was a Steven Tyler. One time I hit a twenty-footer that stopped an inch short of going in and Sponge hit me with his perfect Walter Cronkite impression. "And, sadly, that's a Nelson Rockefeller! Laift dead in the hole!"

He taught me to love playing the ball low. He taught me there was no dishonor letting the ball run the last twenty yards to the flag, not trying to fly it in there. He taught me to listen for the whip of my club to gauge my tempo, not by how the shot went. And toward the end, he taught me to love Macallan.

We were coming in for our thirty-sixth hole. We'd gone through all twelve towels he'd stolen from a neighborhood B&B. We were sopped. We looked like two guys who'd just been rescued from the *Titanic*. And I was feeling so happy about my game—66 on the front eighteen, 65 on the back—and about all I'd learned in one day from this curiously tall, curiously young, curiously wise, curiously orange caddy, and the fact that I really, honestly believed I could actually qualify for the British Goddamn Open the next day, that I asked him for a bump from his flask.

"Oooh, that's damn smooth," I said with a grin.

"Ay."

"You been drinkin' Macallan your whole life, Sponge?"

He took a big swig, wiped his mouth, and said, "Not yet."

A man comes to these forks in the road and this one wound up changing my life.

On the left, the night in the Fiat. On the right, a few beverages in The Spoon. I was beat and needed my sleep, tortured as it was. On the other hand, in the mood I was in, it was like choosing between a new BMW and an arthritic mule. I was on a stool in five minutes, toasting with Bob to bizarre caddies and emotional turnarounds and, especially, friends like him.

He could hear it in my eyes. He looked a little choked up, but got over it with a big pull on his Guinness.

It was exactly then that I saw someone across the bar who knocked the very breath from my lungs.

Maddy.

CHAPTER 13

Maybe I should give you a little Maddy 101.

Maddy was my month of Sundays, my Powerball winner, my five-leaf clover. She was the tornado that went through my trailer park. She was this compact little curveball with sassy chocolate hair and these pink lips that you're still thinking about two days after her face is gone from yours. She had light blue eyes they never made a Crayon for and more than her share of tits and a quick little wit that always seemed to trump anything I had to say.

Maddy was my microwave tragedy. I met her, loved her, and lost her inside of two months. She was the daughter of one of my best friends, the immortal Chunkin' Charlie, the only Chop in history who (we found out after he died) was also secretly a member of the Mayflower. Not that he ever went there. He actually *chose* Ponky over the Mayflower every day. Imagine that? He chose Velveeta over Brie, polyester over mink, Boone's Farm over 1954 Lafitte Rothschild.

He chose us I guess because we made him laugh and he was looking for all the laughs he could get. He had cancer the last two years with us— the Big Uglies, he called it—and yet he played Ponky almost every day. Of course, like an idiot, I squandered the last month he was alive. I was forehead-deep in The Bet, trying to beat Two Down and Dannie out of two large each by getting on the Mayflower first. Who knew we could've just asked Chunkin' Charlie?

One of the ways I tried to get on the Mayflower was posing as a caddy there. And that's how I met Maddy, who was the beverage-cart girl. She spent most of her days trying to keep the octogenarians from sticking their tips too deeply in her front pocket. She never once mentioned that she was Chunk's daughter. Guess he'd sworn her not to.

Everything about us meshed like Velcro—the laughs, the books, the sex—except this one thing. She hated the fact that I lied to her about what I was doing at the Mayflower. She hated the members there and couldn't get over the fact that I was selling out my best friends to try to get on there. Her father, the person she loved more than anybody on earth, was a *member* there and didn't want to hang around with these snobs, and yet here I was turning my back on Ponky to do it. In the end she took an overseas archaeology job with some university and left me.

In a way, that was lucky because it slapped me in the face. Right in front of me, I had a woman who loved me and who I learned to love back— Dannie. FBs became Mr. and Mrs. And though my love for Dannie and Charlie went deeper than what I ever felt for Maddy, the genome project proved scientifically that all men are equipped with an extra dickhead gene. No matter how good things are, a man can't help but wonder about life on the other side of the fence. There are millions of examples of this, but you only need one: Halle Berry's husband cheated on her.

And besides, I was starting to worry that there was nothing on my side of the fence right now. I kept thinking, "If it's over between Dannie and me, could I ever find Maddy? Would she take me back? Would I move to Europe? Would I help her on her digs? Would she move back to Boston?" You think about these things when you're trying to sleep at a right angle in a scratched-up Fiat and your mind is hopping around like a monkey on ephedra.

And suddenly there she was, twenty feet away, across the bar, under the hanging goblets, looking radiant and luscious, like she should be on the cover of *Women You'll Never Get*. She robbed me then and there of my ability to speak, swallow, or step. And just then she looked over and saw me. I could see it shocked her at first. Some guy was talking to her and she obviously wasn't listening and the other guy looked over at me and then I could read his lips, "Who's that?"

I made my way through the people and she picked her way toward me and we met at the corner of the bar. Her eyes were glassy and my mouth wouldn't work. We each put our drinks on the bar and just held on to each other for a while, remembering. I smelled that same perfume and spun back a few years, when all we'd do is laugh and watch old *Andy Griffith*s and try everything known to man to take the word "virgin" out of olive oil.

"Are you following me?" she said at last.

I swallowed hard. "No, I'm looking for a one-armed man. You seen one around?"

"You look nice," she said.

"You look train-stopping."

And so it was for the next hour we talked and laughed and drank. I introduced her to Blind Bob and he seemed to really like her. Then he decided it was time to hit the ol' car and it was just those two columbine-blue eyes and me.

She was between digs for a month, but loving the work. She said she was in St. Haggus because her boyfriend was trying to qualify. "He's a pretty good player, but he just doesn't have any self-confidence. He doesn't think he's good enough. And no matter how many times I tell him, or other people tell him, or other *really good players* tell him, he doesn't believe it. He's sort of the opposite of you—he has all the ambition but none of the belief in himself. You have all the belief in yourself but none of the ambition. Would you guys like to switch places?"

By now I was pretty drunk, so I asked, "Depends—do all the perks transfer, too?"

She laughed and looked into my eyes for a long time. "Ahh, well, neither of us have been getting any 'perks' lately from each other. I'm about on the gone side of leaving him. We've been dating for almost a year, but something needs to happen. He's so goddamn mopey about his golf and so apologetic about not playing well that it just gets annoying. I keep wanting to bitch-slap him. I'm like, 'Grow a sack and go out and start making birdies, like you do every day in practice! It's just golf, not stem cell research!' He just needs one big break and I think he could make it on the European Tour, but he hasn't gotten that break or, better yet, *made* that break."

"Where is he tonight?"

"Oh, he's got this stupid superstition. The night before final rounds, he and his caddy share a room. They visualize all the great shots they'll hit tomorrow. Set target locations. Meditate. Go over the course, shot-by-shot, 'imprinting' them in their minds. Maybe they loofah each other, I don't know. It's all this New Age bull. I tell him, 'What you need is to get laid and sleep like a baby all night,' but he really believes in this guy. Meanwhile, I'm not getting laid, and I'm not even *entered* in the stupid tournament."

Now, I don't know much about women, but if that wasn't a page—"Mr. Hart? Night of wild sex? Mr. Hart?"—I don't know what was.

I kept thinking: *If Dannie was trying to tell you on that phone call that it's over, that she's met someone and fallen in love, and you're divorcing, then you'd be in the Fool Hall of Fame if you didn't take this chance right now. On the other hand, what if Dannie was just bluffing? On the other hand, LOOK at her, you idiot! She'd make the pope bite through his pointy hat!*

"Ray?" she said, tugging at my elbow.

"Oh! No, no. I was just, you know, reminiscing."

She moved closer. "You too, huh?"

"Not often, really. Just weekdays, and holidays and weekends, and leap days. You know? Other than that I'd completely forgotten you."

She threw down a twenty-pound note on the bar, took my hand, and led me out, whispering the following in my ear: "Wanna go set some target locations?"

Years from now, maybe scientists will have a name for the disease that beset Dom, the World's Most Sexual Man. Perhaps his brain's red wire crossed the green. Perhaps testosterone staged a bloodless coup. Perhaps his ego just couldn't cope with finally coming up against a woman he couldn't nail. Whatever it was, he went over the edge, stopped making sense, overshot reason by three exits.

Kelly the Coke Machine had not toppled over yet. In fact, she had hardly even rocked. And there was no living, golfing, laughing, thinking, talking with him until it was done.

Armed with the proceeds from selling his old Porsche ($6,450, Blue Book), he got a cab to a rodded-up part of Boston known as the Junkyard and found a couple acquaintances of his, who knew of a guy, who knew of two guys, who agreed to meet with him at Tito's Tacorama and hear his proposal.

It certainly was the first of its kind in the history of Dorchester crime. What Dom told these two gentlemen was that he wanted a copycat crime committed, without guns, without robbery, without violence. He threw down a copy of the *Globe* article detailing the weird robbery/sex job pulled at the Hungry Dutchman in Hyannis.

"Yo, Dominic," said Freddy, the littler one. "How stoopid would that be, yo? If we hit the Dutchman so soon after it's just been hit, they'd be all jumpy and shit, right?"

"No, no, not the Dutchman," Dom said. "I want you to hit a place called Don's Mixed Drinks, in Dahchestah. You know it?"

He looked at the bigger one, called I-Rod, who was listening to his iPod on giant Koss headphones. I-Rod just stared at Dom, smiling.

"Sure, dude," said Freddy, "we know it, but there ain't gonna be no high rollers in there, yo. It's beat."

"It's not about the money. Any money you take yah gonna accidentally 'drop' as you bolt. It's about this—"

"Wait, wait, bra. You want us to go in and rob a place and *not* keep the money? You're loco, *cabrón*. No way. No deal. Not for no $6,400."

Freddy motioned to I-Rod that they were leaving and Dom had to settle them back down.

"Okay, okay, keep all the money. Fine. Okay?"

Freddy sat back down.

"Damn straight, *vato*," Freddy said.

"The thing is," Dom continued, "is that you have to hit it exactly at eleven tomorrow night, Sunday night. She's always thah Sunday nights. It's karaoke. I want you to come in, dressed just like the guys in Hyannis, all black, evahthing black, ski hats. I want you to come in, hold evahbody up, lock the dahs behind you. Then when you get all the money and shit collected, I want you to fahce evahbody in thah to have sex."

"What?" said Freddy.

"I want you to make them all have sex."

Freddy got antsy again. "Yo, I ain't no rapist, bra. I'm a professional!"

"Not you! You just *watch* them have sex!"

"Why, bra? What if they're ugly?"

"No, listen! This is the whole thing! There's this wicked hot babe, okay? And I've tried everything to third-leg her, but nothin' has worked. This is my last chance. I want you to come in and rob evahbody, and I'll be sitting right next to her and then you'll say, 'Okay, I want evahbody to staht krunkin', right heah, right now!' And then I want you to point your gun right at this girl and me and make us staht hammahin'! See? She won't have any idea I know you guys. She won't have any idea I had anything to do with it! And that's how I'll finally boff this Betty. And it's okay, 'cause I love her. And once she's had me, she'll want more, you know? We'ah really doin' her a favah, you see? And when we'ah done, you go out the back and have one of yah boys waitin' in the alley and yah gone! I'll invite you to the wedding! But you can't in any way let on that you know me or have evah even met me, evah, nevah, okay?"

Freddy curled his lip a little. Dom looked at I-Rod for sympathy, but I-Rod stared back from under his headphones, smiling at him.

"Sounds fuckin' weird, *cabrón*," Freddy said. "Have you tried flowers and candy?"

"Yeah, man! I've tried everything, okay? This is my last chance. Will you *please* do it?"

Dom pushed the envelope of cash forward.

"Half now and then half again tomorrow, here, noon. Okay?"

"Have you tried speaking to her from your heart?" Freddy asked again.

"Yeah! For Chrissakes! I've tried every goddamn thing! I mean, this thing is drivin' me crazy! I can't think about anything else! I'm a wreck! Please? I'm beggin' heah!"

Freddy looked at I-Rod, who hadn't stopped staring and smiling at Dom, then back at the squirming Dom. "I'm not all that fired up about it, bra, but I-Rod seems to be into it. I guess we can do it."

"Yah in?"

"Yeah, we're in."

"Okay, here's the numbah of the bar. I want you to call it once, just be-fah you come in, and then hang up. That's my signal that yah comin'. Once yah in, just look for me. I'll be sittin' right next to her. She's about five-eight, dark hair. Maybe twenty-five years old. Nice big hogans. Point right at us and make sure we start bumpin' Brillo, okay? You probably oughta point at three or fah other couples besides us, just so it doesn't look suspicious. Hell, point at evahbody—but just make *shah* you point at me and her."

"Got it. Dark hair. About twenty-five. Five-foot-eight. *Buena lechería*."

"Yes, beautiful. That's it."

"It lacks romance, though. I mean, it ain't exactly *Romie and Hoolio*, bra."

If you were to plumb the depth of hatred the Chops had toward the Mayflower Numerals, you would need to go to Home Lumber and ask for the thousand-foot line, at least. For forty years Mayflower members had insulted, ridiculed, and mocked Ponkyites. Mayflower officials never failed to hose poor Ponky in the paper. It was Chops who cut Mayflower hair and suffered silently at their barbs. It was Chops who fixed Mayflower sinks and absorbed their snooty looks. It was Chops who washed Mayflower Bentleys and saw their palms go tipless year after year. And in the dark days of The Bet, a Mayflower member and his muscle had come to Two Down's door and turned Two's inner workings into a sort of Latvian goulash.

So it was no problem for Two Down to find a volunteer to help him nail Mr. Laird Fredericks, the man who was designing to put our beloved, rat-infested Ponky under six inches of concrete. Unfortunately, that volunteer was Cementhead, he of the ten-gallon heart and ten-cc brain.

They were staked out across the street in Cementhead's plumbing truck at Fredericks' daily breakfast haunt, Go Nuts Donuts, waiting for their mark to arrive. It was 8:00 A.M. They were both dressed pitifully in their version of business wear. Two's blue suit was passable, if out of a 1988 Jos. A. Bank catalog. Cement's thick neck was trapped in a Nehru shirt that should've been thrown out during the Johnson administration (Andrew), and a tie he must've last worn to the Soap Box Derby awards dinner. On top of this was a double-breasted black blazer that seemed to have been left behind by Robert Goulet at the Sands.

Bored, Two Down was looking through Cementhead's glove box when he found a wire clothes hanger.

"What's this for?" Two asked.

"In case I ever lock my keys in my truck."

"What?"

"Yeah, in case I lock my keys in here, I can use that to get in through the window."

Two stared at him.

"Hey, anvil-brain. If the door is locked, you can't get into your glove box at all."

"Sure I can."

"How?"

"I've got a hidden key in a little metal magnetic box just next to the radiator."

"And what will you do with that key?"

And they said the next sentence together: "Get the hanger."

Just then the mark pulled in and got out of an old BMW. He was by himself, but he wasn't in a suit, as they expected. He was only in khaki pants and a white mock turtle.

Two and Cement approached him quickly, Two from the front and Cement from the behind. Two flashed a phony badge.

"Back in the car," Cement said menacingly, thinking of himself on *NYPD Blue*. "Unless you want to drink from a straw for the next month."

"I drink from a straw already," the guy said, confused.

"Oh, well," said Cement.

"Just relax, Mr. Fredericks, open the car door, and get back in," Two Down said.

"Fredericks?" the man said.

"Oh, sure, play dumb," Cementhead said, flipping the back door open.

"Okay, what the fuck's going on here?" the mark said. He was about to start rearranging dental fillings. "Who are you guys?"

Cementhead readied his pocketknife in his right hand. Two Down got his camera phone ready.

"Now!" Two hollered. And in one perfectly orchestrated move, Cementhead cut the guy's belt, Two yanked his pants down and snapped a picture . . .

. . . of his tidy whities . . . and his catheter.

Understandably surprised at this development, Two and Cement were caught staring at the man's under-regalia when his right hand managed to smash into both of their heads—Two Down's first and then, without breaking centrifugal force, Cementhead's behind.

The guy pulled up his pants as best he could and stuffed himself back in his car as Two's mouth and Cement's left eye started to swell.

Two spit out a tooth and looked up at him as he pulled away. "You're not Mr. Fredericks, are you?"

"No, you fuckin' perverts!" he said, driving off.

One quick visit to the dentist's office and the stakeout began anew the next morning. This time they had a better description of Fredericks, thanks to a Cementhead stakeout—2003 blue BMW, always in a suit, lonely peninsula of hair separating the world's largest forehead.

And, at last, here he was, Laird Fredericks himself getting out of his BMW to get his habitual donut. Only he was accompanied by another businessman. Fredericks himself was sixtyish with an American flag tie on, a bit of J. Edgar Hoover in the jowls, and a gut that put him at about ten months pregnant. His companion was nondescript, more or less the same age only thinner, with a gray suit on that was so dull it was nearly not there at all.

Two and Cement jumped out of the truck and jogged over to them.

"Mr. Fredericks," Two said.

"Yes?"

"Mr. Laird Fredericks?"

"Yes!"

"A word please? Privately?"

"Excuse me?" Fredericks said.

"We need you to come with us right now, Mr. Fredericks. It's very important."

"What?" he said. "No!"

Two Down grabbed him from behind firmly by the back of the jacket, the belt, the pants, and the underwear. He whispered into Fredericks' ear the following: "Maybe your associate would like to see which page of the Victoria's Secret catalog you're wearing today?"

The color left Fredericks' face. Flustered, he turned to his companion and shot him a guilty glance.

"Oh, yes, you want to talk about the uh, the uh—"

"Yes, the Victoria situation."

"Yes, yes, the situation in Victoria. Right. Get yourself a donut, Edgar, and I'll be back in a few minutes."

"Uh, actually," Cementhead said. "We need to take you down to an emergency arbitrage meeting on this. Can he meet you later?"

Two Down stared at Cementhead in disbelief.

Fredericks stammered a bit and then said, "Yeah, Edgar. I'll just meet you back at the office later. I've got to take care of this. It's very, uh, very—"

Two jerked him a little harder by his thong strap.

"Elastic," Two said.

Fredericks threw Edgar the keys and Edgar went into the shop, staring at the threesome as he went.

Two and Cement walked Fredericks toward a nice Range Rover, waited for Edgar to disappear from sight, then quickly bolted toward the plumbing truck. They shoved him into the cab and drove off.

"We want you to forget buying Ponky," Two Down hissed. "Or we rat you out to everybody you know in town."

"Please!" Fredericks said. "You think I can be blackmailed?"

"Fine," Two said, pulling over into a parking lot. He then looked at Cement. "Igor?"

And Cementhead pulled Fredericks out of the cab, yanked the businessmen's pants down to his knees, and stomped them to the ground while Two Down yanked up his shirt and tie. Then Two quickly took two pictures with his cellphone. Today the upstanding president of American Radio, LLC, was featuring a Brazilian lace thong with rosebud embroidery.

"Nice," Two Down said. "They'll love this shot when I tack it up on the Rotary Club bulletin board."

Fredericks was past embarrassed. He pulled up his pants, straightened his shirt, and said, "Okay, you win. We won't buy Ponkaquogue. It's over. You've got your picture. Now just let me go."

"Oh, sure," said Cementhead. "Like we're just going to *let you go*!"

"We are going to let him go," Two Down said. "All we need to do is make sure I can e-mail these pictures to my computer. Then we're done with this guy."

Two Down fussed with his phone, trying to send it over and over but always getting the "Message Unsent" reply. It was sort of awkward, Cementhead thought, so he tried to make polite conversation.

"You're not gonna try to get my license plates or anything, right?" he said.

"No," Fredericks said. "I don't want to ever have to speak of this incident again. Not to the police. Not to anybody."

"Oh, good, good. So, how are things at the Mayflower?"

"Fine, fine."

Long pause.

"Say," Cementhead tried, "just, you know, out of curiosity, if a guy wanted to become a member there, you know, how would he go about that?"

"Well," Fredericks said thoughtfully, "you could just simply tell the membership committee that you were the one who *kidnapped and extorted me!* That ought to work!"

After another twenty minutes of fussing, Two Down had Cement drive to Sy's Syber Cafe. Once parked, he gave Cementhead the phone.

"Okay, cell service sucks inside, so when I get in there, try to send me the two photos to my e-mail. As soon as I see them in my account, I'll come back out and we can let him go. I'll give you the high sign from the window when I'm ready."

"Got it," Cementhead said.

But Two Down could not figure it out. The waiting went on for ten, twenty, and thirty minutes. No high sign.

"I'm starved," Cementhead finally said. "I could really go for a pizza."

This made Laird Fredericks' eyebrows raise a little.

"You like Domino's?" he said.

"Oh, man! That would be sweet. What time you think they open?"

"I know one near here that opens at ten. Should we get a couple pizzas?"

"Sweet! I'll call info," and he started to dial on Two Down's cell.

"No need!" Fredericks protested. "I know the number by heart."

"How?"

"I own it!" Fredericks said, holding his hand out for the phone. "In fact, I own eleven Domino's! Plus, it'll be free!"

"Cool!" Cementhead said, handing the phone to him.

All over the world, billions of men, women, and children of all ages and intellect could've seen right then and there that handing over the phone was not a good idea. You don't hand over the microfiche before you get the princess back. You don't stop for red lights when being chased by mafia killers. And when you have incriminating pictures of a man on a cell-phone, you do not hand that same man that cellphone. Sadly, Cementhead was not among these billions.

And so it was that Laird Fredericks simply deleted the two pictures, then dialed Domino's. Then he handed the phone back to Cement.

"Okay, it's ringing. Will you order? I gotta take a leak."

"No prob," Cement said. "Pepperoni, sausage, and hamburger okay?"

"Yeah," Fredericks said just before he closed the door. "And add a lit-tle Canadian bacon, too!"

"Sweet!" Cement said as Fredericks climbed out.

And you are also among the billions who would've seen right then and there that Laird Fredericks was never coming back. Can we all bite our knuckles in unison?

When Two Down came back, he was somewhat surprised to find their guest of honor missing.

"Where's Fredericks?" Two Down said.

"Takin' a leak," Cementhead said. "Must've had to go bad, though, be-cause he's been gone an awful long time."

"You let him go?! You bonehead! And you think he's coming back? God-DAMN!"

Cementhead just blinked twice at him.

"Just gimme the damn phone," Two snapped. "Let's go to the Verizon store. Maybe they can show us how to download those two pictures. As long as we've still got the pictures, we've still got him."

"Yeah, good point."

But then Two Down couldn't help but notice the two pictures were also gone.

"Cement, where are the pictures?"

"In the phone?"

"No, they're *not* in the phone. They're gone. Did you mess with the pictures?"

"No."

"Did you let Fredericks touch this phone?"

"Uh, well, just for a sec."

The features of Two Down's remarkable face all seemed to fall into a sinkhole. Even his fully extended hair seemed to drop two inches.

"We're hosed."

Two took a deep breath. Cementhead blinked twice at him again.

"Okay, which way did he go?" Two said. "We gotta catch him and do it over. Let's go! Drive!"

"Uh, Two?"

"What? Drive! We gotta go!"

"Do you mind if we just wait another minute?"

"Why?"

"See, I've got some pizzas coming and—"

It didn't matter that I didn't get back to the Fiat until four. It didn't matter that Sponge was pissed I didn't get to the range until twenty-one minutes before my tee time. It didn't matter that Bob was riding me like Eddie Arcaro the whole way. I knew this was going to be my day.

What was the point of hitting balls? I was just stacking them up in a pile out on the range anyway. What was the point of putting? Each little balata-coated sphere was trundling straight off to bed.

"Stop, you fookin' fool!" Sponge hollered after the third straight long one went in. "Save those for Sain' Androos!"

And off we went. We were paired with a Swede named Thor or Lor or something and my friend from the Gog Magog, Desmond, who looked like cat spittle.

"What's wrong, man?" I asked.

"Ahh, I'm just not feelin' it today, mate. Troubles with my bird."

"Hey, you'll be all right. Let's just have us a nice walk in the park. Admittedly, it's Chernobyl Park, but it's still a park."

I felt for Dez, but it didn't matter. With Sponge in my corner, I felt like I could even beat The Cablinasian himself, Eldrick Woods. As Dannie used to say, "Boy, you're grabbin' steel and rippin' cloth." And because it was so wet, I didn't need to hit many Musselborough Skitters. I could throw everything in there high with spin, something these Euros weren't used to doing.

Not that I was hot or anything, but I birdied the first five holes. Just like that. Five for five. Putts of three feet, six, eighteen, ten, and a two-putt birdie from twenty-five. Is five-under after five any good? At this rate I was going to shoot 54. Of course, then I'd have to jump from the top of Westminster Cathedral as everything I would accomplish after that would be Des Moines Dinner Theater.

"There's fookin' gold monkeys comin' ou' your arse, mon!" Sponge declared.

I took that to be a good thing.

Meanwhile, I don't know why Dez was talking about "not feeling it" because he was hitting it every bit as good. His problem was he was missing easy putts. And every birdie putt he'd miss left his face looking like a leftover plate of spackle. After he three-putted 8—his second of the day—he lost all control.

"I fucking hate to three-putt!" he screamed, flipping the putter down. "I hate it! I hate it! I hate it! I would rather go back to my hotel room, right now, and find my girlfriend shagging another guy than three-putt another green!"

There was a pause as the gallery stiffened—until Sponge yelled, "Wha's your roooom number?"

I threw a little sporty six-under 30 front nine at them, which was just so French-kiss-the-dog wonderful I felt like Richard Simmons with a new Abercrombie & Fitch catalog. That put me at six-under for the two days, and most people agreed eight- or nine-under would get you in the top three. I figured I needed three more birdies in the next nine holes.

And then the Commodore showed up.

"Mr. Hart, may I have a look at your clubs?"

Oh, shit. What was this?

"Why?" Sponge said, stepping in front of the clubs.

"There may be a rules violation," Worstenheim crowed.

"If there's too many clubs, it's only because you planted one in there, you fake fuck," I mentioned.

But he counted only fourteen and it seemed to surprise and disappoint him. He tried to slow-play me to death by examining each and every club, measuring them with his little tape, checking the putter face, examining my balls, the whole Checkpoint Charlie bullshit. He even let a group play through us.

Sponge was particularly offended that Worsty would think him a golf cheat. "You wan' urine, feces, and sperm samples as well, you fookin' KGB spook?" Sponge said. " 'Cause I can jus' give you me fookin' underwear if i' would move this along a wee bi'!"

Worstenheim glared at both of us and stomped off with a "Lucky boy."

I was so fried-out about it all I fanned my driver into the gunch on the right. As we walked after it, me doing the slow burn, Sponge said, "There *was* a fookin' kid's club in yer bag. A' the bo'om. I took i' out and throo i' ou'."

"The bastard!" I told him. "He planted it! That would've cost me, what, nine times two? Eighteen shots! That fucking nun-raper rapist!"

I was so pissed, I didn't even thank Sponge for the eighteen shots he'd saved me. I bogeyed 10.

As we walked through the tunnel under the M3 to the 11th tee, Sponge fronted me. "Raymond," Sponge said, looking down at me with those bright orange eyebrows knitted into a V, "if you give tha' fookin' tosser another second's though', I'll personally kick you in the fookin' goolies!"

I took that to be a bad thing.

I couldn't help but laugh. That relaxed me. I went back to my sweet tempo again and took off on a tear after that, birdying 11 and 12, parring 13, 14, and birdying 15 and 16, the last the sweetest little two-hop-and-suck chip-in you ever saw, to get me to nine-under. Sometimes golf can be more fun than redheaded twin strippers, you know?

Dez settled down, too, and was at eight-under, until he birdied 17. Meaning we were tied. Although I didn't know what we were tied for. First? Fifth? Tenth? Who knew? St. Haggus had no leaderboards anywhere. But then I saw Bob, who seemed to be waiting for me.

"Hey, stranger," I said, "got any scores?"

"Some hotshot Euro Tour guy at twelve-under. Then there's a guy at ten. Then just you two at nine. Then a buncha guys at eight."

"Beautiful," I said. "So right now it'd be a playoff with Dez and me for the final spot, right?"

"Right. This is our day, Stick. I called Ponky collect last night and they're makin' good progress there, too. They got some line on the Mayflower honcho who's trying to buy us."

"Bless those felons. Who'd you talk to?"

"That's the funny thing—Dannie."

"Dannie?"

"Yeah, Dannie picked up. She'd just played and nobody was answering so she picked it up. She sounded pretty tore up about all this, Ray. Guess she came home from her sister's. She wanted to know how you were doing. She cried."

"She did? What'd you tell her?"

"I told her about Sponge and how much better you were playing with him. And how you ran into your old friend Maddy and it really seemed to relax you."

Silence.

"No. You didn't."

"What?"

"You told her I ran into Maddy?"

"Yeah. Why? I mean, you said she was an old friend, right?"

"No, you blind bonehead! She was an old *girl*friend, right before Dannie!"

"Damn," he said. "Sorry, man. I had no idea."

"What'd she say after you told her?"

"Nothin'. She had to go after that. I'm sure she didn't think anything of it."

"She had to go? Right after that?"

"Yeah."

"Sure, sure, no problem. I'm sure it's just a coincidence. She was crying and then she heard about Maddy and then she had to go and you didn't think anything of it. [Pause] I'm fucked."

"Soooo sorry, man. If I—"

Sponge cut Bob off. "Hey, Tom Brokaw. Enough with the fookin' news." Then he turned to me. "Ray, pu' all this shi' away for one more birdie, then you can cha' abou' i' all the way to Sain' Androos. Talk of poony is no' allowed on the fookin' golf coorse."

So I stepped up on 18 after Dez smoked his, and tried to clear my mind. I made a nice slow backswing and just as I was about to unload, there came a *beep-beep-beep* from a golf cart right next to the tee. I slid on the shot like I was doing the merengue and skyed it high and so far left it nearly landed on the M3. In fact, it hit the fence guarding the cars from the course and ricocheted back into the salad, thank God. Sponge and I spun to glare at the driver, who happened to be Mr. Royal and Asshole himself, Worstenheim.

"Dreadfully sorry, old bean," he said with a smidge of a grin. "I'm afraid I placed it in the wrong gear." And then he drove off.

My ball was in the trees, with a patch of weeds right behind it. I could either wedge out sideways and try to get it up and down from 180 yards for par or try to punch a 4-iron through that tiny hole and maybe get near enough to the green to get it up and down. But it was one-in-ten I'd get it through that hole, and I still wouldn't hit it far enough to make it to the green.

I guess I was lost in thought, so Sponge went into his Houston mission control thing. "Houston to Glenn, Houston to Glenn. You copy?"

The way he said it flung me back to the brutal days of the gamblers, when Big Al and Dewey smoked us every way but over mesquite. "You copy?" And looking at that lie reminded me of the witchlike things Dewey could do with that 6-iron of his. And I remember that he'd *purposely* put a clump of weeds behind the ball on tee shots to make it fly low and straight and thirty yards farther than it was supposed to. Hell, I already had the clump right behind my ball. And that's *exactly* the shot I needed here.

"I'm going for the green," I said.

"Donna be fookin' daft, lad. You canny ge' there anyway and beside, the hole is tae small. A fookin' anorexic robin couldna ge' throoo there!"

"Sponge, you've been right every time, except now. Watch this."

I lined it up, took a deep breath, exhaled, and then put my best Dewey swing on it—staying low, hands ahead, never looking up. Sponge said it barely missed the tree on the left but it took off like a rifle shot. It not only rolled all the way to the green, it rolled slightly over.

Suddenly Sponge was Texan: "Wail, hail. Tha's just purdier than a firs' place bel' buckle."

"Dewey," I said to myself, "wherever you are, we're even."

I knew I could get it up and down from there, but my big problem now was that Dez was within twelve feet for birdie to knock a certain lonely greeting card writer out of the tournament.

I chipped up stone dead for my par. Now it was all up to Dez. He was starting to stalk his putt when I noticed Maddy standing behind the green. She seemed flabbergasted to see me standing there. I nodded at her. She quickly looked away.

What was that about? Then, to my shock, Dez looked at her and said, "Hello, darling." She gave him a half-armed little wave—very sheepish—and then looked at her shoes.

Holy Christ, I thought. Maddy was with Dez? The golfer boyfriend with no confidence? The one she was about to break up with? I felt small gerbils eating away at the lining of my stomach. I wondered how much he knew. How much had she told him? And why was my life constantly turning into an episode of *As the Titleist Turns?*

Seeing her seemed to push his buttons a little. Hell, maybe she installed them. His birdie try was three feet right and three feet short. Otherwise, I don't know how it didn't go in. He barely wiggled that three-footer in for his par.

We were tied.

"What happens now?" I asked Sponge.

"Four-hole playoff," he said. "Jus' like the Open champeenship."

Oh, yeah. I liked my chances in a four-hole playoff, especially with Dez suddenly looking more nervous than Donald Trump in a wind tunnel.

"You coming for the playoff, lambkins?" Dez asked Maddy, half convincingly.

"Oh, no, not unless you want me to," she said nervously.

I knew Dez didn't want her, but what could he say? "Oh, absolutely!" he faked. "It'll be a hoot! You must!"

"Well, I don't know," she said, trying like hell not to look at me. "Maybe I shouldn't."

"I insist!" he said.

"Well, uh, okay," she said.

And that was when I knew it was over.

The playoff covered 1, 2, 9, and 18, and Dez stepped up on that first tee and put a double-cross hook on it that was so far into the gorse he'd need two wedges and a Humvee to get back to the fairway.

"Does Bob have a seein'-eye dog wi' him?" Sponge asked.

"No," I said.

"Because humans canny find tha' one."

And we never did. Dez made double bogey and I two-putted from thirty feet for par. Just like that, I led by two. Maddy's face fell flat.

Dez walked over to me, looking like a man hoping to be fit for a noose, and whispered, "Why for fuck's sake did I invite my bird to come with me?"

Crap, I thought. We're going to go there.

"Trouble at home?" I asked warily.

"I don't think she came back to her room until four last night," he said. "I called her on her cell all night."

"You don't, uh, share a room?"

"Not the night before final rounds. Little superstition of mine."

Wonderful. My only buddy in Great Britain was in love with Maddy.

"I think she's about to dump me," he said. "I can't blame her. I'll never be good enough."

"Hell, you're better than me!" I said. I wasn't lying. He hit the ball better and farther than me, had a better short game, a more pure swing. He just didn't have the confidence. Or Sponge.

"No," he said, defeated. "If I don't qualify for the European Tour this year, I'm done. My money will be all gone. I'll have to move back to Surrey and work for the hated mother in abysmal real estate."

He played the second hole like he was already in real estate school. When I parred it, he trailed by three.

Then Worstenheim sent one of his stooges to harass me again.

"Mr. Hart?" this little guy in a cart said. "I've been told to warn you that you're on the clock for slow play."

"In a fookin' playoff?" Sponge said. "Who are we holdin' up? Pol'ergeis'?"

"These were my instructions," the guy said, holding out a watch.

This Worsty was shameless. Still, I tried to pretend the guy and his watch were just Two Down making shadows with the flagstick while I tried to hit. I welcomed it. I bogeyed 9 with a bad 5-iron. I still led by two. But on the last playoff hole, I hit this 7-iron toward the green that was just so crisp and lovely I could've cried.

"I think I'm moist," Sponge whispered.

It finished a foot from the hole, a goddamn leaner, a sneeze-in. Bob could've knocked it in. The one hundred or so people on the green applauded like I was an astronaut. Felt kind of good, actually. Then Dez hit a clanky 9-iron to forty feet.

As we walked to the green, Bob was beating on my back and hollering, "You did it, Stick! You saved Ponky!"

And I looked up above the green, in the bay window of that heinously ugly clubhouse, and saw, looking down at me with his hands on his hips, surrounded by other ancient and dandruffs in their ugly blue blazers, Commodore Worstenheim.

And I got a terrible, sinister, delicious idea.

CHAPTER 14

itanic Tuesday arrived for Resource Jones, holding the promise of a new life or a new life sentence.

He was on the course at the usual time—7:15, worked his way methodically from the bunkers on 3, then 2, then finally the bunkers on 1 fairway. His hands shook, his brow poured, his lungs barely cranked in anticipation of seeing Mr. Malcolm Baker, the man in the Panama hat, playing golf gloriously by himself.

He went over for the one hundredth time all the things that could make him abort the Malcolm Mission:

1. The Prison View starter could've put a single with Malcolm Baker— or put Baker into some other group.
2. A guard could wander by for no reason and against all of Resource's planning and time schedules.

3. Baker could've brought somebody else to replace Mr. Hornbecker.

4. The tower guard could suddenly and inexplicably decide he wanted to make like Jim Nantz and watch golfers that morning.

5. Malcolm Baker could have one of those rare butts that doesn't succumb to a well-placed needle.

Resource rattled his head back and forth to shake the toxic thoughts out of his mind, took three tai chi breaths, and tried to relax. And within ten minutes he saw a very lovely sight, a lone stocky golfer bobbing along in a golf cart, coming over the steep hill toward No. 1 green, a Mr. Malcolm Baker, dressed in khaki shorts, a blue-and-yellow golf shirt, and big straw Panama hat.

Just my colors, thought Resource Jones.

When playing in a twosome, Malcolm Baker was fast, but by himself, he was nearly invisible. He looked like a man who was double-parked somewhere. He took a whack at his ball, lying as it was about eighty yards from the 1st green. Resource figured it for his third shot. It ended up in the bunker left of the green, and he skulled it out of there in no time, straight into the bunker on the right side of the green, the bunker Resource Jones happened to be standing next to, flopsweat streaming off his brow. He had planned to get him as he planted the flag back in the hole, but this was even better. The guy was coming straight to him! Baker quickly raked the one bunker and stomped across the green to the other one. He climbed into the new bunker and Resource circled discreetly behind him. As Baker prepared his shot, Resource prepared his, a syringe filled with Rohypnol, otherwise known as a "roofie," only ten times the usual dose.

If Resource Jones had called Acme Victims and asked for someone to knock immediately goofy with stolen drugs, they couldn't have sent a better setup. Baker had a habit of sticking his butt out like a football center on his sand shots. It was like Hannibal Lecter meeting Star Jones. Resource checked 360 degrees again for anybody and found nothing. The time was now. Just as Baker made contact, so did Resource. Sadly, Baker

never saw one of the best sand shots of his life. It rolled up to within five
feet.

The big man went down like a redwood—his knees buckling and his
face pitching nose-first into the soft sand. Again, no sound made there. He
did not even make a groan. He was either dead or very, very asleep. Resource checked again for witnesses, hopped into the bunker, took Baker by
the arms, and started to drag. This was tough sledding. Baker's bulbous ex-
offensive-guard body just sank deeper into the sand every foot. Resource
hadn't accounted for this. Time was wasting, as the next group would be
coming to the crest of the hill very soon. Resource was practically hyper-
ventilating the entire thirty seconds it took to get Baker out of the sand, the
twenty seconds it took him to schlep Baker into the cart, the ten more it
took to drive the cart behind the lightning shelter, and the twenty more it
took to get him out of the cart and into the shelter.

Inside, Resource worked feverishly, stripping Baker down to his Calvin
Klein orange-striped undies, himself down to his prison-issue white briefs,
putting all of Baker's togs on himself, including the shoes, which were a
size too big. He gagged Baker, just in case, and emerged again into the
harsh sunlight. He admittedly forgot to check whether Baker was living or
dead. You know, time constraints.

He peeked around the corner of the shelter and saw, to his horror, that
the next group was driving toward the green from about seventy-five yards
away. And then he saw his colossal mistake. He'd forgotten to rake the
bunker. And it was a very big rake job: It looked suspiciously like somebody had dragged a moose through the sand. He fetched the ball, then
jumped in and raked as fast as he could without looking desperate.

"I know what you did," hollered one of the foursome descending upon
him, an older gentleman.

Resource's heart fell into his feet.

"You do?"

"Yeah, I do. Do it myself. From the looks of that bunker, you must've
left a few in there."

Resource remembered to breathe again.

"Oh! Yeah! Isn't that how it always is? Well, I'll just finish raking. Then I'll buzz out of your way!"

The old guy waved thanks. Resource jogged to his cart and drove to the No. 2 tee box, trying to drive with black spots in front of his face.

My God, that was close, he thought to himself as he planted a tee in the ground. Trying to not look panicked, he took a very slow and deliberate pass with a 3-wood, his first swing of the golf club in three years and—lo and behold—it described the loveliest arc right down the middle, true and long. He laughed at that, actually laughed, like a little boy who, after years of trying, finally sticks the rubber dart right on his sister's forehead. He peered over his shoulder quickly and allowed himself a cantaloupe grin. In all his meticulous planning, he had never once thought about that: The eight holes he was going to play—albeit in a mad rush—might actually be fun. He had always thought about the eight holes as a necessary evil to keep up appearances, the only way out, his fertilized escape route. He never once realized that he was going to actually get in some golf.

He floored it to his ball and eyeballed the distance. Baker never checked distances, so he couldn't. Everything had to resemble Baker. Looked like about 160 yards. He tried 8-iron. No waggle, no practice swing. Just get this over with. But again, he hit it flush in the middle and the ball took off beautifully toward the pin as though he were in some Buick Open somewhere. It actually spun back a few feet and wound up within ten feet of the hole. Three years in the can and he had tour jizz? thought Resource. Incredible.

He walked the way Baker walked, ambling and stiff-legged up to his putt and, without a practice stroke—Baker never used one—knocked it cleanly and beautifully into the hole. Birdie.

Again, he laughed to himself and shook his head. He took a furtive glance around, but still nobody was watching. He got back in the cart and couldn't help himself. He wrote "3" on the second hole and circled it. Been a long time since he'd done that.

At the next tee box he searched Baker's bag for his car keys, wallet, and cellphone. They were right where Baker always put them, in the big pocket. The cellphone showed it to be 8:32. Baker's tee time must've been 8:10, which meant he'd be through nine at about 9:55, in the Explorer by 10:00, at the Brockton bus station by 10:45, in a cab by 11:00 to a mall, where he'd buy new clothes, steal a car, and be hell-bent for paradise.

Preoccupied by these thoughts, he barely noticed himself hitting the 3-wood again on 3, but this, too, was creamy, a draw. From the fairway he hit 3-wood again—as this was a par-5—and this one was even more perfect than the last, eventually rolling onto the green in two. He laughed out loud at that. He nonchalantly two-putted for birdie.

What the hell? Take three years off and then birdie your first two holes? Where was Two Down when you needed him?

And so it went. He became so thrilled at unearthing this sapphire of a golf game, he actually forgot to take the buried food out of the bunkers on 3 and 4. On 5, he didn't even notice that one of the inmates/groundskeepers gave him a rather long, quizzical "Don't-I-know-you?" look. And why should he notice? Through five holes now, he was two under par!

On 7, two guards were sneaking in a game of gin and never noticed him. That allowed Resource to exult in the full joy of golf now. He spent a good deal of time lining up his forty-footer for birdie there, stroked it, and watched it disappear. He gave it the full Tiger fist pump. It was all he could do to keep from screaming like a little girl upon arriving at the Barbie factory. He was now three-under for six holes.

He made himself a lovely up-and-down out of a bunker on the 8th hole for par, actually hollering "Damn right!" when his twelve-footer went in, never once noticing the guard in the tower there.

And so, if you could've been sitting in that cart with Resource Jones as he came up to the 9th hole, you would have never guessed you were sitting next to a man who had just filled a man's bloodstream with The Babe Roof of syringes, bound and gagged him, assumed his clothes and identity, robbed him of his wallet and car keys, and was in the midst of escaping from a federal penitentiary. All you would've thought was that you were with a golf maniac, one who, in fact, was wondering if it was too late to give the Senior Tour a try in fifteen years.

In all his planning, Resource knew the 9th hole would be the most dangerous, as cart boys and assistant pros near the clubhouse might get a look at him. He had even planned on not putting out on the 9th green to avoid the risk, keeping a wide berth around the clubhouse, and heading straight to the parking lot.

But now, all that was Alpo long inside Rover. Resource Jones was interested in only one thing on 9—making par. Looking at his scorecard, he decided to give himself par on the first hole. It killed him to break the rules, as Resource Jones was faithful to rules the way Lassie was faithful to Timmy. But it was such a simple hole and the way he was playing, par was a layup. Hell, the way he was playing, he might have birdied the hole. So that meant a par on the 9th could give him 32, the best nine of his life.

But his sand wedge into 9 left him only six feet from the hole, and as he walked to the green he didn't even think to pull his Panama hat low for protection. In fact, in reading the putt, he took the glasses *off*—too dark to get a good look at the break—and even putted with them hanging from his shirt collar. His golf mind had bound and gagged his criminal mind. The putt went in the hole as if pulled by a string for a birdie. He'd just shot 31 on a single round of golf.

He looked to the heavens. This was . . . unfathomable, preposterous, maddening! He had played golf his whole life. It was his one true passion. He loved it more than sex, food, even grifting. And now, the day when he had no possible chance to play eighteen holes, he was a dead mortal lock to break the impenetrable 70, the Holy Grail of his life. It seemed too cruel to be possible.

And then a very horrible thought occurred to him, a very self-destructive, stupid, and insane thought.

Does anybody know why murderers return a half hour later to pump one last bullet into their victims? Why ex-boyfriends climb lattices just to see their true love humping their best friend? Why fat women suddenly see tight red Capris and think, "I'd look good in that!" No, these are mysteries to us. And so there is no reason why Resource Jones would think the unthinkable, at the worst possible moment: *Why not play all eighteen?*

And the more Resource Jones thought the unthinkable, the more thinkable it became. *Well, why not?* he said to himself. He could do it! There had not been a single second glance at him. No guard had so much as taken his eyes off his cards, much less recognized him. Nobody was pushing him from behind or holding him up from in front. Baker was not scheduled to come back from Roofundland for another four hours. And don't forget, he was bound and gagged. It wasn't like he was going to suddenly jump up and begin singing Rodgers and Hammerstein tunes. Plus, the cellphone said it was only 9:45. He was well ahead of schedule. He'd played that nine in 1:35. He could play the next in 1:30 and be in the Explorer by 11:15. Baker wouldn't even have been knocked out for three hours, really. And was anybody calling on Baker's cell? Anybody asking questions? No! And didn't Baker *usually* play eighteen? Wouldn't playing just nine be suspicious? How could he let a 31 just *sit* there like that? He knew he'd never have this chance again, as long as he breathed, as long as he played golf. He *owed* it to himself. He *owed* it to everybody who'd ever *dreamed* of playing like this and never had! Goddammit, it was his duty!

And so, Resource Jones did not go to the Explorer and escape. He did not give a thought to the fact that if he were caught, he'd be seeing striped sunshine the rest of his life. He instead went straight to the 1st tee, kept his head low, and teed off *again*.

There were no eyebrows raised by anybody, of course. The tee was open. Baker had paid for eighteen holes. No point in waiting. He hit his 3-wood right down the middle. What he didn't know is that the head pro couldn't help but notice something.

"Damn!" the pro said to his cashier. "That big black guy must've gotten a lesson or something. That was a sweet move!"

He parred 1. He didn't even spin the cart by the lightning shelter to see if he heard rumblings. He had only one thought on his mind—69. Onward. He made a bogey on 2, a par on 3, and another bogey on 4, which might explain why coming through 5 again, he didn't see a friend of his from the inside, an inmate who worked weeds.

" 'Source?" he said, shutting down his Weed Eater. "That you?"

It rocked Resource out of his trance. He looked quickly at the inmate and then away.

"Shhhhhhh," he pantomimed, finger to lips. "I just *had* to play this course once, dude! It was drivin' me crazy!"

"I dig," said the inmate, "but ain't you playin' it twice?"

Resource shrugged. "The handicap computer won't take partial scores," he said, and moved on, making a shaky bogey on 5. He was now one-under. He had to par the last four holes to shoot the revered 69.

Resource's nerves were starting to fray like a Goodwill sweater. And now he ran into more peril. For two holes now he'd been playing behind a turtlish foursome—two young bucks and their two girlfriends, who were hitting it so hideously they all seemed to be using the wrong side of the club. After parring 6, he came to the 7th tee only to find them still standing on it. There were waggles, changings of clubs, discussions, more waggling, some hugging, laughing, more waggling. Resource slowly began to lose his previously facile mind.

"Hey!" he said to the kid. "You ever use that driver before?"

"Sure!" the kid said back with a smile.

"Then step up and hit the motherfucker already!"

The teens were stunned into silence. The kid didn't know what to do, so Resource did it for him. He grabbed Baker's 3-wood, marched to the tee, and played through. Then he scorched off in the cart.

If he was going to serve a life sentence, it wasn't going to be on a fucking tee box.

He managed an up-and-down par on 7 and another on 8 and *still* there seemed to be no suspicion, no movement among the bulbous guards. *He was going to pull this off!* he thought. He hit a beautiful drive on 9, followed by a three-quarter sand wedge that was just so delicious he wanted to sniff the divot. He missed the eight-footer and settled for par and his glorious 69.

But something seemed hollow about it. Resource Jones may be a violent criminal, a dangerous weapons dealer, and an unscrupulous con man, but he is not a golf cheat. He was Ponky's golf ethicist, and all arguments among men and women there had been settled by the simple sentence: "We'll ask Resource."

And now that honesty was sticking in his briefs like a tumbleweed. *He had not played the first hole.* He had lied to himself. He could tell himself the rest of his life that he broke 70, but he'd know that as long as he didn't actually play the first hole, that 69 was as false as a plastic surgeon's pool party.

Again, freedom beckoned. He wanted to get to the Explorer and go, but his scruples wouldn't let him. If he was really going to accomplish his lifetime dream, he had to play that one last hole.

And so, against all reason and sense and self-preservation, Resource Jones snuck the cart over to the 1st tee and stuck it in the ground again. He hit it cleanly, if low, and jumped back into the cart, only to see a familiar face five feet from him.

It was the black second-string assistant pro he'd befriended.

"Wanna get a brew after work?" the man said with a slight grin.

It was too late. He had never put the sunglasses back on. They'd made eye contact.

"No," said Resource, "just the golf, thanks," and he lead-footed it down the fairway.

The assistant pro sprinted to the pro shop.

At that moment, Resource Jones's expectations for success dropped well below 85 percent. In fact, the hounds were on him. The bust was coming and Resource knew it. There was only one thing left to do—par this one last hole, the last hole of his life, and at least take that 69 with him into that endless life of fuzzy cable and concrete meat loaf.

His heart was beating just slightly faster than a coked-up hummingbird's. He tried to calm himself long enough to hit his wedge onto 1 green, but he thinned it and it ended up by the temporary home of Mr. Malcolm Baker in the lightning shelter. He raced there, urging the cart forward, rocking it forward, willing it so. As he looked back, he saw four golf carts coming after him, two with staff and two full of guards. The siren at the prison blared. Dogs barked. Cellmates put their cheeks to their bars.

He screeched the cart up next to the shack. From within, he could hear banging and grunting, probably coming from a groggy doppelgänger with a very powerful headache. He had to hit this chip close, but concentration was a little difficult just then. He popped up the sand wedge too high, but it got a lucky hop and lurched forward until it finished about five feet from the hole, nearly the same putt Baker would've had before Resource separated him from his consciousness three hours before.

Over megaphones from the pursuing carts, he heard, "Prisoner! Stop and drop immediately! We will not ask you twice!"

They were only fifty yards away and he still wasn't to his ball. He was never going to make it. From the tower he saw that two guards were training rifles on him.

"I'm strapped with dynamite!" Resource screamed as he inched toward his ball on the green, putter in his right hand. "You shoot me and I blow up everything within five hundred yards!"

As he said it, he lined up the most important putt of his life. The carts were now surrounding him from the edge of the green, every one of them training guns on his temple.

"Where'd you get dynamite, prisoner?" said the megaphone.

"Man, can't you see I'm putting here?" Resource said. "Just, you motherfuckers can just start meetin' my demands! I want a chopper, $10 million in fifties, and a Learjet waiting for me at Brockton Airport! I'm not fuckin' around here!"

"Settle down, prisoner. Let's talk!"

Resource took one last tai chi breath, read the line again under the cruelest conditions possible, and stroked the putt. It wiggled right, then wiggled left, then hung on the lip, took a little look inside, considered for a moment, and then decided, reluctantly, to drop in.

"Goddamn right!" Resource screamed, throwing the putter twenty feet in the air, his head back, and raising his fists to the sky. It was the greatest single moment of his life: A legit 69, with borrowed clubs no less, under duress with armed witnesses. Suck on that, you slobs.

Unfortunately, what Resource Jones didn't realize was that his exultant gesture revealed his midsection to be nothing more than Resource Jones—no dynamite, no guns, not even a money belt. Within three seconds of this sight, eight men had him under a dogpile.

At the bottom of the mass of men and guns and helmets, with clubs and boots and fists battering him, Resource Jones had just enough strength and presence of mind to reach into the hole and grab the ball.

Hey, even cell walls need memorabilia.

CHAPTER 15

Lying one foot from the hole for birdie, with a two-shot lead in the playoff, my $250,000 locked up, Ponky secured—that was fine as far as it went, I guess.

But there was one little itch I had to scratch yet before I could feel holed—Commodore Worstenheim. I could not take my eye off him and his potbellied pigs, the blue-jacketed, blue-haired members of the Royal and Ancient. I could see him up there, pointing at me, tsk-tsking back and forth, his jowls swaying in the air conditioning. Something about that guy just gave me the serious postals. It was not enough to qualify; I wanted to give that six-foot turd something to remember me by.

"What'r you wai'in for?" Sponge said, taking his last glug of Macallan. "Kno' i' in and le's give our livers a swim."

"Driver," I said, holding out my hand.

"Wha'?"

"Driver."

He looked at me like I was asking for a bowl of baby toes.

"Ohh, I ge' i'," Sponge said. "Hail, why no'? Pu' wi' yer driver! You could three-pu' this wee bastar' and still win!"

"Something like that," I said.

Sponge walked back and got my driver, presenting it to me like a knight presenting Excalibur, whipping the headcover off at the last minute with a flourish, and bowing deeply.

"Thank you, knave."

A murmur went through the crowd. I faced the bay window and Worstenheim and his cronies. I held the driver up over my head with both hands. They looked down on me like I'd just head-butted the queen.

I set up over that one-footer, took a wide stance, waggled once or twice, looked up at Worsty, smiled, and then let it rip with a full swing. I smoked it flush, making sure not to take anything out of the green, giving it all to the ball, low and hard, driver off the deck. I hit that thing so hard I swear it changed colors.

You should've seen that bastard's eyes as that RPG came boring in right at him. He dived like Greg Louganis. They all did. It smashed the window dead center, shattering the glass with a glorious din. The ball bounced off the back wall and went ricocheting off the mahogany and Waterford and Chippendale.

"Eleven o'clock news," I said to nobody in particular.

There were no longer any faces to see up there, only occasional glass pieces falling randomly. By then, they were all on the floor. There was openmouthed silent screaming from everybody—the window, the room, and the gallery—until at last Worsty himself peeked up, like a man coming out of a cave at the end of World War II. On his head, a toupee sat cock-eyed, like a napping ferret.

That did it. Desmond collapsed in a heap on the green he was laughing so hard. Sponge was in shock. I was simply staring eyeball-to-eyeball at

Commodore Worstenheim, smiling like a man who'd just married Bill Gates's daughter.

"Guess I hit that one OB, Sponge. Another ball please. And my putter."

Sponge's mouth still hung open like a drawbridge, but he fetched me another ball and my putter. I held the ball out parallel to the green and dropped it in approximately the same place I'd hit the driver.

"Four," I said.

Then I took the putter and buried the 12-incher.

"Five."

By now Worstenheim realized what I'd done, as did the entire gallery, as did Sponge. Some were booing, some were applauding, and most were roaring.

Sponge grinned.

"I love you, Brian Piccolo," he said in his best Gale Sayers, hugging me and picking me up eight inches off the grass. "Ya daft shite, ya!"

By now Worstenheim was screaming, "I'll disqualify you for this! You'll never play another round in England!"

"Under wha' rule?" Sponge was yelling. "He took the two-sho' penal'y, y'arse!"

Dez came up and grabbed my hand like a paint-shaker.

"Well done, Ray!" he said, still laughing. "Well bloody done! Finally, somebody stood up to those self-important wankers!"

"Don't go anywhere, Dez," I said. Then I turned to Sponge and said, "Figure out the damages and tell them I'll send them a check."

I quickly signed my card and went to find a pay phone. I had some people to call.

To the side of the green, looking like a man who'd missed his bus, Bob was saying to anybody who would listen, "Will somebody please tell me what the hell just happened?"

Mrs. Opel Hickenlooper was a very forgetful eighty-seven-year-old widow, some days first-stage Alzheimer's, some days not. She usually recognized friends and family, no problem, but she'd often forget small facts like *Yes, I have already eaten lunch* and *No, I never served under Ike.*

And so it was not a large problem when, a few days after Big Al stole the Lincoln that Two had stolen, she said to Two Down: "I believe I'd like to go for a ride in my Lincoln. Will you take me?"

This was during a game of fifty-dollar mah-jongg and it stopped Two Down cold. He swallowed uneasily, stared into Opel Hickenlooper's glassy eyes, and regained that composure he's so famous for.

"Oh, Opel," he said, patting her hand. "You sold that car two years ago, dear. Remember? To the nice collector man from New York. He put it in a museum. He lets kids sit in it for free now."

"Oh?" Opel said, considering this. "I did?"

"Yes, ma'am. You got $27,500 for it."

"I did?"

"Yes you did. That's woo."

And that seemed to be the happy ending of the matter until the next afternoon, when there was a knock on Opel's door while Two Down happened to be inside, playing a little ship-captain-crew dice with her at five dollars a throw. A man in khakis and a white mock turtle entered. In a bit of bad luck Two Down had suddenly become known for, this man just happened to be the catheter-wearing unfortunate that Two and Cement had mistakenly pantsed outside Go Nuts Donuts in the catastrophic Laird Fredericks incident.

"There's my boy!" Opel said to the man. "This is my friend Two Down. He got the name for his love of crossword puzzles. Isn't that nice?"

From the cold-steel expression on his face, the man did not think it was very nice at all.

"So you're the tool that plays cards with my mom?" he said.

"Yes. Isn't she just a wonderful woman—"

The man pushed the door completely open and held it against the wall with his huge mitt.

"Where's her goddamn car?" he said, regarding Two's skinny body like it might be a javelin he could throw.

"Is this the Lincoln she keeps talking about?"

"Yeah, a 1964 Lincoln Continental."

"She told me she sold it two years ago," Two said, a small trickle of sweat rolling down his temple. "She told me that many times. It's just lately the poor thing seems to have forgotten and keeps talking about wanting to take a ride in it!"

"That's funny," the coach said, taking a menacing step toward him. "Then what the FUCK was I driving in the Fourth of July parade last week?"

Nervous, overcologned, and shaved almost hairless, Dom, the World's Most Sexual Man, took the 41 bus to Don's Mixed Drinks. He was there by 8:00 P.M. and spent the next two hours sitting in the White Castle across the street, anxiously pestering a Coke and waiting for his true and unrequited love, Kelly van Edible, to show up at the bar. This was going to work or he was going to ball himself up in a Tibetan monastery until death.

He reconfirmed the time, the address, and the instructions with Freddy. "You point the gun at me and the brunette. I'll be sitting right next to her. When we're done, you escape out the back, got it?"

"Christ!" Freddy complained. "I *did* get my GED, bra!"

By 10:15, Dom was too nervous to wait anymore and wandered in, trying to appear casual. It was a slow night at Don's Mixed Drinks, where the décor was nearly as imaginative as the establishment's name. It was your kind of place if you liked red Naugahyde booths with Ponderosa-style wood trim, teacher's-lounge-style tables with silver-legged chairs and red-buttoned upholstered seats, not a lamp or chandelier in sight that wasn't a gift of a beer, liquor, or smokeless tobacco company, an Asteroids game that had not moved in thirty years and not worked in fifteen, a shuffleboard table that long ago lost its last piece of sawdust, a jukebox featuring the latest hits from 1989, a pool table where the last precious pieces of green felt were clinging on for dear life, four wooden backless benches surrounding it, and a bar with ten aluminum stools with black seat cushions, almost all of them fighting losing battles to hold in their foam.

It was on one of these stools that Dom took a seat and checked his Fauxlex. The karaoke was in full painful form, with a longhaired man in a Boston Bruins jersey belting out his weekly favorite, Led Zeppelin's "How Many More Times?"—and the crowd asking themselves the same question.

Having been here perhaps half a dozen times the same night as Kelly, Dom had a working knowledge of her karaoke m.o. She would usually come in with another luscious named Amber and they would sit at one of the four-chair tables, facing the karaoke machine. Seeing as Amber could also make a bulldog break his chain, the third and fourth chairs would be snapped up within ten minutes by some swinging dick or other. There were three empty four-tops open now. Dom knew that if he took a seat at one of the tables, they'd take one of the other two. That's why his plan was to sit at the bar and be ready to pounce on the chair next to Kelly the minute they sat.

What he hadn't counted on was the Human Stain, who rode in on his godforsaken scooter at 10:40, parked it in the corner, and took the bar stool next to his.

"Greetings, Dom," he said, picking a zit on his arm. "Any foxes in here tonight?"

"Foxes?" Dom said, trying not to look at him.

"Certainly," he said. "Babes. Beauties. Looks a little thin to me so far. But then, I'm a little more discerning than yourself."

If it's possible for a man's eyes to roll clean out of their sockets, Dom's would've. He took a large pull on his adult beverage and said, "Yeah, well, some guys got it and some don't."

"Ahhh," Stain said. "Don't be so hard on yourself, mon ami. You've just got to get over Kelly and move on. Babes are like streetcars, my friend. There'll be another one along in five minutes."

And another woman did come along just then, in fact, though hardly a

babe—Blu Chao. She walked in warily, wearing some kind of Aunt Beahive hairdo, large pearls, Wal-Mart's best paisley frock, black stockings
with a cheesy seam, too-high heels, and a handbag you could've smuggled
a small farm animal in. It was the first time either man had ever seen her
without her cooking apron, to say nothing of out from behind the Ponky
counter. She spied them sitting on the stools and slunk over.

"I sit?" she said to Dom, pointing to the empty stool next to him.

"Uh, shah," Dom said.

She was a squat woman whose form most resembled that of an Algerian
wrestler, maybe five-foot-even and 200 pounds, so it was no small achievement for her to scale the stool, what with the steamer trunk of a purse and
the heels and all.

Stain looked over and said, "Blu Chao, we are honored. I wonder, as
long as we are in such an informal setting, if I might, before the night is
out, trouble you for the recipe for that *divine* chicken cordon bleu you
make, with the gorgonzola sauce, the stuffed parmesan-crusted squash,
and the sun-dried tomato risotto? I simply *must* have it."

Blu Chao looked at him quizzically.

"Screwdrive," she said.

"Absolutely!" Stain said, then turned to the bartender. "A screwdriver
for the duchess, please."

It was 10:48 when the night's central character walked in, Kelly van
Edible, looking twelve city blocks past hot. She wore a red leather
miniskirt, a painted-on about-to-burst white T-shirt that read I SEE YOU'VE
MET THE TWINS, a double-chained belt, long, tan legs you would happily be
strangled by, and black pumps she must have borrowed off a dominatrix.
She immediately caught sight of the threesome at the bar and came eagerly
to Stain, taking the stool next to him.

What the hell? thought Dom.

"Thanks again for coming!" she said to Stain. "I brought my eight-by-
ten." She dug it out of her purse. "Do you think your brother at *Vogue*
really has some gigs?"

Dom spat out his beer.

"Oh, absolutely," Stain said with just slightly more grease in his voice than that required by a 1979 Jeep Wagoneer. "Of course, you and I should get together and decide—"

Suddenly at 10:50, the door of Don's Mixed Drinks slammed open and a single gunman barged through it, pointing not one but two guns everywhere at once and bellowing, "Nobody move! Everybody get their hands over their head, godammit! Hands over your fuckin' heads! Now!"

It was not Freddy. It was I-Rod. He wore a ski mask, black jacket, tight black jeans, black German army boots, and a DKNY backpack. He felt the door behind him and locked it. He had his iPod phones in his ears.

"Oh, shit," thought Dom as loudly as a man can think a thought. He began to sneak off his stool so that he could scurry over and sit next to Kelly.

I-Rod pointed the Glock straight at Dom. "Nobody fuckin' move, I said!"

"But I—"

"Shut up! Every fuckin' one of you, throw me your cellphones. Every one of you!"

The fifteen or twenty customers did so, to the unaccompanied karaoke instrumental of Neil Diamond's "Song Sung Blue."

I-Rod worked his way behind the bar, yanked the phone out of the wall, opened the cash register, and put all the money in the backpack. He yanked the watch and wallet off the bartender and the bar-back, emptied three more purses from a promising-looking table to his left, and then decided it was time to move on with the proceedings.

"All right, people!" he screamed. "I want to see some sex! Right now, in front of me!"

He pointed the gun at Dom and Blu Chao.

Dom was horror-struck.

"You two. Start fuckin'! Right on the bar. Hurry up!"

Dom was stammering now. He rose, irate. "No! You got this all wrong! This is a terrible mistake! You've—"

"Oh, I know what I'm doin', baby!"

He fired a shot at Dom's feet that launched him three feet in the air. "Get busy! Get her clothes off, let's go!"

Then he pointed at the next couple at the bar—which happened to be the Stain and Kelly van Edible.

"You two! I want to see sex. Get busy, right now!"

Kelly began whimpering. Dom was frisbee-eyed. "Dude, you got this all—"

Another shot from the Glock, this time into the Hamm's mirror behind the bar.

"Everybody! Start screwing! Find the person next to you! I don't wanna hear talking! I just wanna hear humping! Let's go, people! And don't gimme a bunch a foreplay! This ain't *Blind Date!*"

He pointed to a couple near the pool table. "You two! Do it on the table!"

There seemed to be nothing left to do but begin conjugal relations. A couple on their first date turned to each other and shrugged. A married couple began their routine on a bench. Two strangers near the karaoke machine began to fumble nervously with buttons. A teenage couple with fake IDs was already half done. A grandmother looked longingly at a grandfather, who kept her at arm's length while watching the teenagers.

For Dom, it was hell incarnate. For the Human Stain, it was the chocolatiest moment of his vanilla life. For Kelly, the most hideous. For Blu Chao, the most confused. Why was the man from the golf course suddenly feeling her up and yet weeping at the same time?

And that's when Freddy came through the back.

"Everything all right in here?" Freddy said.

I-Rod nodded proudly. He seemed eminently pleased with himself.

Dom pretended to make out with Blu Chao so passionately that he had her on her back on the bar, right next to where Freddy was standing. He turned his head and whispered angrily up to Freddy: "This idiot's got me with the wrong gahl!"

"What?" whispered Freddy. "You said you'd be sitting next to a brunette."

"Not this one!" Dom whispered. "The hottie! And why the fuck is he so goddamn ehly? And whah was my damn one-ring call?"

"He was in a hurry. He wanted to get back in time for *Oprah*."

And that's when six Boston cops busted down the front door and four more came barreling through the back.

It took them three minutes to pry Stain off Kelly.

First thing I did after my smash finish at St. Haggith's 18th was to find a red phone booth and Touch-Tone my life right again.

As usual I couldn't get Dannie, so I tried Ponky, collect. Hoover answered and accepted the charges. What did he care?

"Hoov, it's Ray. Is my wife there?"

"No. Cementhead's here. Are you fluent in Cement?"

"Hoov, this is life-or-death: You've got to get a message to Dannie. Tell her I qualified."

"You, uh, you did?" Hoover said, a little oddly I thought.

"Yeah! I qualified! Tell the Chops, too. Tell Froghair I'm buying Ponky."

"Oh, uh, sure, I'll get right on that."

"But the most important thing is, you've got to tell my wife that nobody means anything to me except her. Okay? You've got to tell her: Tell her: okay? Not Maddy. Not Kelly. Nobody. Tell her I've just made us a bunch of money and I'm going to keep working hard. I want to support her and Charlie forever. Tell her all of it, okay, Hoov?"

"Uh, Stick?"

That sounded ominous.

"What?"

"There's something you should know."

"What?"

"I just drove by your house this morning. There was a U-Haul in front."

"Funny, Hoov."

"No, Stick, this is true. One of those U-Haul trucks people rent. Kind of medium-sized."

That stuck in my gut like a hot fondue fork.

"God-DAMMIT!" I said, slamming the phone on the change slot.

I took a deep breath.

"Hoov?"

"Yeah?"

"I'm coming back there. Today. Find Dannie and tell her I'm coming back on the next flight and not to do anything until I get back."

"Okay, I'll try."

"Okay."

"And Stick?"

"What?"

"Congrats. On qualifying. Way to go."

He sounded almost regretful about it.

"Thanks, I think."

I hung up and sprinted back to the course to find Dez, who was lying down, his head resting against his bag, looking blankly at the sky, possibly thinking jump, hose, or rope?

I ran up to him and said, "You got plans for next week?"

He laughed bitterly. "Oh, most certainly. I'm addressing Parliament all week."

"Too bad. I thought you might want to play in the Open."

"Sure, love to, cracking good," he said. "The West Linksbury Open or the Upper Slaughter Open?"

"The British Open. In my place."

He looked at me like I had a third eye.

"I'm serious," I said. "I'm withdrawing. I've got to get back to the States and save my marriage. I never wanted to play anyway. I just wanted to prove I could qualify."

"You're mad! You can't pass up a chance like this!"

"I can and I am," I said. "I don't want to play competitive golf. I *hate* competitive golf. I just want to go home and play for fun. That's all I've ever wanted to do. All this shit has been everybody else's dream *for* me, not my dream. My dream is to write and laugh and be with my wife and my kid and have a few beers and get laid now and again. And if I don't get back right now, I'll never be able to do that again. So take my place, please?"

"Well, I suppose if you're not going to win it, I might as well inherit the task," he said.

"Great. Beautiful. Go win the thing and take the trophy and the medal and Tiger's nanny and everything, cool?"

"Cool," he said, and he held out his hand. "Mate, thank you so much. If there's ever *anything* I can do for you, anything, you just let me know, anytime, ever."

"Okay, how about right now?" I said. "I need you to follow me and Bob to the airport and buy my plane ticket home. My Visa's toast. I'll pay you as soon as I get home."

"Let's be off then!" he said, grinning madly.

When I found them, Sponge and Blind Bob were jawing with some blue blazer about something or other.

"Bob, we gotta go, right now," I said. I turned to my caddy. "Sponge, I love you, man. You changed my life."

"Save your fookin' speech for Sain' Androos," he said, "afta you've won."

"I'm not going, Sponge. I gotta get home and win something better—my wife and kid back."

Sponge was dumbstruck, no small feat for a guy like him.

"Fook your marriage!" he said. "I'll ge' ya laid a dozen times in Sain' Androos. You canny pass up the Open! You cou' make stoopid money thair!"

"Sorry, buddy," I said, hugging the big beanpole around his chestbone. "You're the best. You saved my ass. I can never repay you, but I'll send you that $3,000 as soon as I land."

"For fook's sakes!" he wailed.

When we got to the Edinburgh airport, Dez bought Bob and me a ticket to Gatwick, and then a ticket for us from Gatwick to Boston. Good lad.

We still had a half hour to kill at the gate when I heard over the loudspeaker, "Paging, Mr. Hart. Paging, Mr. Raymond Hart."

It was Maddy.

"Stick?" she said.

"Miss Earhart?"

"I just wanted to thank you for what you did for Dez and me."

"Hell, I was going home anyway. He was the one who played himself into the right spot."

"No, you know what you did. And I just want to thank you so much."

"Ahh."

"And I want to thank you for last night, too."

"Thank me?"

"Yeah, for keeping me from doing something stupid. It's just that, you were right. I know I love Dez and I know we can work this out. So thanks, I owe you one."

"Did you say 'doing *something* stupid' or 'doing *someone* stupid'?"

"Either way."

Bob whacked me on the shin with his cane.

"We gotta either go now," he said. "Or find that kid from Cambridge again."

I rubbed my leg.

"Maddy, I gotta go, but can I tell you something?"

"What?"

"It killed me to stop last night."

"Yeah. But you were right to. Besides, you were always against those."

"What?"

"Mulligans."

CHAPTER 16

aving been abandoned by claps and whoops, not to mention shoes with built-in weight transfers, mercury-loaded drivers, an on-course relaxation tape-headphone system, and even his life coach, Hoover could not break 100. In fact, he could not even scare 100. To be honest, 100 didn't know Hoover even existed.

And so, as the final day dawned in the bet, his wife gloated, "If I don't hear you've broken 100 by tomorrow, you and I and mother are going to Arthur Murray!"

That sent Hoover off to his thirty-six holes with a shudder. He'd taken to playing thirty-six a day for the last week in hopes of doubling his chances, but it was simply polishing brass on the *Titanic*. It was hopeless. The second eighteen was always worse because he was tired and also because there is only so much time any human being should be forced to spend with the Human Stain, and that time should be limited to ten seconds per day. Of course, now it was worse after Stain's lucky sexual adventure with Kelly van Edible at Don's Mixed Drinks. Not a shot, beer, or card game went by without some mention of it.

"It's not unheard-of, you know," Stain said in the Pit of Despair one day. "Gorgeous people falling in love with plus-sized people. Mariah Carey and Tommy Mottola. Celine Dion and that French guy."

"Free Willy and the boy," Hoover said.

Their relationship was tense by then. Hoover felt that the Stain had done everything in his power to screw him over—pumping cart brakes, asking him whether he inhales or exhales on his backswing, mocking him whenever possible. "You know, Hoover," he'd say. "You are the only golfer I've ever seen who consistently is able to hit it right-to-right. Not a lot of players have that shot." Since Stain had been his constant guardian, Hoover's game had only gotten worse, and the notion of never getting to play golf again depressed him beyond Paxil.

And so it was, on that final day, second eighteen, on the 8th hole, lying 57 with eleven holes to go and looking slightly more frustrated than a toothless man with a candy apple, the end came.

"Has anyone ever told you," Stain said, munching the last of Blu Chao's Vietnamese tacos he'd brought along, "that you swing like a caveman trying to kill lunch?"

That about capped it for Hoover. That was the curtain-closer. He did not often speak out against his repulsive brother-in-law, but this was the push off the building ledge. He spun around on him, beet-faced, and barked, "Has anyone ever told *you* that they wished you were *dead*?"

"Good, good, Hoov!" Stain said. "Get mad! That's your problem, you never get mad and take your problems into your own hands! Look how wimpy you swing! Look how wimpy you live! That's why you settled for my fat sister and I ended up with the most delicious girl in Dorchester."

Hoover was so pissed you could've melted titanium on his head. He swung very hard on that tee box, so hard that he nearly broke a vertebra. It was the first time anybody ever remembered him getting the club higher than his right shoulder. Maybe that's why, for the first time in his life, he hit a shot flat-out in the dead center of the clubface, with such force and purity that it rocketed off, sure to go three hundred yards at least.

But on 8, that is exactly the shot you *can't* hit, owing to the *Boston Globe* billboard that overhangs the hole from the street. You must hit a cut around it or a punch beneath it or a skyball over it. Hoover had always unwittingly done one of those three things, or dribbled it, or shanked it way left, or missed it entirely.

But this shot—arguably the best of Hoover's life—hit the base of that steel billboard with awesome force and ricocheted backward at almost the same speed, striking the Human Stain square between the eyes. The Stain never even had time to move. It hit him so hard it actually knocked him off his scooter backward, sending his legs up in the air, his hat flying off, and his taco flying in bits toward the sky. The ball made such a pop hitting Stain's skull that people heard it two holes over.

It took a fraction of a second for Hoover to realize what had happened. He ran to his brother-in-law, who was lying flat on his back, eyes wide open, taco-stuffed-mouth agape, dead as a Sears hammer.

I didn't sleep a second all the way home, fretting about moving vans and divorce papers. The sentence that kept my stomach turning went something like, "Okay, Mr. Hart, the court has decreed that you'll have Charlie weekends and every other Thursday." How does a guy fly off to England, pull off a Lourdes, and then fly home as a cadaver?

Blind Bob, bless his heart, could tell what a wreck I was and offered to stay and get the bags at Logan while I jumped in a cab right away. It never occurred to me I was leaving a blind man to get my bags, but what the hell. I gave the cabbie my address and asked him to drive like he was in a movie.

"Uh, well, if you don't mind me asking?" said the little guy driving the cab. "What's the hurry? Your house on fire?"

"No, my life's on fire," I said.

We made eye contact in the mirror. There was something familiar about the little guy that I couldn't quite place.

"Oh, uh, well, if you don't mind me asking?" he said. "What seems to be the problem?"

This was really bugging me. I *knew* I'd met this guy somewhere.

"Hey, you ever play golf at Ponky?" I asked.

"Uh, well, uh, no," he said.

That's when it hit me. The face, the mannerisms, the running start to every sentence.

"Yeah, I think I know you," I said. "You brought me my dad's will. Remember, if I qualified for a golf major, I'd get $250,000 inheritance? Kind of an unusual clause, remember?"

He suddenly looked like a chicken in an airport searchlight.

"Uh, well, see, I don't think so. No."

"Oh, I think so. Business a little slow down at the law firm these days?"

"Uh, well, oh, hmm, no," he stammered. "I mean. I don't know what you're talking about. I'm a cabbie."

I reached around, grabbed him hard by the nipple, and started twisting.

"Yowwwww!" he screamed.

"Dude," I spit into his ear, "you better tell me right now what the hell you were doing with that will or you'll be the only one-tit hack in Massachusetts. And I want it in twenty-five words or less." I twisted harder.

"Owwwww!" he said. "Okay, okay! Two Down paid me to pretend I was a lawyer!"

My breath left me.

"Why?" I said finally, increasing the twist.

"Because he had a thousand-dollar bet with some guy! He bet you could qualify for a major! He said he needed to light a fire under you! He gave me fifty bucks!"

My mind reeled. This whole thing had been for a *bet*? There was no $250,000? There was no *goddamn* money? No will? I wasn't going to buy Ponky? I might have lost my wife for a fucking *bet*?

"Mister! You're killin' me here!"

I let go. I needed a drink. I needed an oven to stick my head into. Two Down, my best friend, had ruined my life? It seemed beneath even his gamblaholic's ass. When were they going to tell me? When I bounced a $250,000 check to buy Ponky? Hell, if I'd known this, I'd have stayed and played in the British Open! Maybe I could've made enough to at least pay Sponge back. Or Dez. Or to refill Charlie's college fund. Or some goddamn thing.

I flopped back in the cab and put my fists over my eyes.

"Take me to the Ponky clubhouse instead," I said. "You *are* a real cabbie, right? This isn't just another episode of *Punk'd* or something?"

"Uh, well, no, I am," he said, still rubbing his nipple.

We pulled up to Ponky and I got out, yanked open his car door, and pulled him out with one hand.

"Uh, well . . ." he said, as I dragged him. "I'm not sure I can—"

"Shut up and walk," I said.

As I approached the clubhouse, The Voice came crackling over the loudspeaker: "Hey, aren't you supposed to be winning the British Open right now?"

I flipped off the air and walked in. I marched the cabbie straight over to Two, who was sitting at one of the flimsy card tables, engaged in some bizarre game with the Chops.

"I'd have to say Jaundice," said Two.

"Placenta," said Hoover.

"Bruise," Cementhead said. "No, wait! Hurl."

Two turned his head toward me. "Heya, Stick! Welcome back! You wanna add to the list? Worst crayon colors."

My God, these guys can make your head hurt.

"Let's try a different one," I said, suddenly all Mister Rogers. "How 'bout we do Worst Best Friend?" And with that, I spun and landed a perfect right cross on Two that sent him sprawling over the La-Z-Boy and onto his back.

Two shook the bells out of his head and spit out another tooth. I walked over and stepped on his neck.

"Recognize this guy?" I said, still holding the cabbie by the collar.

"Schtick, I can echplain," he said, trying to push my loafer off his voice box.

"You moral-less hairball! You wrecked my life!"

"Schtick—"

"It was all a *bet*? You tricked me into going clear across the ocean, nearly getting killed on those goddamn left-hand roads, had me sleep in a damn Fiat, ruined my marriage, so you could win a *bet*?"

"Look," he said. "It's not that shimple."

"No, no, no, it's that shimple," I said. "Tell me something. Who knew? Did Dannie know?"

"No," he said, rolling out from under my foot. "It was just a bet between Dom and me. I bet a grand you could qualify for a major and he bet you couldn't. He said you wouldn't even try."

"Who knew?"

"You know, the usuals—Cementhead, Hoover, Froghair, a few Chops, but not Dannie."

"Blind Bob?"

Two looked down in shame.

"Yeah, but he wanted you to qualify so you'd finally know—"

"So Ponky's not really for sale?"

"No, that's real. That's sort of what was behind the bet. I was hoping you'd qualify and then go win the thing or something and then buy Ponky yourself."

"Sure! No problem! Maybe solve the Palestine thing, too, long as I'm over there."

"But, Stick, look how good you were doing! Why didn't you stay and play?"

"Because I didn't want to! I didn't! Me! And you know what *you're* going to do now? You're going to call Dannie right now and tell her it was all a bet. You're going to tell her how much fun it was to screw with her life—"

"Stick, think about it—"

"No! And you're going to tell her all about Hide and Seek, too. That's over. You're going to tell her about the condom. Everything. You've got one minute to call her before I get to the house or I'll come back and turn your face into leftover spaghetti. How's that for a crayon color?"

"All right, all right," Two said. I handed him the phone, then started dragging the cabbie back out with me.

"I was trying to help you!" Two hollered as I left. "And I was right! You *did* qualify, right?"

I threw the cabbie back in the driver's seat and crawled in the back. I gave him my address again.

Five minutes later we pulled up to my formerly happy little two-bedroom, but there was no U-Haul anymore. I had a supersized cup of bile in my gut. I figured I'd walk into a place that was missing furniture, toys, TVs, wives, and kids. This was it. I fully expected to hit bottom in the next two minutes—and me with no crash helmet.

I dragged myself out of the cab, leaned in the window, and said, "I'll pay you when my big inheritance comes in."

"Well, uh, I don't think—"

But I was at the door of my house by the time he'd finished his sentence. I took a big deep breath and tried the door handle. It turned. Hey, that's at least one good thing: She hadn't changed the locks.

Slowly, I opened the door. Saw the same entry table with the mail stacked up on it. At least that wasn't gone.

"Hell-o?" I tried.

No answer.

The furniture seemed to all be there. So she hadn't burned that.

"Anybody home?" I tried again.

Zip. A picture of me with Charlie was still hanging. So she hadn't cut the eyes out of every image of me yet.

I walked down the hall. Our bedroom door was closed. I dreaded what I'd find if I opened it.

I leaned into the crack of the door and yelled, mostly to myself, I guess, "Husband's home! Wish somebody would give him a big wet one!"

Just then, an ice-cold splash hit my butt from behind. I spun around to see Charlie, laughing hysterically, his empty apple juice glass in his hand.

The kid is very literal.

"Studly!" I said, sweeping him up in my arms and kissing every piece of exposed skin on him. "Daddy's so glad to see you!"

He giggled and screeched and turned to point into his bedroom, where Dannie was standing, smiling sheepishly, looking prettier than a kick-in birdie.

"Ray?" Dannie said, tears running down her cheeks. "I've been tryin' to tell you somethin' for the longest time."

"No, wait," I said. "I've been wanting to tell *you* something for the longest time. Did Two call you?"

"Yes, but I have to say this—"

"See, I've been so stupid—" I said.

"See, I've been so stupid—" she said at the exact same time.

I felt like I was trying to talk while listening to UN translators.

"I found out something while I was gone," I said.

"I figured out somethin' while you were gone," she said right on top of mine.

"I found out that there are people who need me and—"

"I figured out there's somebody who needs me and—"

We both laughed nervously and said, "You go."

"I found out what makes me happy is making other people happy—" I said at the exact same time she was saying . . .

"I just couldn't be happy if I didn't step up and do something," she said, "so—"

"I'm redoubling my commitment to you and Charlie, because I learned that when I get outside my own stupid self—"

"I've decided to bring someone back here, to live with us, my daughter—"

"—that my own stupid self grows—WHAT?"

"Yeah," she said, weeping now. "My daughter."

She motioned with her hand and to her side came a little girl with red curly hair and peach cheeks, a checked jumper, and bright shiny tap shoes. She jumped into Dannie's arms.

English suddenly failed me. It took me a good long time to even make a noise. I kept starting and stopping, like a kid trying to drive a stick shift the first time.

Finally I looked at Dannie and said, "Wait. On the phone, on the plane, you said you'd met somebody."

"I did," she said, wiping away tears from her cheek. "This is her."

"Start over. This is who?"

Dannie pulled the curly hair off of the little girl's face. She looked like she was about seven, cute as a kitten calendar. Dannie took a deep breath.

"This is the somebody I met—Jolene," Dannie said. "My daughter."

With four hours sleep in forty-eight hours, I knew I was exhausted, but now I was hallucinating.

She said the next part very quickly while I stared at both of them without blinking. "Ray, I had no choice. I tried to not let it bother me, but it did. I know I hardly talked about her, but not a day went by I didn't think of her. So a couple of months ago, I got a call from social services and it turns out the people that adopted her weren't takin' care of her and they said would I be willin' to adopt her or she'd be placed in foster care, but there wasn't a snowball's chance she'd even be placed with a foster family for a few years because of overcrowding and in the meantime she'd have to just sit in this awful orphanage I visited on that first trip to Roanoke and it turns out my sister Joey has kept a line on her all these years without tellin' me and I didn't even know she was alive!"

She took a big breath in and let loose again. "And as soon as I saw her I knew I couldn't let her go again and that's why I've been so nervous about how little money we have and I'm sorry I've been so hard on you but I was so tossed upside down about all this and so I started the adoption paperwork and I know that's *way* wrong without asking you first, but you were in England and I didn't know what else to do!"

With that, she started the full-scale waterworks and held Jolene even tighter. Guess she was making up for all those years she didn't get to.

I took a deep breath and looked at Jolene, who was, at that essential moment in her life, exploring the deepest riches of her left nasal cavity.

"I just have one goddamn question," I said firmly.

She looked into my eyes, scared.

"Does this mean you're not leaving me?" I said.

"No!" she wailed, collapsing into my arms. "I love you, you big stupid mule!"

I grabbed her and held the two of them so close neither of us could breathe.

Finally I pulled back and looked into that perfect face. "You know nothing happened between me and Maddy, right? Turns out we're both in love with somebody else."

"I know. Bob called and set me right on that."

"And I don't give a box of shaved butt hair about Kelly."

Charlie laughed uproariously at the mental picture, falling backward, his legs and arms flopping around like landed groupers.

"I know."

"Then why'd you start moving out?"

"What? I didn't!"

"Well, what was with the U-Haul?"

"Oh! Jolene came with stuff! A bed and a lamp and some toys! And my sister gave us a dresser and some clothes."

It was like having a FedEx truck lifted off my shoulders. I felt great. I started laughing and crying at the same time and so did she.

"Yeah, but did she come with a dowry?" I added, laughing like a monkey. "Because we're flat broke!"

"I know!" she said, laughing hysterically. "I am going to *remove* Two Down's eyes with a fork!"

Ten minutes later we were back in the Ponky clubhouse, all four of us, walking straight up to Two Down.

"Uh, Two, buddy?" I said. He looked up. "Dannie has a little gift for you. Honey?"

And Dannie stepped around me, took a big step forward with her shag bag, and coldcocked Two Down, hitting him right in the mouth.

It was such a sweet shot that Two Down's bar stool didn't even move. His head went straight back and his feet shot up in the air and he landed perfectly on the Jell-O green linoleum.

The whole room went dead silent, with everybody staring at Dannie wide-eyed and slack-jawed. Two Down spit out yet another tooth.

Jolene stared at this and then whispered to me, "My birthday's coming up, but I don't want any gifts, okay?"

Five days later Two Down and Cementhead were hip-deep in the Funeral Game while Dannie and I and Charlie worked on a plate of Blu Chao's Spaghetti Saigon and Jolene hit putts into Bob's open mouth.

"I'll take one car," said Two. "Not counting the hearse, of course."

"One car?" Cementhead said. "That's it?"

"One. An all-time low. Fifty bucks."

"I'll say two cars," Cementhead said.

"I don't think it'll get over one," Two insisted, "not counting the hearse. Maybe not *even* one."

"What kind of person only has one car full of mourners? It'll be at least two."

"Bank?"

"Bank."

With that, Cementhead rose. "Well, I'm gonna make like a tree and head out."

Even Jolene stared at him.

"Cement," Bob said, clearing one ear out. "It's 'Make like a tree and leaf,' or 'Make like a baby and head out.' But it's not both."

"You sure?"

"Holy Christ!" I said. "Check this out!" I was holding the *Dorchester Bulletin*.

Everybody gathered around. It was a tiny mention in the business section.

PONKY SOLD

"Ponkaquogue Municipal Links and Deli was sold to an overseas buyer Monday who wants to remain anonymous," I read aloud.

" 'I have a friend who keeps me from doing stupid things,' the buyer said Monday. 'But he wasn't around to keep me from doing this.'

"The new owner said Ponky will remain a golf course and deli and not become a parking lot for the Mayflower Club, a new city dump site, or a motocross track, as was rumored."

We all stared at each other in disbelief.

"Hell," Bob finally said. "If I bought Ponky, I'd stay anonymous, too. Who wants that on his record?"

Whereupon, the Pit of Despair became the Pit of Delirium. We all whooped and hugged and dogpiled. The Ponky employees seemed especially giddy. Kelly came out and kissed everybody, and she was just about to lay one on me when she caught sight of Dannie and gave me a handshake instead. Blu Chao came out and kissed everybody, although she seemed a little disappointed there was no Dom. There was a smile on Bob's face you couldn't have taken off with a sandblaster.

"Damn, Bob, looks like you're stuck at this dump for a while longer," I said.

"Could be worse," he yelled happily. "I could have to *see* the place."

Fifteen minutes of celebrating later, the phone rang. It was for me. "Somebody in Scotland," Kelly said.

I knew who it was.

"Maddy?" I said.

"Dr. Schweitzer?"

"Buy anything stupid lately?"

"Just a shitty golf course. Wanna run it for me?"

I had to catch my breath.

"Only if it's not next to those snobs at the Mayflower."

"I have only one request: You don't change anything."

"The health inspector's not gonna like that."

"I'll pay you $50,000 a year to run it and I'll keep everybody else's salary the same. If anybody can make that dump turn a profit, it's you. God knows why you love it."

"Maddy, you got enough to do this?"

"Ohhhh, yeah. Daddy was *way* more flush than even I knew."

"So how'd you know about Ponky being for sale?"

"Bob called me. Explained everything, even that lousy trick they pulled on you."

"I *have* to find a new set of alcoholics to befriend."

"I don't know. Seems to me they got you to do a little archaeology. You dug down under all those layers and found something in yourself you didn't even realize was there."

Hmmm. Hadn't looked at it that way.

"I owe you one," I said.

"No, we're even. I've never seen Dez happier. I think this is the break he needed."

"Would you tell that homosexual something for me?"

"What?"

"Tell him he already got the break he needed."

"What's that?"

"He met you."

When I got back to the Pit of Despair to tell everybody the news, Two Down was baying at the window, railing about "Rules infraction!" and "Inquiry!" and "You set me up!"

I looked out the window to see the Human Stain's funeral procession. There were two cars in it. One was driven by Stain's wife, with Hoover in the front seat.

The second was driven by Cementhead himself.

EPILOGUE

 It was another day of Chops contesting their matches with their usual quiet respect for the game and its traditions.

"What'd you have on that hole, Hoov?" Dannie asked as we walked down the fifth, searching for Hoover's seventh lost ball of the day.

"Diphtheria," he said dejectedly.

"You know what your problem is, Hoov?" I said. "You have delusions of adequacy."

Hoover slumped. "I can play better, I just never have."

Hoover found a ball near the fence and set up to it.

"Hey, that's not your ball, you Iraqi!" Cementhead yelled at Hoover. "That's mine."

"Not true!" Hoover said. "Yours is over the fence."

They saw Two Down on the other side of the fence and asked him to identify that ball for them. Two picked it up and looked at Cement.

"What are you playing?" said Two.

"A range ball with a red stripe," said Cementhead.

"And what are you playing?" Two asked Hoover.

"Same thing," he admitted.

"Okay, what number?" Two Down said.

Just then the voice came over the loudspeaker. "Just throw it back, prisoner, and get on with your exercising."

Two Down looked up at the guard in the tower, hitched up his bright orange prison jumpsuit, and heaved the ball back over the fifteen-foot-high fence with the curled barbed wire.

"Who taught you to throw?" sneered Dom, standing right next to Two. "Beyoncé?"

"Shut up, slob," Two Down said. "Or I won't give you the digits of that tall swarthy one in Cellblock D."

"Get bent," Dom said.

"Don't say that around *here*, you moron!" whispered Resource, who was standing next to Dom.

What Two, Dom, and Resource had now was a regular threesome at Bridgefield State. We'd drive up every Tuesday to see them—Dannie, me, Cement, and Hoover. We'd play eighteen at Prison View, teeing off at the perfect time to catch them on the fifth—the hole that borders the exercise yard—and visit quickly with them during their one-hour exercise break.

See, Two Down didn't realize that assisted-living homes have security cameras everywhere—even in the basement garage. All Opel Hickenlooper's son had to do was complain to management, who checked the tapes, who saw Two driving out with a different gorgeous, classic vehicle every day, the last of which was Opel's 1964 white-and-blue Lincoln Continental with the suicide doors.

We tried to find the gamblers and the car for a few weeks, but both had disappeared like Enron, so Two got a one-year all-expenses-paid ride to Bridgefield, with a chance to graduate in three months. It wasn't so bad, he admitted. He had Dom and Resource to hang out with and played a lot of dice and cards, caught up on a lot of movies, and stood every day in the yard and made bets on what the next hack would do, with slightly reduced bet sizes. "Five cents says this chop leaves this in the bunker," he'd say.

"Five cents!" Dom would say. "Are you batshit? That's a day's pay!"

What Dom didn't realize was that even people having sex have ears, and three of them heard Dom talking back and forth to Freddy, who wound up rolling over on him like a sumo wrestler. Freddy got a reduced sentence for fingering Dom as the brains-less behind the plot. Dom pleaded stupid and got two years, with a chance to be out in six months. After all, nobody lost their money or their virginity. Okay, one lousy pregnancy. Dom, though, wasn't as thrilled with prison as Two. No girls. No golf. Nor did he make good on his promise to be a pickle-kisser if Kelly didn't bed him, though I-Rod, who made eyes lustily at him every day in the mess hall, seemed bent on changing that. Dom shuddered at the thought.

"Yo, why you gotta be so picky all a sudden, bra?" Freddy kept telling him.

The one who really lucked out was Resource. Turns out Mr. Malcolm Baker was on the Bridgefield State Prison parole board.

"Somebody shot 69 with *my* clubs?" Baker asked when his head finally stopped thumping. "Let me meet this guy!"

And not only did Baker forgive Resource, but insisted the board not add any time to his sentence—after all, it was never clear that Resource was trying to escape; it's just that he wanted to play golf. But Baker attached a string to his generosity—Resource had to give him a playing lesson every Tuesday before his round. Since they were the exact same size and build, Resource could relate to his problems. "You get me down to a single digit," Baker told Resource. "And I'll vote yes on your parole."

It's been only two months as I write this and Baker is already down to an eleven. I told Resource as soon as he got out, there was a teaching job waiting for him at Ponky. I like employees with ethics.

Yeah, Ponky continues to live on, in all its gory. I run the golf end and Dannie runs the business end and Charlie and Jolene run like overcaffeinated gerbils through the clubhouse. It's not like they're going to wreck anything. Everything at Ponky comes pre-wrecked.

Sure, some people think my job is about as thrilling as jumping off a pancake, but for me, I feel like a wino locked inside a Liquor Mart. Besides, I've prided myself on granting my boss's wishes. I've changed nothing. We still feature the same SPAMwiches. Still use just enough fertilizer so you can call them "greens." Still gotta put your ball in the pipe—no computerized reservations. You gotta *want* Ponky.

Okay, I made a few changes. Green fees are free now if you're blind.

"But only if we play at night, right?" Bob asked when I told him.

In fact, yesterday, only two months after Stain died, Hoover finally broke 100. Turns out Hoover's wife secretly hated her brother, anyway. That was part of the reason she came up with the bet—to get rid of him. Besides, she found something darkly dangerous in having a husband who could hit a golf ball so hard it could kill a thickheaded ape like him. His dragon slayed, Hoover floated in with a smile like a cantaloupe slice: "99!" he screeched. It was the first time I'd ever seen him drunk—or happy. Only later did I find out that Cementhead and Dannie had done the same little hide-in-the-woods-and-toss-out-the-bad-ones favor that Dom had done for Two Down against the gamblers. We all vowed that the first person who told Hoover would be made to absorb full drivers from fifteen paces.

At Dannie's suggestion, I had Kelly van Edible and Nuke, the mattress-wearing range boy, switch jobs. Kelly quit within two days of the switch. Imagine that. Of course, life wasn't too bad for her now—Stain was dead and Dom was in jail—and word was she was going to go down to Tampa and get the receptionist job at Froghair's nudist colony. Too bad, though. Always liked her T-shirts.

Dez never did make it on the European PGA Tour, owing to the way his windpipe constricts at inopportune times. He missed the cut at St. Andrews by two counties and never made it back to the big leagues. Last I heard, he and Maddy were on a dig in Bali. She looks for prehistoric fish and he goes to the golf course and looks for live ones. Wonder if he's used the two-caddy trick yet?

The best shot I ever hit in my life—through that window—cost me $1,746 by the way, but it was worth every shilling. Not that it slowed the wack Worstenheims down. Daddy is doing a two-year term as president of the R&A right now, presumably trying to pass legislation that all Americans should be barbecued upon clearing customs. Young Worstenheim made the European Tour and even won a PGA stop at Castle Pines in Denver this year, proving once and for all that karma died with Mother Teresa. Still, after he won, he managed to piss off enough members at the winner's party that he wound up duct-taped at the wrists, ankles, and mouth and was left hanging by his belt loop from the moosehead over the fireplace.

As for Sponge, he didn't want his $3,000. Instead, he wanted a ticket to Boston and a place to live. When I picked him up at Logan, he dropped his bags and went into a very nice James Cagney: "Made it, ma! Top of the world!" The Big Orange has his own apartment now and is already taking citizenship classes. He looped for a while at the Mayflower, until he got the bag of a certain Mr. Fredericks.

"Well, Mr. Fredericks, I see you continoo tae win the figh' again' anorexia," he said, then launched into everybody from Ted Koppel to Aunt Bea. Fredericks loved him so much that he fired him as a caddy and hired him as a voice-over and impression man at his radio stations. He's making six figures now, which means he's upgraded to the twenty-five-year Macallan's. Still sleeps on a tarp on the floor next to his bed, though. Whatever he does for a living is fine with me, as long as he keeps coming to Ponky and giving Charlie six-foot-eight shoulder rides.

Besides, without Two Down, we're short one bizarre human. We miss him. Every now and then, just for laughs, we'll put a phony notice in the *Bulletin* . . .

HOLE IN ONE

Two Down Petrovitz—No. 4 at Ponkaquogue, 86 yards, driver.
Witnessed by: Stain Dalton, Blu Chao Ng,
and Bingsley Colchester.

Then we'll send it to him in jail, just to slag him off a little.

I forgave him within a week for trick-fucking me on that bet. I finally realized it was his way of getting me off my ass and seeing how good I could become. It really was a gift in a way. Thanks to that bet, I saw that I could have a pro golf career if I wanted. It'd be a lot of Red Roof Inns and Grand Slam Breakfasts and smiling wanly to the Worstenheims of the world, but I knew I could have it. Of course, the best thing was that it also showed me how badly I *didn't* want it.

Oh, I dust my game off now and then and go out and win a Massachusetts amateur. Finished sixth in the U.S. Mid-Amateur last year, which was pretty good for having played an entire practice round the day before with my maniac son on my shoulders.

I never was mentioned in my dad's will, not that it mattered. Turns out he *wasn't* as flush as I thought he was. He made some brilliant investments—luxury laundromats, for one—and was up to his pocket square in debt when he croaked. His second wife got whatever equity was left in the house and I got zilch, which was sort of fine with me.

Still, I don't see how I could be happier. I found out that I was running so hard away from where my father wanted me to go that I completely lost track of where I wanted to go. Now *that's* lifesuck.

I even got a new card out of it. On the outside, this husband dressed as Santa is kissing his wife under the mistletoe. There's a fire in the hearth and presents under the tree. And it says, "Hey, Santa, do you know the best thing you made me this Christmas?"

And inside, it says . . . "Happy! Merry Xmas."

I finally finished that book, too. No, not that one. The one you're holding in your hand. Got a little stackable jing for it, too, and used it to pay off Dez, refill Charlie's college fund, and start one for Jolene, who is just so damn cute she oughta have her own cable show. Yeah, she's a handful sometimes with her abandonment issues, but we're working through that and she loves it when Blind Bob babysits. They play a very even game of Hide and Seek.

I guess happiness has me up six, four, and two these days. I love and

I'm loved and that's about as good as you can get out of a muni life like mine.

It's like the great philosopher Cementhead said the other day.

"One man's trash," he declared, "is another man's treasure."

And we all looked at him in complete shock.

"Cementhead!" I said. "You got one right!"

"You sure?"

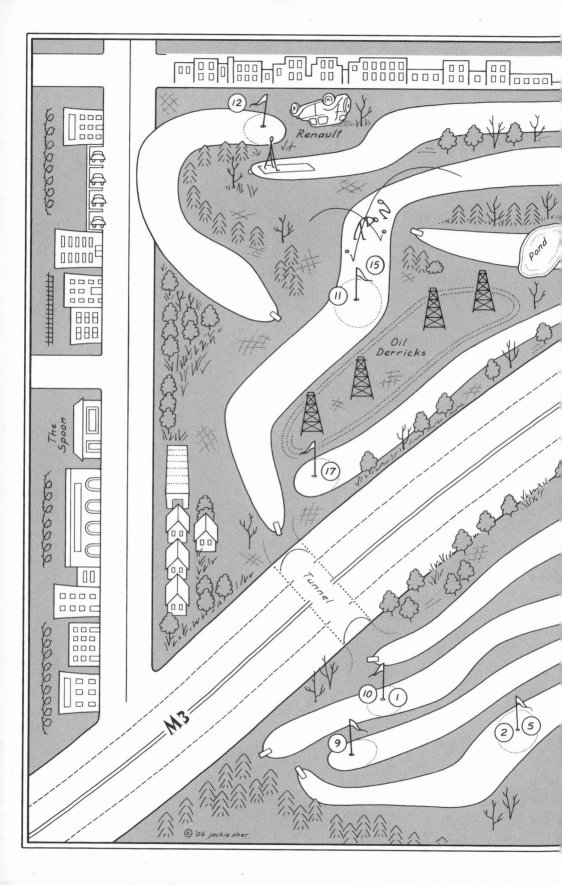